CURSED PACK

SHELLEY MUNRO

MUNRO PRESS

DEDICATION

For Paul, my partner in crime and fellow adventurer.

INTRODUCTION

Two misfits with little in common...

The paranormal species have come out to humans, creating havoc and unease, but Princess Malikah doesn't care. She's too busy trying to survive the foreign world in which she and her fellow gargoyles have arrived by mistake. Several youngsters in their fledgling clan have succumbed to a mystery disease, and the adult gargoyles blame her. She can't find a job, and they're surviving on handouts. Malikah has no time for the annoying wolf who follows her when her entire world is imploding and she's making one mistake after another.

Werewolf scientist Seth's life is in upheaval. Honor dictates that he steals a formula with potentially dire consequences for his fellow wolves, his werewolf boss is hunting him without mercy, and he's developed weird, stalkerish

1

tendencies, trailing an attractive woman around the city like a lost puppy. Then, there are the peculiar dreams, which make no sense. Yeah, he's losing his mind.

Malikah is understandably wary when Seth approaches her, but they have more in common than they realize. Their uneasy truce grows into friendship and more, but fate is a fickle witch, and she has other plans to test the unlikely pair.

1

SHADOWCLAW CLAN, NORTHERN ENGLAND.

MALIKAH TIPTOED ALONG THE passage, her overnight bag in hand. She stepped over a creaky floorboard and carefully approached the open door of the manor house reception room. If she were lucky, she'd avoid her mother.

"Malikah, is that you?"

Or perhaps not.

Malikah's shoulders slumped because she'd intended to sneak out to party with Alfred and his friends. Her parents disliked him, expecting her to marry into a powerful gargoyle family to strengthen their position, not waste her time with a lazy, disreputable human. Alfred was not good enough for a princess.

"Malikah." Her mother's stern voice made her straighten, and she quickly squashed her annoyance before

3

entering the main reception room.

Her mother sat in a high-backed chair, surrounded by a group of equally regal gargoyles—her ladies-in-wait. They were taking a tea break, but given the numerous papers on the oak coffee table, it was apparent they'd been planning a royal event. Each woman turned to Malikah as she entered their domain. *Best to hold her tongue.* She waited and held still, despite the nervous flutter in her chest.

Her mother's black eyes glistened in the sunlight, as hard and unyielding as onyx. Malikah recognized this expression. It was the one that announced *I am not pleased.* Her mother's gaze swept her from head to toe, took in her ragged jeans and skimpy blue top. She tutted.

"What is it, Mother?" she asked, trying to keep her voice steady. Her gaze drifted past the deep royal blue damask curtains to the rose garden and the gorgeous sunny day beyond. When her mother cleared her throat, Malikah jumped to attention.

"What are you wearing? You resemble a trashy human when we expect guests this evening. The crown prince from Denmark is arriving for talks with your father."

Malikah's stomach hollowed with churning fear. *A crown prince?*

"W-what sort of talks?" She hated her telltale stutter because her mother noticed. The queen observed everything, which made her an excellent ruler.

"Discussions to determine our kingdom's future," her mother replied, her voice sharp. "We must impress our visitors. Your father and I have discussed potential matches and believe this is the perfect opportunity to introduce you to the prince."

Malikah's heart sank. She'd always known her parents would push a political marriage, but being placed on display like a museum artifact made her stomach lurch.

"I understand, Mother," she said, her voice barely above a whisper. "I will do my best to represent our kingdom."

"Excellent. Now, prepare yourself. You must look your best for tonight's dinner." She waved a disparaging hand at Malikah's clothing. "Change into something more worthy of a gargoyle princess."

Malikah dipped a quick curtsy and left the room at a suitable princesslike pace, her overnight bag still clutched tightly. Dread settled in her chest, a noose tightening around her neck that not even gargoyle strength could break. When she was with Alfred and her other friends, she felt free. She felt alive. But her parents loathed the human who still knew nothing of her world. And now, her mother had clarified their wishes. She could soon expect a loveless marriage for political gain.

In her bedroom, she placed her bag on the bed and walked over to the window to stare at the blue lake and the oak forest. She couldn't imagine spending her life in a Danish palace, playing the dutiful wife to a foreign prince.

She had to wriggle from this closing trap.

A firm knock on her bedroom door had her stiffening, anger flooding her.

"Yes," she snapped.

"The seamstress has arrived. The queen wishes you to try on the gown she commissioned in case we require last-minute alterations," a lady-in-wait said.

5

Malikah clenched her hands at her sides. "I'll be there in ten minutes."

"The seamstress is waiting in the small reception room. Her Majesty told me to tell you to go immediately."

"Very well." Malikah stomped to the door and flung it open, not troubling to hide her displeasure.

The lady-in-wait bowed her head and stepped aside, allowing Malikah to pass. Somehow, she must meet Alfred at the bonfire party in the forest.

Possible escape plans circled her mind. She could climb a tree near the palace walls and jump over or sneak through one of the side gates. The latter seemed more sensible, so she focused on that avenue.

Malikah entered the small reception room, full of determination. It was her favorite room, but today, the cream-colored walls and the oil paintings of flowers and landscapes did nothing to blunt her bad mood. She tromped past an elegant maroon chair and ignored the sun streaming through the windows to glare at the seamstress.

The seamstress, a middle-aged woman with kind eyes and a warm disposition, stood near a full-length mirror, a puddle of green and gold silk on the table beside her. Malikah noted her simple yet impeccably tailored dress and growled.

"Your Highness." Her expression didn't change from friendly and accommodating, but Malikah saw the quick up-and-down scan of her jeans and sleeveless top. The curl of her top lip.

"Make this as fast as possible," Malikah said.

The seamstress inclined her head. "The dress is ready for

you."

Even her voice was calm, and that irked Malikah. She was a royal princess and should have more say, given her heir status. With bad grace, she stripped and donned the gown. The green silk shimmered and flowed around her body, fitting almost perfectly.

Madam Bernadette made minor adjustments, her manner meticulous.

Malikah fidgeted, silent while the seamstress worked. She twisted ideas. Plans. And all she decided was to escape after dinner once the gentlemen retired to their cigars and port. She'd tell her mother she'd like a spot of air and invite the other young ladies to go with her. They wouldn't accept her invitation. The royal court's disapproval of her was palpable, yet they spent time with Malikah because of her position. They felt obligated.

All went to plan. Dinner was excruciating, full of boring discussions of the Stonehurst clan and their creeping, grasping ways. Gossip about European families—who was marrying and those single and eligible.

The crown prince flirted with Malikah and hinted his discussions with her father had gone swimmingly. His slimy smile, when his gaze slithered over her breasts, made her want to vomit. None of the delicious meats and vegetables, the berry wine, or the triumphant and towering dessert tempted her to eat. Instead, a hard knot collected in her stomach.

Finally, after her father's nod, her mother stood with a swish of her rose-pink gown and gestured for the ladies to withdraw to the reception room for tea.

Malikah rose with alacrity, eager to escape to the garden. Once she'd gone, her mother wouldn't create a fuss. Oh, she'd express anger tomorrow and punish Malikah in a diabolical way, but it would be worth it to see Alfred.

Once the ladies took their seats, Malikah wandered to the open terrace doors. The scent of roses and a buttery note from the oak forest drifted inside.

"It's such a beautiful evening," she said. Nothing less than the truth. "I might walk in the garden. Would anyone like to join me?"

Several of the girls stared at her, their expressions aghast.

"But it's cold," said a blonde beauty.

Yes, because her shoulders were bare, and her breasts almost poured out of her scarlet gown.

Malikah smiled, wide and genuine instead of her usual twist of lips—the fake smile where emotion never reached her eyes. "That's okay. I'm only going outside for a short time."

Without waiting for a reply, Malikah departed. Her heart raced as she hurried down the stairs to the garden. Stars studded the night sky, and a half-moon lit her path. She ran through the gardens, inhaling the rose and jasmine in the air. Freedom called with each step she took. At any other time, she might've shifted to gargoyle and flown over the moon-speckled countryside. Outside the estate, she took a well-trod path toward the clearing in the middle of the oak forest. A tinge of smoke carried in the wind. They'd already started.

As Malikah grew closer, voices drifted to her.

"I'm gonna be rich. Malikah is hooked, and once I have

the marriage contract signed, I'll give away my garden center job."

Malikah halted, anguish darting her chest along with a blast of heat. She recognized Alfred's voice, and his arrogant bragging sent a tremor through her. *Ooh!* Her vision blurred as she hovered behind a giant oak trunk. Her parents had been right.

Male and female laughter rang out, cruel at her expense.

"Jenny and I have a game where she pretends to be her. It's so funny. We laugh and laugh." Alfred lowered his voice to a suspenseful whisper. "And the sex is smokin'."

He had another girl.

Malikah's heart twisted in searing pain, and she clamped her teeth on her lip to keep the tears away. The heat in her chest whirled and grew. Alfred had deceived her with his smooth talk and soulful glances. His handsome face. He'd betrayed her.

Malikah closed her eyes, centering herself and gathering tight control, as January, her gargoyle guide, had taught her. The heat in her chest retreated. When she opened them again, her eyes glowed with an otherworldly light, and her transformation to her gargoyle form was instant. She spread her wings wide. The voices from the clearing ceased, replaced by shocked gasps, as she took a flying leap into the air, her speed rattling the tree branches.

"What was that?" Alfred demanded.

"Sounded too big for a bird," a woman said, her words rapid and pitch high.

Malikah's lips curved but didn't come close to a smile. She was more than a joke, but after three swift wingbeats, she was too far away to hear the commotion.

The wind buffeted her body, the updraft lifting her until the trees were a smudge on the landscape. The stars sparkled like jewels while the moon did its best to light the rolling hills.

She flew for half an hour before steeling herself to return to the manor. At least she was calmer, the angry fire in her chest a mere ember. If she saw Alfred again, she might punch the conniving wretch. He didn't know she was a gargoyle, and she was so thankful she hadn't confided this secret.

Reluctantly, she turned back, her heart heavy with shame, embarrassment, and anger, some aimed at herself. Headstrong and determined, her father had informed her. Right now, she understood her bloody-mindedness had impeded her judgment.

Without warning, a loud screech pierced her reverie.

A distress signal.

A call to arms.

Immediately, she dived toward the forest. She landed with a thump and shifted smoothly. Her gown rustled as she hustled to the forest's edge, battle cries and shouts carrying to her.

Malikah skidded to a halt, gaze scanning the manor. What she saw chilled her. Gargoyles swarmed the sky, diving and shrieking in victorious cries. Giant winged beasts, much bigger and stronger than she wielded swords and battleaxes.

A woman rushed into the garden Malikah had suggested they wander through after dinner. An immense slate-gray gargoyle swooped and slashed with his sword. In that one sweep of steel, her head separated from her torso, and she dropped.

Horror filled Malikah as she spotted several gargoyles splitting off and flying toward the village. Did they mean to murder everyone?

Malikah thought quickly, that cursed heat flaring through her chest. She should...no! Given the number of the enemy, they'd surround her before she could use her power to save anyone. What would her guardian advise? She sucked in a head-clearing breath. January would tell her to save as many gargoyles as she could. Malikah squared her shoulders and focused. She wouldn't make it to the village in time to shout a warning, but several outlying houses existed. She could alert them of the danger.

Instead of flying, she picked up her skirts and dashed through the forest, hoping to remain undetected. She ran like she'd never run before until each breath emerged in a hoarse, whistling pant. Her legs ached, her flimsy shoes no protection against the forest floor stones and twigs. They rubbed, a blister growing, but when she might've given up in the past, she kept racing across the uneven ground.

Finally, a house appeared in the distance, and she flitted from tree to tree, hoping to escape notice. In the distance, screams rang out from the village. Inhuman cries that had horror rising up her throat. Malikah forced her legs onward. When she finally reached the thatched cottage, she burst inside.

The family was having dinner, and a bulky male leaped to his feet.

"What do you mean by invading our home?" he demanded in a deep, gravelly voice.

"The manor house and the village are under assault. Hurry, you must hide before the attacking clan extends their search."

"Attack?"

The adults exchanged a glance.

"It's the truth. Step outside. You can hear the screams."

After another exchanged glance, the adults stood and hustled toward the ajar door. It was clear they didn't believe her. Malikah had seen them around and, to her shame, recalled her rudeness. She'd stared straight through them because she'd considered them coarse and uneducated.

"Please believe me," she said. "Where is your nearest neighbor? I must warn them." A shudder worked through her. Horror. "They're killing everyone."

The couple stepped outside, and she spotted the second they believed her.

"Children, quick. Come now," the mother said. "We'll go to the old barn. It will be safer than our house."

"Take the children," her husband said. "I will warn the others."

"Which way is your closest neighbor?" Malikah asked.

The gargoyle gestured to the right. "At the end of the lane. Tell them to come to the dilapidated barn. It appears disused and will make a satisfactory hiding place.

With a nod, she ran in the direction he'd indicated, pushing every scrap of pain to the back of her mind. A blister, aching legs, and oxygen-starved, burning lungs were nothing compared to life.

Once again, she had difficulty persuading the gargoyle family she was telling the truth. She clasped the woman's arm and dragged her to the door. Flames and shrieks and battle cries flared from the village. The color fled the woman's cheeks as crazed enemy laughter reached them.

"We'll go to the barn," the woman said. "Another family lives that way."

"I'll warn them," Malikah promised.

The woman nodded and sprang into action.

Fire licked the village when Malikah and the last group entered the barn. The gargoyles stared at her, but Malikah didn't care what they thought. The barn represented safety even though it smelled of musty hay and mouse droppings.

She sank into a corner, exhausted, every muscle aching, and closed her eyes. She immediately opened them again and shuddered, rubbing at her breastbone to massage away the ball of heat collected there. A sliver of guilt ran through her at her lack of action. Of course, she'd tell her guardian, but she'd hardly saved anyone, and they might all die yet.

Her mind slid back to the carnage and refused to stop replaying the beheading. The gargoyle slayer's face had been full of unrelenting glee and satisfaction. The horror of it made her stomach swirl, and she pressed her fingers into her sternum to the point of pain.

Shouts and laughter came from overhead, and none of their group spoke or moved. Malikah held her breath and prayed as she never had before. The night seemed to still, and the flap of wings, the taunting calls of gravel-deep voices carried on the night air, sounding way too close.

"No one at that house," one called.

"The others are empty," a gruff voice reported.

"Should we search, captain?" the first asked.

"No, the flare will take care of them. Return to base so we're behind the wards when the magic occurs."

The flare?

Malikah puzzled over the gargoyle's words. She glanced at the others, and their confusion was plain even in the blackness of the barn's interior.

The flap of wings and chatter, the laughter and the screams faded, but still, their group scarcely breathed. The wait was interminable, but like the others, Malikah remained silent, disbelief filling her mind.

Another five minutes passed, and one of the male gargoyles stepped toward the door.

Malikah opened her mouth to protest when a bright flare seared her eyeballs. She raised her hands, but her muscles locked.

The light confused her. Malikah couldn't discern anything in the barn. She felt a wave of intense heat, and her skin prickled as if it were on fire. When the brightness faded, Malikah found herself frozen.

Then, her world faded to black.

2

AUCKLAND, NEW ZEALAND.

SETH WALSH WINCED AT the violent pounding on the door of the apartment he shared with his best friend and two other wolves. His nostrils flared as he gathered clues about his caller's identity.

"Open up, Walsh. I know you're in there."

Seth's shoulders slumped. Raoul expected him to work in the lab, carefully measuring ingredients to create the scent inhibitor. Despite the tests going well, there were flaws to address, like increasing the drug's longevity. After an hour, the drug's effects dissipated. Unacceptable, according to Raoul. Seth had tampered with his paperwork, making it impossible to replicate his work.

As far as he knew, Raoul hadn't uncovered that bit of skullduggery.

Yet.

Then, there was the other formula he'd developed by mistake...

The thunder of fists came again, and Seth realized he'd run out of time and luck. He'd evaded Raoul during his first day off, but now his boss expected him at work on a Saturday night. *Unreasonable bastard.*

Seth strode to the apartment entrance, fear of the upcoming meeting radiating off him like a tangible force. Raoul was an intelligent bully, and he'd taken the credit for Seth's best inventions to date. Not that Seth cared. It was the work that was important.

Not giving himself a chance to wimp out, he opened the door. A meaty fist caught him on the jaw, and Seth crashed onto the faded blue-and-white linoleum flooring. His glasses went flying and hit the wall with a distinct crack. He saw stars and a red cartoon bird flitted across the back of his eyes before he pushed up to glare at Raoul.

Bastard.

"What did you do that for?" His words were almost indecipherable, and he tentatively explored the tender spot on his lip with his tongue. The metallic taste of blood told him Raoul hadn't held back. Thank the stars for his wolf heritage, otherwise he'd feel a lot worse.

Raoul and two grinning underlings—thugs wearing jeans and leather jackets—stepped over Seth, the last slamming the door shut to avoid witnesses.

Seth glared anew and used the hem of his T-shirt to blot away the worst of the blood before staggering a few steps. If it hadn't been for one of his strange trance-like fits, he would've left long before Raoul arrived.

Bloody hell, his luck was crap lately.

Seth wiped his mouth again and scowled at the blood soaking into his T-shirt. He rubbed his face, carefully avoiding the rapidly swelling left side, and attempted to focus. A glance told him his glasses were past saving, and he muttered a curse.

"Why are you here?" he asked Raoul, blinking at the man's expensive suit and black hair spiked with gel. "My next rostered day is Monday."

Raoul's intense brown gaze made Seth want to backpedal. However, he straightened and rose while the silence lengthened. Seth refused to break first.

"I made it clear I expected you to put in extra hours on the weekends to perfect the formula."

"Can't one of the other scientists work on the project until I'm back? I struggled to stay awake during my last shift and made stupid mistakes. Anyway, I can't focus if I'm physically impaired." Seth gestured at his face and relished Raoul's jaw clenching as he ground his molars. Seth had Raoul because he couldn't work with a swollen right eye.

Another knock rattled the apartment door. Iain was in Ohakune, visiting his aunt. Their other two flatmates were working, one in a bar and the other as security at a nightclub. His visitor's impatience was palpable, each knock growing louder and more determined.

Raoul shot a glare at Seth. "Who is it?"

"I'm expecting a visit from a university friend," Seth lied. Fortunately, he'd had practice during the past six months. His poker face was excellent.

17

Raoul scowled. "Get rid of them."

"It'll raise his suspicions since I invited him," Seth countered, taking sly pleasure in Raoul's frustration. He stepped toward the door and contained his pained wince until his back was to Raoul and his cohorts. Man, his face throbbed like a nagging tooth. A mouthful of aching teeth. He dragged in air before reaching for the door, immediately intrigued by the non-wolf scent.

He opened the door to a tall stranger.

"Hi, I'm Fergus Murray."

Seth glanced upward to meet the man's intense and piercing gaze. He was much taller than Seth and broad of shoulder. *Interesting*. Why was the dragon visiting him? Seth hesitated. No, he couldn't involve an innocent dragon in his messy life.

"Oh." Seth assumed a puzzled expression. "I thought you were my friend. How can I help you?"

"I'm Elspeth's brother. She and Iain were worried when they couldn't reach you. I promised I'd check on you." Fergus's focus was on Seth's swollen face. "Do you have a problem?"

Seth hesitated again, fully aware of the three wolves at his back. No, he needed to get rid of Elspeth's brother. "No, I'm fine."

"Can I come inside?"

Seth hesitated again. "Sure."

He stood back and allowed Fergus to enter. It was easy to see the dragon's suspicions as he took in the three silent wolves and the blood on Seth's shirt. "Iain is worried about you," he repeated, pitching his voice too low for the wolves to hear. "If you need help, I'll do whatever I can."

"Tell Iain I'll call him. Wait, is Elspeth with Iain in Ohakune?"

"Yes."

"You don't mind?" Seth had never heard of a wolf and a dragon hooking up romantically. Not with the current climate between the paranormal species.

"Elspeth is an adult and capable of running her life. It's not my place to tell her what to do," Fergus replied. "I haven't met Iain, but I've spoken to him on the phone. He's not a self-absorbed prig, or he wouldn't worry about you or even have friends."

A laugh burst from Seth, and it hurt like a bitch. He pressed his fingers to his mouth, testing the results of his self-healing. A grunt escaped. Like his shift, his recuperation powers were slower than the typical wolf. Yet another area where he was a failure. "Thanks, I think. Look, I promise to call Iain tonight."

"Make sure you do." Fergus pulled a piece of paper out of his pocket. "This is my number if you change your mind about needing help."

Seth accepted the paper and shoved it into his jeans pocket. "All right. Thanks. I'll contact Iain as soon as my visitors leave." Since he had backup, he turned to Raoul. "I'll be at work on Monday morning."

Raoul sent him one scorching glare before sharply motioning to his companions. "Make sure you are because you won't enjoy the consequences if you disobey."

"Are you threatening him?" Fergus asked, taking half a step forward.

19

"No," Raoul said through gritted teeth. "That was a promise." He stalked to the door, flung it open, and disappeared. The two wolves followed.

Seth didn't speak until he could no longer hear their footsteps.

"Thanks." He forced a smile at the dragon, even though his face still throbbed. "Excellent timing."

"Are you positive I can't do anything to help?"

"Getting Raoul to leave was all the aid I needed. Honestly, I'm not in trouble. I'll call Iain tonight."

Fergus chuckled, his amusement zapping away his earnest expression. "If you're sure, I'll leave you to your Saturday night. Nice to meet you."

"Same," Seth said, offering his hand in friendship.

Fergus didn't hesitate, his firm grip full of confidence.

Seth approved. Although this was their first meeting, this guy appeared genuine, as had his sister when he'd met her at the dragons' nightclub.

"Will those guys come back?" Fergus asked, hesitating on the threshold.

"Possibly, but I won't be here. I'm grabbing a bag and leaving, although if you see them outside, please don't tell them of my intentions."

Fergus made a buttoning motion across his lips and lifted a hand in farewell. An instant later, long strides took the dragon down the hall.

Seth locked the door, wasting no time in grabbing the go bag he'd packed only last weekend. He'd known it'd come to this, and he wished Iain was here so he could talk to his friend. Unfortunately, that wouldn't happen because involvement with a dragon meant Iain had his own problems.

Seth opened the apartment door a fraction, and once he saw the corridor was empty, he slipped out of his place and into the one next door. If Raoul and his henchmen did return, this might throw them off.

Seth made a quick phone call to Iain. "Hey, Iain," he said, babbling, because this call needed to remain short. He couldn't risk anyone tracing him. "No, I'm fine. Just busy. Stop bothering me. I'll call you soon."

Iain spoke just as a familiar voice shouted Seth's name. Seth hung up and scarcely breathed, thankful he'd had the foresight to use the scent-inhibiting tablets. Iain's father was the last wolf he wished to tangle with tonight.

Seth heard another shout, and something crashed into the ground before silence fell. No point checking on his apartment. He'd wait an hour before he left to go to the place he'd rented under a fake name in another part of the city. He'd kept a few of his pills, thinking they'd come in handy when he wanted to avoid Raoul or other wolves tasked with hunting him.

The clock ticked slowly, but Seth was patient, sitting still. He'd always been a fidgeter in constant movement, but recently, without warning, he'd started sitting Buddha-like with nary a twitch. Weird.

Another thunderous crash jerked Seth from his trance. His lids flickered up and down as he slowly cast out his senses. Ah! Raoul had sent more than one wolf to grab or beat him. Seth remained in position, focusing on sensing what the intruders might be doing.

A phone rang inside his apartment. Muted words transmitted to him through the thin walls, but not enough to make sense of the conversation.

At some stage, Seth dropped into one of his weird trances. His body stiffened, his limbs becoming heavy and unresponsive. His mind drifted to an unfamiliar place. Forest-clad hills gave way to snow-tipped mountains. Streams cascaded down slopes, toppling and churning over rock cliffs and sparking tiny rainbows of color in his gaze. Somehow, Seth settled on a rock and scanned his surroundings with peace and happiness. A sense of belonging.

Below him, he spotted an approaching flock of birds. As they arrowed closer, he saw they weren't birds, but something else and familiarity flooded him. These creatures were his friends, his ancestors.

His mind stalled at the rightness of this thought, the shock of it.

No, that couldn't be right.

3

AUCKLAND, NEW ZEALAND.

"IT'S YOUR FAULT WE'RE stuck in this place, isolated, with no way of returning home. Your boyfriend sold us like pieces of garden statuary. We didn't have an option, Princess," Tamaini snapped. "You promised to keep us safe." She gestured at the warehouse interior, her lips curled enough to show sharp teeth. "We have no money. No food."

Malikah kept her face impassive despite each accusation flailing her like a whip. Guilt slivered through her. Anger at herself. At the man she'd thought loved her. Somehow, Alfred had discovered them in the barn. He'd seen a money-making opportunity and sold them to the local garden center while they'd been in stasis.

He hadn't even recognized her or what he was selling.

That hurt the most. An overseas buyer had purchased them as a group lot. The arduous ship journey from

England to New Zealand had taken months, and thankfully, they'd remained in a state of suspended animation.

Malikah's memory of events remained fuzzy, and she recalled little from when the flare struck. Waking in an Auckland warehouse had been a shock, but they'd escaped and sought fellow gargoyles for help.

On meeting Samarak Ironwing, the head of the Auckland gargoyle clan, she'd assumed he'd welcome them. They were a group of fifteen, seven of whom were children. But Sam had rejected them, citing the risk of illness and contamination. When it became clear they were healthy but weak due to lack of food and the long journey, he'd still refused them shelter. His vague reasons had ruffled her temper. But in a first, she'd kept a grip on her anger to maintain the tenuous relationship between her people and Sam's clan. No bridge-burning this time.

And this had paid off.

Sam had asked careful questions on their behalf, which was how she'd learned of Alfred's part in their plight. The Stonehurst clan had annihilated her family and their people. Even if they'd had the finances to leave Auckland, they had nothing to return to in Northern England. A few gargoyles in their group—like Tamaini—resented her, blaming her for their dilemma. Thankfully, some of the gargoyle adults understood she wasn't at fault or cast blame for their predicament at the feet of their enemy.

Malikah didn't bother with excuses or point out that she was as much a victim as Tamaini. Instead, she'd set about trying to find a temporary home. The warehouse Sam had suggested was a drafty dump. Easy to discern the reason for the building's vacant state, but they'd been desperate.

This new life was the opposite of the luxurious one she'd had as a royal princess. She'd never have let a servant speak to her thus.

"I've been out this morning trying to find a job," Malikah said.

Tamaini's dark brows winged upward, her slate-gray skin darkening with her emotions. "And did you find employment?"

Malikah fought her scowl and lost. "No."

"How will we feed the children?" Tamaini snapped. "I have a part-time job. Flint and Jasper have jobs, and Talon thinks he has secured one. Why can't you?"

It was a well-worn argument. The truth—she had no skills. "I'll try again this afternoon. Meantime, I have food." Once, she might've rubbed Tamaini's nose in her success, but she'd stolen this food. Shame cut through her, but she'd do it again if it meant her group survived. Her thievery was for the children. It didn't matter if she went hungry, but the children deserved better.

"What sort of food?"

Malikah's patience fizzled out, and she thrust the sack at Tamaini. "Does it matter? It's decent and suitable for children. I'm going out and will return for dinner."

She strode to the warehouse door, cautiously opened it, and slipped outside. So far, they'd been lucky. No one had ventured near the building, possibly because they'd pooled their failing gargoyle magic to cast an avoidance spell. If they remained healthy, they'd have enough power to fuel the ward.

Malikah strode through the lower part of Queen Street, forcing aside her worry. Since the pandemic, dozens of shops and businesses had closed, although Sam had told her the humans were returning to the city. She sidestepped a group of foreign students heading for the language school at the end of the block.

Along with traffic fumes, a delicious coffee aroma, and a faint whiff of body odor, Malikah caught the brine of the sea. The harbor was beautiful, and she looked forward to a day when she could fly for fun. Currently, she focused her energy on keeping the makeshift clan alive.

Another robust, earthy scent with a faint metallic undertone had her growling in frustration.

The wolf was following her again.

She hesitated, the hitch in her long strides barely perceptible even as her temper spiked. The stupid animal had spied on her for the last two weeks. No matter how hard she tried, she couldn't evade the silly mutt. The question was why. Why did this animal keep following her, and how concerned should she be?

Was she putting her clan in danger?

That worried her. She was responsible for their safety and refused to let a mangy wolf wreck their lives when they'd barely established themselves.

Sam's clan—who'd settled in New Zealand over one hundred years ago—had started to accept their presence, or at least didn't attack on sight. The lingering fear in her people, the stress and anxiety, had lessened, and now they were on the verge of living instead of struggling to exist.

Then, this wolf had come along and rattled her growing confidence in their security.

She couldn't allow that to happen.

The wolfish scent intensified. Bother, the stupid, determined mutt.

She darted from the alley and turned left, putting on a burst of speed before sprinting down another path. Once the shadows concealed her, she halted and watched to see if she'd evaded the mangy cur.

He trotted past, but she cursed inwardly because he glanced to his right at where she hid. After a brief hesitation, he continued past. She lingered until several other people wandered past in groups or singly. Their inane chatter calmed her angst, but she waited another five minutes. The wolf didn't reappear, and the tension slid from her shoulders.

A glance at her watch told her she needed to hustle or be late for the job interview. She cursed and strode to the end of the alley. She peeked out, reassured when she neither saw nor sensed the wolf.

The job interview was at a restaurant. She didn't care what job she got if they had money coming in while her group regained their strength. A large group had already assembled for the interview. There were eight spots available, ranging from chef to kitchen porter. *Son of a dung beetle!* How would she get this job when she sensed the same determination in the other applicants waiting to speak with the recruiters?

Her shoulders slumped before she straightened again. If she didn't get this position, she'd try for another. Bar work, perhaps. Anything because they needed medicine to treat the three youngsters in their group. They were suffering from a respiratory disease, and despite trying every traditional treatment, the youngsters weren't responding.

It was worrying, and although no one had mentioned anything to her, she was sure they were thinking evil thoughts. It was her fault they'd ended up in this unforsaken place. Leadership was a heavy yoke, but she must continue with her plans. It was too late to return to the place they'd called home since the Stonehurst clan had moved in their people. They'd been lucky, even if the others didn't see this, because all those who'd gone into stasis in the village had died. The Stonehurst soldiers had beheaded them. Helpless men and women and children. Just thinking about it sickened Malikah, and the vision haunted her dreams.

Winged warriors! Why did this have to be so complicated? She held her head in her hands for an instant before she heard someone call her name. She straightened and pinned a pleasant smile on her face.

Showtime.

SETH WOKE GROGGY AND his mind blank. He took his time, inhaling and exhaling until his senses returned. A wispy memory came to him, and he frowned.

God, he had gargoyles on his mind because of the woman.

That was why his dreams were heading in weird

directions. He glanced left and right, surprised by his surroundings. Oh! Right, he was in his neighbor's apartment. His go-bag sat on the floor at his feet. Time to leave. He forced his stiff limbs to move. He couldn't stay here or in his apartment. It wasn't safe with Raoul on the rampage.

After checking for loitering wolves, Seth climbed down the fire escape and dropped the last three feet. Then he set off at a jog, intent on heading to the apartment he'd rented as a bolt-hole. About three hundred meters from his apartment, a now-familiar scent drifted to him, and his pulse jumped. He smiled. The smoky, metallic fragrance with vanilla and a tinge of crisp magic hit him. Some of the tension in his shoulders smoothed away.

The woman.

Somehow, he found her easily, even though every night, every day, he told himself he wouldn't look for her again. He was almost positive she was a gargoyle and a secretive one. But the worst thing was this driving compulsion to speak to her, to learn everything about her, and to have her in his bed.

It wasn't natural.

Not normal for him, yet she intrigued him, confused him. He found himself stalking her, and nope. That wasn't him.

Hell, he wanted to go caveman on her arse and tell her to stay home, where it was safe. He knew where she lived, and some part inside him sensed her whenever she was out and about, mainly at night. Maybe she avoided direct sunlight. His eyes didn't do well with bright illumination.

A mournful cry split the air, and the hair at the back of Seth's neck stood on end. Every muscle in his body tensed as horror pulsed through him. What the hell?

Seth instinctively drew into the shadows when another animal released an answering howl. Whatever was going on, he did *not* want a part of this madness.

A chorus of unearthly song pierced the air, and Seth shuddered, his wolf wanting to join with the mournful howl. It was a call to arms. He took two steps in the direction he'd come from before he forced himself to halt.

No, he must hide. Go to his apartment. That would be much safer.

His inner wolf snarled. *The woman.*

"Not now," Seth muttered. "If we follow her, we might place her in danger."

Woman. This time, his wolf sounded more subdued, and Seth relaxed a fraction. Neither of them wished to place her in jeopardy.

"I promise we'll find her soon. Speak with her," Seth said.

Woman is good.

Seth took that as agreement and jogged up the street parallel to Queen Street, the principal shopping street in the central city. A loud whoosh sounded overhead, and he froze. The thundering trumpeting that followed had him gawking upward. *Dragons.* Six of them in colors ranging from black to red to blue and green.

Seth's heart thudded against his ribs as he watched the massive beasts soar across the sky, their wings creating a powerful downdraft.

Up ahead, a man shouted, "Did you see that?"

"What?" his female companion asked, tearing her gaze away from the jeweler's shop window and the ring display.

"Dragons. A group of dragons flew overhead."

"Don't be silly, George," the woman replied. "I told you not to have that last drink."

Another chorus of mournful cries rang out, louder and more powerful than earlier. It sounded like a pack was massing, which did not bode well.

The two humans glanced over their shoulders, took one look at each other, and ran in the opposite direction.

Seth didn't blame them. He wanted to flee, too.

His gaze settled on an alleyway between two buildings, and he darted inside, pressing himself against the wall. The steady *whop-whop* of dragon wings came again, and the flare of fire and loud trumpeting as they passed overhead. Seth held his breath until they had flown out of sight before cautiously stepping out of the shadows.

The street seemed empty now, but Seth knew better than to take chances.

Still, he hesitated before cursing, undecided about the best course of action. Several beings with luminescent skin appeared in the next intersection, and the surrounding air charged with magical energy.

He gaped and shook his head, but they didn't vanish. His brain rapidly filtered through everything, and a glimmer of understanding came. Recently, the paranormal species had discussed coming out to the humans. Most of the species agreed to the proposal, apart from the wolves, who wished to cling to tradition and secrecy. Seth didn't understand why, but he was a minor cog in the pack and not privy to decision-making.

Tonight, it appeared the humans were learning firsthand of the others who shared their city, whether they were ready or not. This distraction could work to his advantage because something peculiar was happening to him along with his work situation.

He wanted to call his friend, but Iain had enough problems, given he was consorting with a female dragon. Seth loved Iain like a brother, but Iain's father was cruel and all about the power of wolves.

Seth caught the terrified expressions of the two women running toward him. Humans. They'd spotted otherworldly beings and were in panic mode. A wave of designer perfume struck him before they detoured around him. Their fearful expressions told him they half expected him to pounce. He raised his hands and kept moving because he wanted to return to the tiny apartment he'd rented under a false name. A reaction to difficulties at work and Raoul's odd behavior.

He hadn't known what a godsend that private space would become. A hideaway when he urgently needed it. He continued moving, the women's adrenaline spike no longer reaching his sensitive nostrils.

His thoughts turned to Iain. Yeah, he wasn't sure how his friend would react to his strange symptoms, but Seth would tell him... No, Iain had enough drama. Iain's father would shit a brick when he learned his son was dallying with a dragon. Ewan McKenzie was a cruel bastard, and especially to his son. Seth didn't understand their relationship. Then there were the new pills and serums Ewan and the council had them trialing. Until the other paranormal species had outed themselves, the wolves would've taken advantage of the suppressants. Seth wasn't sure what the pack had intended, but knowing Ewan McKenzie, it'd be nothing good.

When he neared his apartment, he slowed, his approach stealthier. He'd hate to meet a wolf. Because he'd tested the suppressants on himself, they'd fail to follow his scent trail, but that didn't mean they couldn't gain a visual and track him.

The strange lethargy that had assailed him of late crept through his fingertips and into his hands. Alarmed, he put on a burst of speed and thumped through the rear door of the building. The residents seldom locked it, even though it was a secure exit. He sprinted up two flights of stairs, his pace slowing because it felt as if his blood had thickened and wasn't pumping through his veins. At his apartment door, he fumbled with his keys, grimacing with pain.

Fear slithered through him. His brain ticked over, but no plausible explanation occurred to him. His mind wasn't working at normal speed, which worried him most.

A hot shower was the only thing that helped with his lassitude and aches and pains, so he headed straight for his tiny bathroom. He flipped on the tap and stripped. Seconds later, he stepped beneath the spray.

The water temperature increased, and steam filled the tiny bathroom. Still, weariness inched over his muscles. His toes turned numb, the lack of feeling traveling snail-like up his legs and thighs and along his arms. Seth groaned and, while he could, turned off the water. He dried himself rapidly before he lost all body sensations. Then he began the torturous journey to his lounge. Dull pinpricks seared his flesh. He grunted, pushing his limbs to move.

He reached the doorway before his muscles turned to immovable blocks. Dull pain traveled up his legs, into his torso, and higher into his shoulders. Bowing his head, Seth gave in because experience had shown that once his body reached this stage, he wouldn't move again until the next day. He let his arms drop to his sides and straightened a fraction.

Too late.

He'd frozen in position, and now the weirdness would move to the next stage. A bizarre stonelike membrane crept across his skin.

His mind traveled to fanciful places, and he saw things. Weird creatures that had him doubting his sanity.

Tall mountains towered over a tiny village in a valley. The scent of pine drifted in the air, filling each breath with a delightful freshness. A creature swooped down, casting a gigantic shadow. Seth stood rooted to the spot with fear piercing his heart and curdling his belly. He tried to run, yet a powerful force fixed him in place.

Aware of the menace but unable to move even his head, he waited for what was sure death.

Then the beast landed in front of him, a sly smile twisting its great maw.

Gargoyle.

The creature was as large as a draft horse, and its gray

body held muscle and bulk. Strength. A massive chest with a stonelike appearance tapered down to a thick waist. A gray panel covered the creature's modesty while powerful thighs held him upright. Two enormous wings flickered back and forth before folding out of the way. But it was his face that snared Seth's attention. Two horns curved from above pointy ears. Harsh cheekbones and a snub nose didn't grab Seth's attention as much as the creature's beautiful violet eyes.

"Why are you gaping like a startled child?" the gargoyle asked, his rough voice echoing through Seth's mind. "Haven't you seen a gargoyle before?"

"Not this close," Seth admitted. "Where am I?"

"You are near the hall of ancestors," came the gravelly reply. "It is the place of history and dreams. Pull in your wings before you knock someone over."

"Wings? Whoa! Why am I here? How?" He backed up rapidly, his body not his own with these weird-arse wings. His balance wobbled before his knees stabilized. He was losing his rationality. That was the only explanation. His foster father had always told him he was too smart for his own good.

The gargoyle scowled, his expression ferocious. "Why are you asking these questions, you silly child?" His violet eyes flashed with impatience. Then slowly, slowly, the displeasure cleared, replaced by shock and enlightenment. "You don't know the purpose of your visit?"

"No." *What the hell?* He had stubby horns. He prodded the foreign nubs poking from his head and gulped, too nervous to check for a tail.

The gargoyle frowned again before giving a clipped nod. It was almost as if he'd communicated with someone else. "Right," he said. "I will give you a tour and explain while you remain in dream stasis."

"Thank you." Seth reached for manners because that was something he could control.

"Follow me," the gargoyle ordered.

Seth started to tell the gargoyle he couldn't move, but his limbs obeyed. He fell into step, even as he wondered if this was safe. It was a dream. Surely, no one could kill him while he was in his apartment and dreaming? Seth hesitated. Anyone could breach locked doors.

"Stop it," the gargoyle snapped. "Your random thoughts are deafening. Most disconcerting! You must listen because we have much to discuss."

Seth paid closer attention to his surroundings and where the gargoyle led him.

"My name is August. I am one of the gargoyle dream world guardians. Visitors are rare, which is why you caught me unaware. You are a chosen case, earmarked for extra help."

"The gargoyle dream world?" Perhaps Seth had spent too long with his chemical substances.

"Come along, child."

Bemused, Seth trailed the large gargoyle into what appeared to be a church. He clipped his wing on a wall and almost tripped. Flustered, he regained his balance and edged inside. No, a monastery. A peaceful green haven. Water tinkled in a fountain to his left, and unseen birds twittered in conifer trees.

Seth hastened to catch up with the powerful gargoyle, this time managing his wings better. "Why am I here? I'm a wolf."

"Patience, young one," the gargoyle chided.

Chastened, Seth followed the gargoyle through the garden and more cautiously into a library. Peace descended on him like a cloak. He'd spent many happy hours in his local library. August headed to the far end of the room and turned a corner into an L-shaped space.

Seth came to a stunned halt in front of a gargoyle statue. A stone mason must've taken months to carve the creature because the detail was impressive, as was the size. The statue towered over August, but that wasn't the strangest thing.

"What—?" Seth began.

"Shush, I must concentrate," August said.

While Seth gaped, the statue slowly changed color until the entire piece transformed from gray to lavender. Then it moved.

4

"YES, YES," AUGUST SAID. "Most intriguing. I wonder how she managed that. To ensure the child's safety. Yes, that makes sense. Those were dangerous times, and it was important to keep the son safe. But what to do?"

Seth blinked when August and the statue turned as one to study him. He pressed his lips together to keep his mouth firmly shut.

Were they discussing him? Was the statue communicating with his mind? That hypothesis made sense since August restarted his one-sided ramble. It was like listening to a string of unconscious thoughts.

"He's half-wolf. Do you think that will be a problem? A mate? No, that's impossible. He can't have discovered a mate, not with the depleted number of gargoyles in his part of the world. He lives in the southern hemisphere, and the gargoyle population is low—merely a handful when we did the last census. Oh, it was that long ago? My. Time has passed rapidly."

Seth's ears pricked, and his mind slipped to the dark-haired woman with the flashing violet eyes, whom he felt compelled to watch, to follow. The weird yearning to ensure her safety and watch over her had appeared from nowhere, almost hitting him over the head. He'd spotted her slipping through the shadows early one morning when he'd found sleeping impossible. From that moment, she'd figured large in his thoughts, and he'd turned into a sneaky stalker because of his concern for the aloof and beautiful woman.

His mate? He shook his head, bemused. Confused. No, that couldn't be. The pack elders had been adamant. Because of his weak wolf, he would never have a partner, let alone a mate.

"I see," August said. "That is indeed interesting. I will pass on your wisdom, Oracle. Yes, of course. Thank you for your counsel." August turned to Seth. "Let us retire to the lounge where we will eat, and I will impart advice."

Answers? Hell, yes, he wanted answers to his many, many questions. The first one was, what had happened to him? Why was he here? He wasn't a gargoyle.

Aware that he'd receive no information until August was ready, he followed the gray gargoyle. They strode through a series of rooms, and Seth noted the lack of furniture and the high doorways and ceilings. Was this because gargoyles were giant and, like him, less agile in confined places? Huh, yet another conundrum to add to his extensive list.

Finally, they reached what Seth thought was a lounge,

and for the first time, he spotted other gargoyles. Most glanced casually in his direction before returning to their conversations.

"Sit here," August commanded once he reached a group of four empty seats. "I will order refreshments from the kitchen."

Seth perched on the edge of a seat because of his cumbersome wings and used the waiting time to covertly study the gargoyles. Some had massive curving horns, while others sported stubby knobs above their ears. They were shades of gray with wings tucked to their backs, but each had blazing violet eyes. The gargoyles wore minimal clothing, so Seth assumed they didn't feel the cold. A shiver ran through him because it was cool in this dream world.

August approached, carrying a tray. Over his arm, he had a square of fabric, which he handed to Seth once he'd set the tray on the table. "I noticed you trembling. Drape this over your shoulders and pour yourself a hot drink while I grab your file."

August hustled away before Seth could even form questions. He had a file? The delicious scents of cinnamon and other warming spices floated from the silver jug, tempting him. He poured the red liquid into a silver goblet and sniffed, unsure of the contents.

By the time Seth placed the fabric around his shoulders and took a tentative sip, August had returned with a thick folder.

"Very unusual," August murmured after opening the file. "Lad, pour me a mulled wine, if you will."

Seth filled a goblet for August, still bewildered by his weird dream.

"You are of high blood, but your parents never formally mated. Ah! Yes, that makes sense. You are half-wolf and half-gargoyle. Your mother was a wolf, and your father was a wealthy gargoyle of the aristocracy. The families disapproved. When they discovered your mother was pregnant, they sent her away. The gargoyle's parents had their soldiers seize her one night and whisk her to another country to place her out of their son's reach. They then forced marriage on their son, although the union was unsuccessful. The gargoyle perished during the first paranormal wars, never knowing what happened to his love or their child." August tsked. "An unfortunate situation has set off an extraordinary chain of events."

"Do you have the correct records? I'm a wolf." Seth grimaced. "My shift has always been problematic, but I've managed." *Sort of.*

August picked up his goblet and took a long swallow. "Oh, that is easy to explain. Lone gargoyles seldom come into their powers early. Our experts aren't sure why, but close contact with others of your species makes magical powers surface faster." He flicked through several pages and hummed under his breath. "Ah, yes. It is as I thought. You have recently turned twenty-six. Much slower than other gargoyles, but your mixed blood explains this."

Seth thought back. He'd been busy with his experiments and tests, and his birthday had come and gone with little fanfare. Iain had given him a present, and they'd had dinner together. His best friend had presented him with a cupcake and a candle. He smiled, remembering. He wished he could discuss this with Iain. Iain would never reject him if he had gargoyle blood.

Wait. Did he believe August because this was a dream? Right? Like other scientists, he preferred to judge proven facts.

"Seth, lad."

August's tone was strangely compelling, and Seth focused on the gargoyle.

"Everything I tell you is the truth. It's here in my folder. You may think you're dreaming, but this is a gargoyle realm."

Seth nodded, but he was a scientist, and that was that. "You think I've come into my gargoyle powers?"

"Yes," August agreed.

"Then why am I befuddled? I can still shift to wolf. Do I have extra powers? Where are they?"

August spluttered as if Seth's words offended or amused him. "Lad, our system has worked since we first arrived from our home planet of Vircan."

Seth blinked. "Wait. We're aliens?"

August frowned. "Not true aliens, since Earth has been our home for thousands of years."

"I see." An overstatement. With each of August's fresh revelations, Seth felt as if he was standing on quicksand.

A buzz of arousal blasted through his body without warning, and every inch of his skin tingled. Seth gripped the arms of his chair, his gaze traveling past August to a new arrival. He did a double-take, and for long seconds, he gaped at the woman he'd stalked through the streets of

Auckland. Her violet eyes flashed fire, and she glared back at him.

The woman broke their visual connection first and stomped after a gargoyle even larger than August, given his impressive horns. He also had a tail with a pointy end, and it swished from side to side as he walked.

"Who is that woman?" Seth asked in a hushed voice.

"Hmm?" August lifted his gaze from his paperwork and frowned.

"Who is she? I've seen her in Auckland." Seth swallowed hard, his pulse fluttering. This was a weird-arse dream. "Something compelled me to follow her. Um, I've been stalking her. It's wrong, I know. I've tried to stop, but my mind goes haywire whenever I see her."

"Interesting," August said, gazing after the woman. "I wonder."

"Wonder what?" Seth asked because information was powerful and helped in a hypothesis.

"Seth, focus, please." August's tone turned sharp and authoritative. "I refuse to send my charge home without giving them my best effort."

"But—"

"No." August was firm. "Can you fly?"

"No, I can't fly!"

"Your wings look normal. We'll have a training session each time you visit."

"Um, sure." Seth watched the mystery woman hustle after her gargoyle and vanish into another room. The burst of adrenaline that had carried him faded. He slumped in his chair, and it was as if everything in his world had turned gray.

"Who is he?" Malikah asked January, her gargoyle advisor. The man was still staring at her, and heat seeped into her cheeks and crept down her neck. She scraped her hair away from her face and averted her gaze, but his appearance and features stayed front of mind.

He wasn't much taller than her, with blue eyes behind those ridiculous round-framed glasses he wore. Whoever heard of a wolf who required glasses? But he'd had wings. And nubby horns poking from his short, sandy blond hair. Since when did wolves have wings? He'd looked good in his ripped jeans, an old, faded T-shirt that hugged his upper torso, and heavy boots, and no! *Just no.*

January glanced over his shoulder and frowned. "Who?"

Malikah scowled. "The weird man who keeps following me. How can he follow me here? Only gargoyles can enter the dreamland to seek advice. Why is a wolf here?" She must've imagined the wings. She *was* tired.

"A wolf? No, you must be mistaken," January replied, leading her to an alcove overlooking the garden.

"I've spotted him at home." The wolf popped up everywhere. What if he was dangerous to her people? Her fists clenched, and fury tinged with fear assailed her, pushing away the fluster that had swamped her on recognizing him. If he threatened her small clan, she'd get rid of him. Her people, and especially the children, had been through so much. All they wanted was to integrate and enjoy a peaceful life. It was all she desired, and she intended to ensure her promises to Tamaini and the others came to fruition. Nothing left for them in Northern England, even if they could get home.

Their survival teetered on the brink, with their meager wages barely enough to support the entire group.

Worry joined her fear and blunted her rage. Her head hung, and her shoulders slumped briefly before she straightened with renewed determination.

This new home must work because they had no other options.

5

SETH CAME TO IN slow degrees. He yawned and shivered, the cold air pebbling his skin. His eyes slowly opened, and he blinked several times to adjust to the glare. His mind took seconds longer to come online, and memories of his weird dream burst over him.

He tried to stretch, and dread hit him as his muscles contracted, yet he remained immobile. Not one limb responded to his move command. His mind whirred so hard Seth worried about his sanity. His life had turned into a nightmare. Even his decision to oppose Raoul was out of character. Not that he wouldn't do it again, but yeah. He questioned his mental well-being. These fanciful dreams were intensifying.

While he struggled to move, a gravelly voice drifted through his mind. A memory or something else? Seth didn't care, and since he was stuck in position and freezing his balls off, he'd take any advice he could get.

Seth batted away his anxiety and inhaled, striving for calm. At least he could breathe. That was something. And heck! There he was, going off on a tangent again. Another sign of something wrong. Iain admired his laser-like focus. Right now, it had gone AWOL.

Seth emptied his mind before mentally pushing away the material holding him imprisoned. Material? No, stone, if the gargoyle was to be believed. He imagined his hands tugging the rock away from his limbs, his torso, leaving his human form behind.

He wriggled his fingers. It was working! As if by magic, the stone dissolved into his skin with a weird prickling sensation. Bit by bit, his gray body turned to tan skin, and finally, *finally*, he could stretch and shift position. He took a cautious step and then another before running his hands over his arms and legs. They felt normal. Looked normal. What the hell? Bruises peppered his limbs.

An urgent need to use the bathroom had him striding in that direction. Seth took care of business before hustling to the kitchen because his stomach grumbled as if he hadn't eaten for days. He wrenched open the fridge, which was empty apart from a bottle of milk. He tried a cupboard and discovered a crust of bread and a can of baked beans. That wouldn't work. Not to appease the hunger stirring his belly.

Seth took a five-minute shower, dressed, and grabbed his wallet before leaving the apartment to hunt for a cafe. At the street entrance to his apartment, he turned right toward his usual cafe, but everything about this decision screamed wrong. Seth froze, his wits returning in a rush.

The last thing he wanted was to confront pack wolves, or worse—Raoul.

Seth scrutinized his surroundings, and the rush of fear seeped away. When he stepped toward the right again, inappropriateness assailed him. With an abrupt turn, he stomped in the opposite direction. It was as if an invisible strand tugged him along. He spied a cafe—a perfectly acceptable one, but that wash of fear struck him in the gut, and he doubled over.

"This is ridiculous," Seth muttered, rubbing his belly.

He checked the street and spied a suit-wearing businessman and two ladies of the night heading to the cafe. Instead of fighting the weird compulsion to step out of his routine, he continued walking in a straight line. This happened twice more when he spotted a cafe, only to have so much dread pulse through his body that his knees trembled.

The road curled to the left, and he spotted the welcoming lights of the cafe when he rounded the corner. He half expected another panic pulse, but this time, it didn't arrive. The instant his hand curled around the handle, a tingle of expectation flooded him. *Interesting.* He wrenched the door open and strode inside, so hungry that nausea tiptoed through his belly.

He took a deep breath, savoring the delightful scents wafting out of the filled cabinet by the till—a mix of sugary sweetness, buttery richness, and cinnamon spice.

A radio played with an announcer breaking into a slow song to announce dragon sightings in the city. "Several witnesses described the creatures gliding over the harbor before disappearing to the north. Other people heard strange cries and saw people who sparkled in an otherworldly manner," the announcer said. "If you saw or heard anything peculiar in central Auckland last night, call and tell us about it."

Seth rolled his eyes, imagining the exaggerated stories to come. All sorts of conspiracies would take root.

"Crazy, huh?" A female server smiled at Seth. "Take a seat. I'll be with you shortly." She gestured toward the mostly vacant customer area. Customers sat in two of the three positions near the window, but Seth wanted to remain hidden from any loitering wolves. He bypassed the empty chairs and headed for the tables in the back. The scent of another person hit him first—a blast of flowers and minerals.

He sucked in a harsh breath, his gaze connecting and holding for long seconds.

The woman leaped to her feet. "Why are you following me?"

"I'm not." Seth focused on her, wondering what about this woman made him yearn to be near her. Her flashing violet eyes held temper, and he couldn't help but stare. She was gorgeous with the blaze of color in her cheeks, her sharp features, and regal air. Today, her skin was a golden shade, not the gray he'd seen in his dreams. Her long brown hair hung over her shoulder in a braid, and the urge to tug on it was so strong his fingers twitched. Not the right time, but maybe in the future.

"Please," he said. "I don't wish to hurt you. Please listen to my explanation. This morning, when I woke, I had no food in my apartment. I came out to get something because I was starving. When I tried to go to my regular place, a sense of fear gripped me, and it continued until I walked in this direction. The anxiety grew at each crossroads until I arrived at this cafe. I honestly didn't know you were here, and I'm sorry, but I can't explain my compulsion to follow you. My name is Seth Walsh."

She searched his face, and Seth wondered what she saw. Her intent manner made him feel as if she were dissecting his soul.

"Let me buy you breakfast," he said, pushier than usual but terrified she'd leave and ruin this chance to speak with her. She was so pretty, and her scent bewitched his wolf. He prodded Seth to step closer.

She hesitated at the mention of food, making Seth wonder if she had money. She was nursing a cup of tea, and that was all.

"Please," he repeated.

Finally, she nodded and resettled in her chair. Seth slipped into the seat opposite before she changed her mind.

The female server arrived, her order pad poised.

"Two full English breakfasts and two cinnamon rolls, please." He studied his silent companion. "Would you like more tea?"

"Yes," she said.

Seth nodded. "English breakfast tea for two, please."

"Is that all?" the server asked.

Seth glanced at the woman, and she jerked her head. "Yes, thank you." He waited for the server to step out of hearing distance. "Thank you."

"Any funny stuff, and I'll leave."

"Understood," Seth said. "What is your name?"

"Malikah."

A strained silence fell while Seth frantically wondered what to say or ask to gain information. Iain was the charming one, and he could've done with a buffer. His inner wolf considered this, and a faint growl rumbled at the idea of Iain meeting this woman. No, Iain's charisma wasn't getting anywhere near Malikah.

The server brought a fresh pot of tea, a jug of milk, and a cup for Seth.

"Would you like more tea?" he asked, surreptitiously glancing at her.

She nodded, her expression betraying her wariness. She looked as if she might bolt at the first opportunity.

Seth refreshed Malikah's tea before pouring one for himself. Now, her face appeared paler under the bright lighting. While she was tall, merely two or three inches shorter than his own six feet, she was thin. Too thin. She sat with her shoulders hunched as if she bore responsibility too heavy to carry. Large purple shadows beneath her violet eyes told of sleepless nights. If he pieced together the subtle clues, Malikah was a woman enduring a heap of stress.

Perhaps she'd lose her wariness if he shared a little of himself. Worth a shot.

Seth sucked in a huge breath and took a sip of his tea. "Until recently, I thought I was a werewolf," he said, his gaze on his cup. "My parents died when I was a child, and

I don't remember them. A childless werewolf couple took custody of me, and I consider them my parents. My best friend is a wolf, and I spend time with him when I'm not working. Our circle of friends are the children of council members, and apart from Iain, they disparage me. They consider me inferior and weak." *Too weak for an arranged marriage, let alone the honor of a mate.*

Seth felt the weight of her gaze, her interest, and he continued, pleased at catching her attention. "Growing up, I loved learning. The pack decided my intelligence might prove useful, and they paid for me to attend university, where I studied science. Once I graduated, the higher-ups put me to work in their laboratory, where I researched and followed the lead on whatever they wanted me to invent.

"About a month ago, I started having weird dreams about flying. Gargoyle-related stuff. Although I can shift to a wolf, my shift is always troublesome."

"Last night was real," she murmured.

His brows lifted, amazement and shock swamping him. *Huh!* His brain tried to make sense of what he'd been told, slotting facts into order. "Well, August tells me I am only half wolf, and the rest is gargoyle."

"How could you not understand your heritage?" she blurted.

Seth's lips twisted. "An excellent question. August tells me I'm the product of an illicit affair. It's a lot to process."

The server arrived with their meals, and Seth bit back a smile when he heard Malikah's stomach grumble. When she hesitated and stared at the laden plate of eggs, bacon, mushrooms, sausage, and toast, he said, "Eat. Don't let your breakfast go cold."

Malikah fell upon her meal, shoveling food into her mouth. She kept sending him darting glances. Did she suspect he'd snatch away the plate? Bemused, he stifled his curiosity and applied himself to his meal. It was standard cafe fare but beautifully cooked and presented. Seth took his time, savoring the crisp bacon and the fried eggs. The homemade hash brown tickled his taste buds, and a dollop of spicy English brown sauce made it perfect. While he ate, he observed her. She continued to eat but took more care now, savoring each mouthful.

"Why are you up so early?" he asked.

"Job hunting," she said. "I'm asking cafe owners about vacancies."

"Any luck?"

Her shoulders curled inward before she straightened to hide her disappointment. "No, but they gave me a cup of tea."

"How many have you tried this morning?"

"Five. No, six," she said.

"What do you do? Cook, server, or something else?"

"I'm willing to try anything. I need a job." Desperation rang in her voice as she pushed her last cube of toast through a puddle of egg yolk. She lifted it to her mouth, averting her gaze from him. She chewed and swallowed.

"Why aren't you with the gargoyle clan? They'd give you shelter while you get a job."

She swallowed hard. "It's not just me. It's the rest of... Never mind."

The cinnamon buns snagged her attention. Seth reached for the plate and shunted it closer.

"Eat," he urged.

"No, I can't. Not when the others go hungry." Her head jerked up, and her gaze flitted over him while color pooled in her cheeks.

"How many of you are there?" he asked, his voice insistent.

"Fifteen," she said. "Eight adults, and the rest are children."

Seth schooled his features because he sensed she'd bolt if he asked too many questions. When the waitress neared, he waved her over. "Do you have fifteen cinnamon buns we can purchase to take with us?" he asked.

"We do," she said, her smile bright.

"Could you put them aside and add them to my bill?"

"I'll do that straight away," she promised and hustled away.

"You can't do that," Malikah snapped. "You can't buy me cinnamon buns."

"I just did." Even though Seth had to watch his money, he didn't regret his offer. Malikah had wolfed down her food. He'd lay odds her people were making do, too, given Malikah's desperation to secure a job. He couldn't help with employment, but he could purchase the buns.

"Eat your bun." He plucked one off the plate and took a bite. The cinnamon spice filled his nostrils while sweetness danced across his tongue. "They're delicious."

She grabbed the bun and tore into it, her eyes closed while she savored the buttery goodness and sticky frosting.

Seth opened his mouth to tease her before halting the impulse. He topped his cup with tea and did the same with hers, content to watch her for now.

She ate the bun in record time and washed it down with sweetened tea. The high color remained in her cheeks, and the angle of her chin told him of her pride. No explanations were forthcoming. It didn't matter.

He'd get his answers, eventually.

Heat filled Malikah's cheeks. Embarrassment mostly, but ruffled pride inched in there. This wolf-man confused her. Half wolf-man. He must be telling the truth because he couldn't enter the sanctuary and receive an exceptional mentor if he wasn't a gargoyle.

But why had he been following her for the last few weeks?

Maybe she should ask.

"Why have you been following me?"

He frowned, and the light reflected off his lenses. "I don't know." He sounded frustrated and out of sorts, vulnerability flashing in his blue eyes. "I've scared you, but it's a compulsion. I need to make sure you're safe. If I didn't know better..." He pressed his lips together.

"Is that why you're feeding me?" The idea stung. She wasn't a charity case.

"No! I wanted to spend time with you." He shrugged, confusion dashing across his features. "This stalking thing is freaking me out. I truly mean you no harm, but something is compelling me to watch you. Watch over you."

"Well, if you're buying me breakfast, I guess it's not that bad. Although I'm not some delicate flower. I can look out for myself." If she didn't count her stupid misstep with Alfred. His betrayal still nagged like an aching limb. But she'd taken charge and tried to help her gargoyles. She sighed and wished she could find a job.

"August told me few gargoyles receive guardians," Seth said.

"Yes, it's a gargoyle tradition started by the council hundreds of years ago. The council helps gargoyles who lack support and require aid with their new powers."

Seth's eyes narrowed. "What new powers?"

Malikah froze, wondering if he was joking. Every gargoyle gained an extra talent or power on maturing—in her case two, but she was an exception. The longer she stared, the easier it was to discern his confusion.

"You don't know," she said finally.

6

"No." SETH TRIED NOT to scowl with frustration. "My knowledge of gargoyle history is minimal. Until last week, I thought I was a wolf." *A weak one.* Now, he was facing the same condemnation from the gargoyles.

He couldn't win, no matter what he did.

"After my recent birthday, I can blend with the background. My camouflage makes me almost invisible to the casual glance. If I wanted to go over to the dark side, I'd make a brilliant criminal," Malikah joked.

Seth scowled because he didn't feel different apart from his weird dreams. "Does every gargoyle have this extra gift?"

"Yes."

Figured. He was out of step. *Again.* "What other talents might a gargoyle receive?"

"Exceptional hearing, the gift of sight and forewarning of future events. Dream walking. Invisibility like me. An extraordinary singing voice. The talents are many and varied."

"So gargoyles always develop a talent once they come of age? In every case."

"That's correct."

"Huh."

"Didn't your guardian describe the extent of your talent and its limitations?"

"I was busy asking questions about other things. You forget this was a shock. I grew up thinking I was a wolf, remember?" *Trying to fly and failing.*

Malikah shrugged. "Ask your guardian."

"How do I contact August?"

Malikah gaped this time. "Don't you know anything?"

"I wouldn't have asked if I had the answer," Seth said, trying to keep the snap from his voice.

"A gargoyle coming into their powers has twelve visits before they graduate. After that, you get an annual visit if necessary."

"How do the guardians know you need them?"

"They just do. I—" Malikah stood abruptly. "I must go. Thank you for breakfast."

"Will I see you again?"

Malikah ignored the question, her entire demeanor full of anxiety as she fled.

"Don't forget the cinnamon buns," he called.

She hesitated before diverting toward the counter. The server handed over a large white box, and Seth caught Malikah's smile of pleasure. Seconds later, she was out the door. He caught his breath and waited for the loss that always struck when he'd forced himself to stop following her.

Yes, it was there, but the edges weren't as sharp. *Interesting.*

Seth finished his tea and proceeded to the counter to pay. He handed over a hundred-dollar note and received little change. He'd need to risk withdrawing more cash. Manageable if he used a bank machine far from his temporary apartment.

He wanted to speak with Iain and discuss everything. His gargoyle blood. He wished he'd had these questions when his parents were alive. Now, he only had Malikah and August to help him.

Seth clenched his jaw. He knew what Iain's father had done, the abuse he'd heaped on his son without remorse. It was part of why Seth had done a midnight flit from the pack and taken measures to prevent others from replicating his chemical formulas. He'd stashed his important research in a safe place without pack ties.

"Thanks," he said to the server and tossed his change in the tip jar. He left the cafe and continued walking away from his apartment. Exhaustion tugged at him, but he'd withdraw more cash and try calling Iain. At least then, he'd know precisely how much trouble he was in with the pack.

MALIKAH HURRIED TO THE rundown warehouse where she and her people had taken refuge. She slipped through the gap in the wire fence and, after checking for observers, entered the largest of the wooden buildings.

"Flint?" Malikah paused, letting her appearance shift to partial gargoyle, her skin morphing to gray. "Flint?"

"Here." Flint stepped from the shadows, black hair scraped back in a man-bun and worry pushing wrinkles into his gray forehead.

"What's wrong?"

"Onyx and Amai are sick."

"Worse than last night?" Malikah asked, concerned. Had treating them with juvenile painkillers been right? Should she have done more?

"Yes," Flint said.

"I'll check on them." She handed over the box of cinnamon buns. "Something to eat," she said. "I'll let you give them out."

Flint lifted the lid and sniffed. His expression brightened. "Food."

Malikah headed to the smaller room on the first floor, where the younger gargoyles slept. Silver and Aurelio, orphans, stood frozen in their gargoyle forms, their color no longer gray but a pale yellow. Clay was also losing his gray coloration, but his skin didn't resemble the yellow of a human's healing bruise. Malikah smoothed her hand over his rock-solid shoulder, biting her lip at his lack of response. It wasn't as if she could take them to a medical practitioner, even if she could pay.

Her most obvious option was to ask Sam for advice. Her breath hissed through her teeth as she considered the ramifications. The cost to her. Foreboding rippled through her and landed like a heavy rock in her stomach.

She sighed because approaching Sam and groveling was her last preference. He'd expect a return for favors. He'd made no secret of wanting her in his bed. Malikah recalled how he'd ogled her and the appreciative glint in his eyes. The gargoyle had a partner of long-standing, but Malikah had heard rumors of his philandering. Heck, she had firsthand knowledge.

With a soft groan, she ran a hand over Onyx's and then Amai's heads. Neither child moved, and claws of worry scratched at her confidence. She prayed their bodies would fight to keep them alive. In the meantime, she'd humble herself and ask for help.

Malikah retraced her steps to their gathering space. She found the adults and other children enjoying tea and a cinnamon bun.

"Where did you get these?" Talon asked, his words muffled by a mouthful. He swallowed. "They're delicious."

"I know," Malikah said. "I met a friend while I was job hunting. He bought me breakfast, and when I enjoyed the bun, he purchased one for each of us."

"You didn't tell us you had a friend," Cameo, Tamaini's daughter, said, her eyes narrowing in nosy interest.

Malikah almost groaned aloud at Cameo's tone. She did *not* wish to discuss her confusing ah...relationship, friendship, or whatever it was with her wolf stalker. But she had to say something. "I met him at the gargoyle sanctuary last night, or at least I saw him with his guardian."

Cameo beamed, diverted by the mention of the

sanctuary. "You didn't say anything about your nocturnal wandering when we spoke this morning. Who is your guardian?"

"January," Malikah said.

"*Ohhh,*" Cameo cooed, her eyes bright with excitement in her gray face. "I've heard he is excellent and doesn't take on novices. That's a coup for our group."

"Yes," Malikah said, in an understatement. January had been her guardian since she was sixteen and came into her second power. He was always encouraging and told her she had excellent instincts. Her gut told her to ignore the other gargoyle group and seek help elsewhere. Seth popped to mind, and she immediately shook her head, nonplussed by the...the...

Oh, curses. She was going to admit it—at least to herself. Seth was an attractive man, even if he was strange. He'd treated her with kindness this morning, and his confusion as he'd tried to explain why he was following her had been apparent. She no longer thought him dangerous. Merely a little peculiar.

Shouts and cheers exploded outside, carrying on the stiff breeze. Malikah stilled, her gaze going to the other adults in the room. One youngster tugged her hand.

"Joyful noise. Scared noise," Aeryn said.

"Yes," Malikah agreed, curious about the uproar. "Let me fly to the lookout point to investigate. I'll be back in a minute."

Malikah shifted fully before unfurling her wings and shooting upward. At the last minute, she darted through a hole in the roof. She flew low across the rooftops, employing her camouflage to help her blend with the tiles. She landed on the tallest building in the vicinity, and her eyes widened.

A pack of wolves loitered on the street below, confused and uneasy. A dragon carrying a passenger landed, with two more dragons settling beside the first. Several of Sam's gargoyle warriors followed. Malikah gasped softly because none paid attention to the gawking audience.

And the place swarmed with humans.

They had their phones out, filming the entire spectacle. She wanted to hear what was happening but played safe until she understood the situation. With that in mind, she arrowed back to their temporary home, taking the same route.

"What is it? What's happening?" Cameo asked.

"I'm not sure. We need to listen to the news," Malikah said. "There are three dragons, several of Sam's gargoyles, and an enormous pack of wolves wandering the street in broad daylight. The humans are filming everything, yet the wolves, dragons, and gargoyles don't care."

"Interesting," Jasper, Cameo's mate, said. "I've heard rumblings the paranormal species want to make themselves known to humans. Last night, I saw several fae not bothering to employ a glamor to conceal their identities."

"Do you think the paranormal folk have taken action?" Cameo asked, reaching for Jasper's hand and reassurance. "What will we do?"

"We need information," Malikah said. "Where is Rosslyn?"

"She is teaching the older children," Jasper said.

"I'll let her know what's happening. Were you and Cameo going job hunting?"

"Yes," Jasper said.

"Keep your ears open. I'll learn as much as I can, and between the three of us, we'll understand the situation," Malikah said. "Stay safe."

"This is exciting." Cameo tucked her arm through Jasper's. "Let's go right now."

Malikah wasn't so sure. She preferred nice orderly plans and a schedule of events. This was not that, and the circumstances made her itchy. Jasper and Cameo left while she spoke to Rosslyn about watching the children. Since this was the standard plan, Rosslyn merely nodded and continued teaching. Rosslyn's presence with the children gave Malikah peace of mind.

Outside the giant warehouse, electric energy floated in the atmosphere. The sidewalks teamed with pedestrians. Malikah—in her human guise—passed dozens of animated, chattering, and gawking humans. Eagerness charged the air, and conversations drifted to her—people discussing events. Some were worried. Scared. Others were enthusiastic about facing a being normally confined to book pages or movies.

"I knew authors weren't making up everything in their books," a young woman said, her hands waving and expression sparkling. "They use too much detail. I reckon some of those werewolves must be writers."

The woman's friend, walking at her side, rolled her eyes.

"Did you see that dragon?" a beefy young man

demanded of his equally muscular friends. "Did you see how that guy calmly climbed on its back and flew away? So cool. Man, I wish I could take a dragon ride."

Malikah snorted softly, not wanting to spoil his dreams. Dragons seldom gave rides to others. They had to be related, which begged the question: Why were dragons and wolves playing nice together?

Malikah marched along Queen Street, the major thoroughfare, and spotted several fae. She drew a sharp breath, shock hitting her with a one-two punch. They weren't even trying to hide their otherness.

Her steps slowed, her gaze bewildered. Two fae women skipped along the street in gowns made of leaves, their wings fluttering. They paid no attention to the humans, more interested in their conversation. The humans, however, openly pointed and stared. They whispered and gaped.

Something weighty thumped overhead, and she started. The harsh bark of laughter at her expense grated on her nerves, and she forced herself to take three deep, even breaths to compose herself.

"Malikah." Sam spread his wings and glided down to street level, ignoring the startled squeaks from a family of four attempting to cross the road. They scattered, the father ushering his wife and two daughters into the nearest store.

"What do you want, Sam?" Malikah asked, careful to keep her emotions concealed.

This gargoyle was a bully, even if he did a fantastic job of keeping his colony safe. Just because he wanted to boast of a royal connection, it didn't mean he could corral her into accepting his protection. Everything he gave or offered her came with strings. Besides, no way did she want to upset his mate. According to gossip, even Sam respected her temper.

"Did you hear the announcement from the leaders of the paranormal species? I've come from the initial outing to the press. The reporter has scheduled interviews with the leaders over the coming week."

For once, Sam wasn't trying to hassle her or flirt. She needed to take advantage of his eagerness to chat, but she had to take care with framing her questions.

"All the leaders came out to humans simultaneously?" She'd heard the wolves had objected.

"Yes, we discussed it at our meeting last month. We made an official announcement once news of the wolves and the dragons' appearance in Downtown reached our leaders. After all, the wolves shifted and showed themselves to humans first. They can hardly complain."

"True."

"Are you still living in the deserted warehouse near the harbor?"

Malikah's chin lifted, but she forced back her snappish retort. He knew she was, but she needed his help, so she held back her instinctive reaction. "Sam, I wondered if I could speak to your medic. Several of my group—children—are sick. I'm worried."

"What's wrong with them?" Sam asked.

"They've gone into stasis, and their skin has changed from gray to a pale, creamy yellow."

Sam took a giant step backward.

"I'm not sick," she said. "Neither are the others. It's the children who are poorly."

"Any other symptoms?" He'd stepped firmly into his authoritative leader's shoes instead of the usual Lothario guise he showed with her.

Malikah told him, her stomach churning because his expression didn't bode well. He intended to reject her request.

He drew up but allowed his giant wings to flutter and displace the air at his back. "I can't take the risk that whatever your youngsters have will infect my people. You could speak to our medic via phone." He pulled out his wallet and handed her a business card. "Call him. I'm sorry, but that's the best I can do."

Malikah swallowed hard, disappointment wafting from her even as she tore her gaze off the thick wad of money in his wallet. "We don't have a phone," she said, attempting to shove aside her money envy. The children could have clothes to blend and food in their bellies. They could find somewhere better to live.

Sam barked out a laugh. "No phone? For someone of royal blood, you're doing a poor job of caring for your people." A tiny half-smile played on his lips.

A chill crept through her, and if she'd been in her gargoyle form, she'd have bared her teeth and hissed to show her contempt.

"Accept me as your lover. I can buy you a phone and give you money in return."

He wanted her as his bit on the side. *Never*. The gargoyle

would never dare to make this disgusting suggestion in the past. Every part of her wanted to snap and snarl, but she pressed her lips together and shook her head.

Once positive she'd gained control of her temper, she said. "No, thank you."

Sam shrugged his big shoulders. "Your loss." He pushed off the ground with an easy show of strength, not fazed by the ohs and ahs from the surrounding humans. His giant wings caught the air, and mere seconds later, he'd vanished.

"Well," she muttered. "Mission accomplished." She spun to retrace her footsteps before continuing to search for a job. They needed the money.

7

BEMUSED, SETH FOUND HIMSELF in the gargoyle world again. He remembered returning to his apartment, unlocking the door, and doing his usual sweep for signs of an intruder. Thankfully, there were none, although he'd glimpsed several wolves who worked security. They'd been scanning faces, and he'd had to circle to get to his shelter. Yeah, he recalled skulking along alleyways.

He'd switched on the portable TV, slapping it on the side to get a decent picture. The breaking news had been enough to startle away his troubles. A news reader reported wolves wandering downtown streets and three dragons appearing from the other side of the harbor.

The report didn't make sense. The council would never allow fraternization, and wolves and dragons avoided each other. The pills he'd developed to mask scent and tested at the nightclub were a sign the council approved only clandestine interaction. It was the push he needed to leave.

Neither he nor Iain had understood the reasoning behind the drug. Their questions had gone unanswered, raising their suspicions. At some stage, he'd blacked out again—thankfully inside his apartment.

"Ah, there you are." August approached. His craggy, weathered features held satisfaction, and he beamed at Seth. "We have much to cover, including another flying lesson. Come, I have prepared a meal and an accumulation of knowledge you must learn to live a long life."

Seth fell into step with August. "May I ask a question?"

"That is what I am here for—to answer questions, my lad."

"I met Malikah yesterday. January's charge," Seth explained when August looked blank.

"Yes?" August said, turning it into a question. His vast wings stirred before tucking neatly into his back.

"Before I spoke with Malikah, I met her in Auckland, where we live. I was stalking her."

August started, his violet eyes narrowing in consternation. "You meant her harm? She is of royal blood."

"Wait. What?" Seth gaped at the large gargoyle.

August's mouth opened wide enough to display sharp teeth while his eyes glowed. Seth took half a step back, alarm seeping into him.

"Did you intend to harm Malikah?" August thundered.

Other gargoyles wandering past halted to stare at August and Seth.

Seth backed up, his hands raised in surrender. "No! This is what I'm trying to explain. I encountered her scent before I knew I was a gargoyle or Malikah was one. She smelled of herbs and the wild freshness of the forest. The instant I caught her trail, everything in me pulled tight, and it was imperative to meet the scent's owner. I discovered Malikah and started following her. No matter how I tried to stop, I couldn't. Malikah fascinated me. She drew me. Yesterday, I wanted breakfast. My favorite cafe is nearby, but a persistent impulse led me to a different one, far from my apartment. I bought her breakfast. We talked, but my compulsion to see her disturbs me. I hate to act like a creeper and scare her."

Seth risked a glance at August. His mentor's breath hissed out, and the tension tightening his broad shoulders receded. He pushed open a door and gestured for Seth to enter.

"Take a seat."

Seth sat in the cluster of chairs, his heart still pounding at August's fury. He hadn't meant to anger him, but he required knowledge.

August claimed a seat and clicked his fingers. A few minutes of silence passed while Seth wondered if he'd erred and what to do next. He opened his mouth to speak several times before leaning back in his chair to enjoy the warmth of the sunshine coming through the window.

A young male gargoyle arrived, carrying a tray of steaming drinks and food. He poured goblets of what smelled like mulled wine and departed.

August picked up his drink with a loud sigh. He took a sip, clearly in thinking mode. "This need to find Malikah, to be in her company, reminds me of something I have read from our gargoyle pasts. You differ from other gargoyles because you're half-wolf. Right now, your two halves are confused about which should take precedence."

Seth pulled a face. "That doesn't sound encouraging."

"In the past, wolves mated for life. Is this correct?"

"Arranged marriages are common in our pack, but the rare wolves who find a mate stay together for life. There is no divorce in the wolf world. Death will end a marriage. The survivor is then free to take another partner if inclined."

August scratched his chin, his eyes going unfocused. "Back in history, gargoyles and wolves had fated mates—the one being who was perfect for them. If they didn't find their one, they remained single. In modern times, this necessity disappeared or grew out of favor. Individuals marry whomever they wish. Yes, very interesting indeed because the oracle mentioned mates. He told me, but I dismissed his words. You are such an interesting case that I got distracted." He beamed. "I believe Malikah might be your destined mate. I must consult with the other guardians, but this answer makes the most sense. You tell me you don't wish to hurt her but answer me this. Do you have romantic feelings for her?" When August watched him this time, his eyes gleamed with humor.

Seth gawked, shock making him speechless. Was he interested in the sharp-tongued, bristly gargoyle woman? If he were honest, he'd have to say yes. He'd enjoyed seeing her eat the food he'd purchased this morning. She was too thin, and it had pleased him to provide for her. His impulse to buy her cinnamon buns had given him intense satisfaction. Witnessing her startled pleasure had brought joy. She hadn't treated him with her usual disdain. She'd smiled, and this softening of her attitude had pleased him greatly.

August prodded Seth with a sharp claw, almost shunting Seth off his chair. "What brought that smile to your face? Were you thinking about Malikah?"

"Yes," Seth said simply. "She is often in my mind, especially since we've spoken. I want to help her, look after her, and make her smile. Care for her as much as she lets me."

August nodded. "That sounds like the actions of a fated mate. This is intriguing. I shall seek an audience with January and learn all I can. If you're mates, it makes sense for me to work in tandem with January."

"Can Malikah be my mate, but I not be hers?"

August pursed his lips. "No, I believe nature makes the attraction mutual to prevent chaos."

Seth nodded, unsure he understood. "Malikah hasn't mentioned how she feels about me." She was prickly and arrogant, but strangely, he found that attractive.

"Malikah cares for her surviving people and struggles to keep them safe. Maybe she hasn't noted the signs because she is under stress."

"Can you tell me more?" Seth asked.

"It is not for me to tell tales. You must earn Malikah's trust and get her to tell you her history. Would you like me to inform Malikah of your parentage and your other private business?"

Seth took his point. His life comprised many secrets, some of which might get him killed or place Malikah and her people in danger. That was the last thing he wanted. He sought Malikah's trust, which meant he needed to advance their friendship at a pace that suited her.

"Enough about your relationships," August said in a mock-stern tone. "We will use the next hour to cram your head full of gargoyle history and facts to help you thrive and survive in this modern world then we'll go flying." His mouth twitched with amusement. "Or crashing, in your case."

Seth sipped his fragrant wine and paid attention.

He felt a new confidence. He'd liked Malikah on sight, and his initial attraction had grown after this morning. The idea of them belonging together thrilled him.

Now, he needed to persuade Malikah to take a chance on him.

ANOTHER CHILD HAD FALLEN ill, the natural blue-gray of his skin bleaching away to a concerning paleness.

"What have they eaten?" she asked without taking her gaze off the yellow-tinged face and bared fangs. Judging by the contorted expression, the kid had gone into stasis while experiencing significant pain.

"Nothing the rest of us didn't eat." Rosslyn paced back and forth before halting in front of Malikah. "I made vegetable soup, and we had toast on the side. Two gargoyle women from Sam's colony visited and brought a caramel slice, and we had that with a cup of tea. The children drank fresh milk after the soup. Everyone ate the same food."

Malikah frowned. "Is it likely the children picked up something and ingested it? Something they shouldn't have?"

"No," Rosslyn replied. "Ever since the first two fell ill, we've supervised the children closely. Everyone has eaten the same food." Rosslyn's brow puckered, and she gave the old warehouse interior a disparaging look. "It could be something lingering on the walls and surfaces. The interior is not what we are used to."

Malikah stiffened. Luckily, her brain engaged before she fired resentment at Rosslyn. Dammit, she was doing her best. She'd finally scored a job and started next week. They had accommodation away from the elements and curious humans. It wasn't the castle luxury or the tidy cottages they'd had in Northern England. The sturdy walls of their homes hadn't kept out the Stonehurst clan, who'd barged in and destroyed everything.

Pain at the memories clenched her chest tight and blunted her irritation. None of this was her fault, despite Tamaini's assertions. Even as these thoughts crystalized, the ever-present guilt pierced her with the accuracy of a champion archer. If she'd followed her parents' orders and accepted one of the many marriages they'd proposed, the situation might've turned out differently. If she'd used her special power, but no. January had told her she'd done the right thing, but maybe she should've—

Malikah swallowed hard and pushed away her remorse. It was more important to discover what was ailing the children and the cure.

Rosslyn resumed her pacing, her ponytail bobbing until Malikah snapped. "Enough! Go for a walk outside or seek the company of other adults. I need to think."

Rosslyn froze, her shoulders tensing in affront. She sucked in a sharp breath and glared daggers. Malikah's lips twisted, her breath catching as she wondered if Rosslyn might forget herself and attack.

Their gazes met, Rosslyn's challenging. It hurt that the adult gargoyles blamed her. Everything inside her compressed tight, and her eyes stung. Malikah swallowed but didn't break their visual connection. It was Rosslyn who backed down first. She whirled and stomped out of the children's room, and only then did Malikah let her head hang and grief come to the fore. She'd honestly tried her best. Not enough when the children were falling sick.

The hovering tears forced their way to freedom. Her sight blurred, and one rolled down her cheek. It hurt to breathe, and the urge to scream her frustration, her pain, her sorrow had her balling her fists. She couldn't show any emotion except confidence. She couldn't show her doubts or insecurities. Her vulnerability. Instead, she'd shelve every tender sentiment and offer the strength that the gargoyle kings and queens had always displayed.

Her ancestors.

Their strength flowed through her veins, and now, she needed to draw on their resilience, their courage and channel it as her own.

Malikah stroked the child's head. Although she hadn't succeeded in mental contact with the gargoyle youngsters, she hoped they heard her encouragement.

"I will help you," she promised before leaving the nursery.

Voices came from her right, but she didn't seek company. Rosslyn would've reported her version of their head-butting, and Malikah wouldn't receive a warm welcome. Her mind slid to the wolf, and instinctively, she knew he'd listen without judgment.

Despite his weirdness, he'd shown kindness this morning by buying her breakfast. She ignored the part of her that leaped with eagerness to see him again. Malikah was almost out the door when Tamaini hailed her.

"Your majesty!" she called.

Malikah hid her grimace and turned to Tamaini with a forced smile. It felt stiff at the edges, but it was the best she could dredge up, considering her emotional storm. She glimpsed Rosslyn, Cameo, and Flint in the kitchen area. "I'm going out for a walk."

"We were listening to the radio. The other paranormal species have come out to humans. The news is all over the internet. A human broke the story, and from tomorrow, she is publishing interviews with each group."

Shock washed over Malikah. Sam had informed her of this earlier, but the reality of coming out had seemed farfetched. She'd known many paranormal groups wanted this, and perhaps it had been inevitable after the wolf and dragon showdown. Hiding was ingrained in all of them.

"That will make our lives interesting," Malikah said in a light voice. "I might go for a flight tonight and check out the situation. Keep me posted if you hear anything interesting. I'll make sure I'm still in communicable range."

Tamaini nodded, her bearing stiff and guarded. She dipped a curtsy, brief, and somehow insolent. "Your majesty."

"Tamaini, you don't have to curtsy or use my title."

Tamaini said nothing, her sullen sneer making her attitude clear.

Malikah forced a smile. "I'll see you later."

Cameo appeared behind her mother, her gray face ashen and her blonde hair a wild tangle of curls. "Do you think your guardian might have advice on how to cure the sick children?" Worry emanated from her because her son was one of the inflicted.

"I have asked. He didn't recognize the symptoms. My... I'm too agitated to go to stasis and thought a flight might relax me."

Cameo's face crumpled, and she sniffed, a hairsbreadth from weeping. "Please, help us."

Malikah's breath hitched as an invisible arrow of guilt struck her heart again. Her youthful age and lack of experience were showing. Her parents would've known what to do.

Tamaini was still watching her, her expression vaguely taunting now, and for the life of her, Malikah couldn't push a word past the knot in her throat. She managed a clipped nod before she strode for the door.

Those wretched tears stung her eyes again as she hustled, walking fast to escape the guilt and frustration that refused to release her.

8

MALIKAH HEADED STRAIGHT FOR her secret place where she relaxed in privacy. Right now, she craved physical exercise. She'd speed through the city and soar until her limbs whimpered. Then she might rest.

She padded across the flat roof of an office building, savoring the scent of fresh bread and coffee rising from the cafe below. The day had been dull, the clouds sullen with threatening rain, and now, late in the afternoon with low light, it was safe enough for her to fly. Once she perched on the roof's edge, she let her body morph into her true form, which was bulkier and a deeper gray with undertones of blue. Her arching horns became prominent, and she grew a tail.

The change slid over her slowly, giving her the luxury of enjoying the emerging differences. Her increased senses. Her greater strength. The awareness of her surroundings, and sweetest of all, the caress of fresh sea air brushing her skin.

As she stared out over the forest of city buildings to the sparkling waters of the harbor, she noted she wasn't the only paranormal enjoying the new freedom.

A thunder of black dragons flew near Rangitoto Island, the dormant volcano that crouched in Auckland harbor. The howl of a wolf carried on the flirtatious breeze, and on the streets below, several pedestrians bore fluttering wings. Their exuberant laughter floated after them.

At least humans weren't running around with guns, trying to shoot those with differences. *Yet.* Cynically, she thought that kind of outlawed behavior would come. *Different* spooked people. So far, the government had come out saying that nothing had changed. The laws of New Zealand bound every citizen in the same way they'd always done. There'd be problems ahead, but she had enough to deal with.

A dark shadow—no, two shadows in her peripheral had her jerking upward and whirling to scan her surroundings. She relaxed on recognizing the newcomers. It was Sam's wife, Esmerelda, and one of her friends, whose real name Malikah didn't recall since everyone called the gargoyle Fluffy.

"Hello." Esmerelda followed her greeting with a friendly wave.

Sam Ironwing's wife was a statuesque beauty, and her elegant gargoyle form mesmerizing with its midnight-blue skin and black-blue hair. Even more unusual were her intricate shoulder tattoos that reminded Malikah of swirling constellations. Fluffy's sleek form and long, midnight-black hair were equally beautiful. Malikah sighed, feeling like a plain Jane in their presence. It made Sam's persistent flirting and his propositions even more disconcerting and confusing.

Malikah waited a heartbeat longer for her ruffled composure to settle before she greeted the pair. "Esmerelda. Fluffy. Are you taking advantage of the weather to enjoy a daytime shift the same as me?"

"Yes," Fluffy chirped. Her chunky tail flicked from side to side. Her luxurious lashes fluttered, and a broad smile stretched her stony face.

She reminded Malikah of a cheerleader. In her human form, she was just as perky.

"I'm glad we spotted you," Esmerelda said. "Sam mentioned some of your children are sick. I'm so sorry to hear this. I had intended to invite you to the manor for the weekend. We're having a party to celebrate our new freedoms." Her bright smile slipped. "But I hate the idea of your colony passing on bugs. The young don't have the same immunity to disease as adults."

Malikah gave a nonchalant shrug. If she were the one issuing the invitations, she'd also act on the side of caution. "Don't be silly," she said, keeping her tone light despite her gargoyle's gravelly voice. "I understand. Perhaps we can visit once the children recover."

"Oh, thank you." Esmerelda's smile grew broad enough to show her sharp teeth. "Sam didn't think you'd understand, but I told him you were a thoughtful woman who'd hate to cause a super spreader event." Her throaty laugh rang out. "Sorry. I couldn't help myself. Those words have been banging around my brain since the last variant of COVID-19 came through the human community in Auckland. I know your young ones don't have COVID since paranormal folk can't catch it."

Malikah bit her tongue, guarding her snappish reply since Esmerelda had rubbed her stone feathers the wrong way. The woman wasn't usually this tactless, but she spoke nothing but the truth. She'd also extended the hand of friendship from their first meeting. She didn't mean anything by her remarks.

"I feel bad about rescinding my party invitation. Let me make it up to you in a small way," Esmerelda said. "I'll drop off food baskets and ask our cooks to add several portions of healing broth." Esmerelda leaned closer and gripped Malikah's forearm. "Let me do this small thing for you. I truly pray your young ones recover soon. It's no fun being sick."

"Thank you," Malikah said. "We'd appreciate the treats."

"It's no problem," Esmerelda trilled. "Well, we'll let you continue on your way. Fluffy and I are taking a flight of the city. I hope we come across humans."

Fluffy pouted. "It's so cold out that most of them have scurried indoors, but I'd love to hear a scream or two."

"It's lovely to see you," Malikah said, biting back her instinctive disapproval. "I must go. I'm meeting with a friend."

"A boyfriend?" Fluffy asked.

"No, just a friend," Malikah said, although truthfully, she didn't know what to do about Seth.

Esmerelda's gaze stripped Malikah bare, intense for an instant before she tossed a bright smile in Malikah's direction. "Fluffy and I will drop off a few treats tomorrow afternoon."

"If I'm not there, Cameo and Tamaini should be," Malikah said. "Thanks again."

"You're welcome. Let's do this," Esmerelda shrieked and, with a burst of laughter, pushed off the roof. Fluffy whooped and charged after her friend. Their high spirits followed them, and Malikah couldn't help smiling. She liked Esmerelda more than Sam. Sam made her uncomfortable, and she sensed he chased her because of her royal status.

She could've told him her bloodlines didn't place food on the table.

Aware she was losing the last light, she centered herself and propelled her body upward. Her wings automatically flapped, and she arrowed through the air. Four strong wingbeats took her over the water, and she enjoyed the rush of power that roared through her. When she glanced down at her hands, she noted her body had automatically shifted to blend with the blue sky. Anyone from below her would have difficulty making out her form.

"Malikah?"

Everything in Malikah froze instantly, and she dropped several feet before remembering to flap her wings and soar with the air currents. Once she'd stabilized her flight, she cautiously reached out with a mental reply. *"Seth?"*

"Wow," he said. *"I can hear you as if we're in the same room."*

"This shouldn't be possible," she murmured in shock. *"How are you doing this?"*

"I don't know," Seth said, sounding bemused. *"I was thinking about you, felt a sense of worry and instinct had me calling for you in my mind."*

"This must be your gift," Malikah said, intrigued.

"But you must have the same gift since you're speaking with me," Seth said.

"No, my power is camouflage," Malikah said. *"With you, I guess anyone you initiate a conversation with can reply. The communication is all you. Didn't your guardian inform you of special gifts?"*

"He did, but he wasn't certain I would receive one because of my wolf blood. What are you doing right now?"

"Flying over the harbor," she said. *"I thought I'd take advantage of the dull afternoon. Bright light and gargoyles do not go well together."*

"I wish I could fly with you," Seth said, and she heard the longing in his voice.

A punch of shock slowed her wingbeats and sent her body on an abrupt downward trajectory. She hurriedly righted her flight path. *"Have you tried?"*

"Yes. My attempts have been abysmal." His chuckle filled her mind. *"I take off and panic because I forget what to do. What goes up must come down, right?"*

"I could go flying with you." She hesitated. *"But I shouldn't. Another of the children has become ill. I should go home after I speak with Sam."*

"Who is Sam? Wait, you told me earlier. He's the leader of the Auckland group of gargoyles."

"*Yes.*" Malikah angled her wings and headed toward the office block where Sam conducted workday business. "*I asked if his colony doctor could visit the children. They've gone into stasis, and January couldn't offer me advice. He hasn't seen anyone with the symptoms I've described.*" She paused. "*I'm worried, and my people are blaming me.*"

"*Why?*" Seth's tone was sharp.

"*Some of them resent the forced trip to New Zealand. Now the children are sick, and we're short of money—*" She shut her mouth, aghast that she'd shared the truth with this man.

But she trusted him, even with their brief acquaintance. He'd received a guardian to help him despite his mixed blood. It told her he was decent because guardians weren't stupid.

The stalking thing...

Well, that was odd. He'd informed her something had compelled him to watch her. Malikah pulled a face. Perhaps she was producing a pheromone to attract gargoyle men. After all, Sam kept coming on to her. If she complained, he shrugged and said he was a natural flirt. Esmerelda didn't seem to notice, but the sexual component of Sam's grubby stares made Malikah uncomfortable.

"*Have you stopped talking to me?*"

"*I'm here. My mind is spinning in a dozen directions.*" Malikah paused and went with the truth. "*I don't enjoy feeling out of control.*"

"*This place is unknown to you, as is leadership. Most people would struggle with your situation.*"

Malikah landed on the roof where she'd started. *"How do you know me so well?"* A laugh escaped her, and she froze because she couldn't recall the last time she'd made that sound.

"I'm a scientist. I observe. It's part of my nature and helped me stay healthy while living with the wolf pack. That and my best friend, Iain."

His dry tone told her more than his words. Survival hadn't been easy, and he was as confused as her. What must it be like to learn that everything you believed about yourself and your family wasn't true?

Before she could speak, he continued, *"If you can't get a gargoyle doctor to visit your place, I could come and see if there's anything I can do to help. I want to meet other gargoyles. I understand if my wolf makes you wary, but I promise I'm no threat to you or your people."*

He spoke so fast she had trouble deciphering his words. When he stopped, she smiled because his uncertainty came through clearly. This made him more approachable and less of a threat, and the last of her reserve toppled to the wayside.

"Would you like to visit tonight?" she asked impulsively.

"Yes." His acceptance was immediate. *"Also, I should tell you I'd like to kiss you very much. I want your friendship, but I also want more, starting with a kiss. I thought you might like the warning and the time to consider whether you'd enjoy the same thing. Have a pleasant visit. I'll talk to you later."*

"A kiss? Wait, how will you know where I live?" Malikah waited for an answer that didn't come.

She walked down the stairs to street level, slightly bemused but smiling. Happiness she hadn't experienced since before the massacre lent a spring to her step. The reminder wiped her feel-good mood away, but the weight on her shoulders had lessened a fraction.

Soon, she'd start her kitchen-hand job. Although it differed from what she was used to, she'd promised herself to smile through her tasks because the extra money was worth it.

She strode along Wellesley Street and entered the lobby of an office building. Sam's office was on the top floor. Instead of taking the elevator, she ran up the stairs, using the dozens of flights as training. No longer a princess, at least in appearance, she required fitness to survive. Her plan included exercise, smarts, and a work ethic. Feeling warmer, she stalked from the stairway with confidence.

The last thing she wanted was to give Sam the impression she might give in to his persistent suggestions in return for money and support.

Sam was the type of man who preyed on those weaker. Any boons he offered held strings—the expectation of payback in the future. She'd suspected that from their first meeting as she experienced his quick summing up of her person and had sympathy for Esmerelda. She wondered if the woman knew he'd propositioned Malikah and probably countless others who'd come before her.

Malikah stopped at the receptionist's desk.

The attractive redhead smiled a dazzling welcome. "How can I help you?" she purred.

"I'm here to see Sam," Malikah said. "Sorry, I don't have

an appointment, but all I need is five minutes of his time."

"I'll see if he's available." Instead of calling Sam, the woman stood and swayed to the door. She tapped lightly, waited a few seconds, and disappeared inside the office, closing the door behind her with a click.

Malikah sighed and waited. Although her hearing was excellent, her eavesdropping didn't pay off. Sam must've soundproofed the rooms. A smart move.

Ten minutes later, the door opened, and the redhead clattered out, her appearance less put together than when she'd entered the office. Malikah's gaze zeroed in on her smeared lipstick. Well, that was interesting.

"Sam has five minutes. He is going to lunch with his wife and her family and doesn't want to be late," the redhead said.

"Five minutes," Malikah agreed. Like the receptionist, she knocked lightly before entering the office. She'd expected to find Sam seated behind his desk. The man did like his tiny displays of power, but he stood in front of a large window overlooking the harbor.

He spoke without turning to look at her, his gaze on a group of black dragons, perhaps the same ones she'd noticed earlier. "The world is changing."

"Yes," Malikah agreed because it was nothing less than the truth. Not only had she come to live in a new country, but the paranormal rules were morphing. On the latest news bulletin, before she'd left, the newsreader had mentioned a segment of humans pushing back. Dozens of humans had rung in after that, stating their horror. According to them, she and other paranormals were dangerous.

"What can I do for you, Malikah?" Sam turned to face her, his gaze doing a swift up and down before settling on her face. "Are you here to tell me you've finally agreed to spend a weekend with me?"

Malikah restrained her *hell, no!* with difficulty. It was apparent Sam was sleeping with his receptionist, and he wanted her, too? Ugh! "I wondered if you'd reconsider letting your medic visit my people. I have four ill children, and I'd like a doctor's opinion." Her heart gave three anxious beats before squeezing in disappointment. His impassive expression implied he wouldn't agree to her request, and she hurried into speech. "If he donned protective gear and disposed of his clothing before returning to your colony, the odds of spreading the virus are slim."

Sam shook his head, his manner sorrowful, but the gleam in his blue-gray eyes told the truth. He'd never say yes until she gave in to his sexual demands. His preference was for her on her knees and sucking his dick. Submitting to his every desire.

It's one tiny act.

You could do it for the kids. You've already sacrificed so much. Did her dignity matter when the kids' lives were in danger?

"It wouldn't hurt anyone or cause a problem with your clan." Malikah battled to remain calm. Collected. In control of the panic that bubbled like a mud pool inside her. She wanted to slap his face and aim a kick at his groin. She could do it too—if she moved fast enough and took him by surprise. Instead, she held still and waited, every muscle tense while silently fuming at his mental games.

"I want a weekend away with you in a private place of my choosing," he said.

9

Now that rumors of the wolf pack in turmoil had reached Seth via the media and eyewitnesses, he relaxed his guard. Ewan McKenzie would have his hands full, trying to gain control of whatever had caused his wolves to mass in downtown Auckland. He'd be too busy to worry about Seth's traitorous actions.

But one thing worried Seth. Iain wasn't answering his phone. He hadn't heard from his friend since he'd called Iain to tell him not to hassle him. Guilt flooded him as he recalled his abruptness during that call. Seth tried Iain's work number. Nothing. Iain might have lost or damaged his phone, but the message each time suggested Iain had turned it off. This concerned him.

He wanted—no, needed—to discuss his situation with someone impartial who understood him.

Seth grabbed the prepaid phone he'd purchased several days before. He dialed a woman he used to work with in the pack's lab. She might betray him, but he'd learn pack info.

Uneasiness assailed him. Immediately, he stretched his senses. No warning scents or alarming sounds. Still, the trepidation persisted, tap dancing up his spine and lodging in his chest. His heart pumped faster, yet the nature of the danger eluded him.

The phone rang, and his hackles rose. His wolf growled, guttural and furious. *Malikah*. Another growl pushed past his compressed lips, and he struggled for control.

"Hello, Geraldine here," a sweetly feminine voice chirped.

"Gerry, it's Seth."

A gasp flowed down the line. "Raoul has a team searching for you. He's accusing you of stealing the formula you developed and paperwork from the lab."

Seth ignored the question in her statement. "Have you seen Iain? I've been trying to contact him."

"Haven't you heard?" Gerry asked, lowering her voice to a whisper.

"Heard what?" Seth asked, not trying to hide his impatience.

"You don't have to be rude," Gerry snapped with a clear sniff. "You're in big trouble."

Seth bit back his groan. "Sorry, Gerry. What's going on?"

Gerry sniffed again. "Everyone around here is more concerned with Ewan McKenzie's death. His wife shot him."

Blood roared through his ears. "Ewan McKenzie is

dead?"

She lowered her voice, and Seth heard a door shut. "It happened the day paranormals emerged from hiding. Rumors are rife. Iain and Finn have left the pack. The council members aren't talking."

"They'll be jostling to take over leadership."

"Exactly, although I can tell you one thing. Iain arrived with a dragon. He ordered the wolves to return home before he climbed aboard the dragon and flew away. What do you make of that?"

Seth's mind darted to the dragon woman he and Iain had met at the nightclub. He'd known Iain was interested and intended to ask her on a date. That had been before he visited his aunt. But he didn't want any of this information passed around. "Iain has never met or spoken to any dragons."

"Oh." Gerry sounded disappointed. "I thought you'd have the inside scoop."

"I haven't seen Iain." Seth wished he'd told Iain of his plans but hadn't wanted to cause trouble for his friend.

"I'm trying to stay under the radar. It's safer," Gerry said.

"You mentioned Raoul is searching for me."

"Yeah, I don't rate your chances if he catches you."

"Was this before or after the wolves came out?"

"Before. I haven't seen Raoul for several days."

Seth heard the frown in her words and imagined crinkles in her forehead, the pinch of concentration on her narrow face.

"Wasn't he interested in grabbing a council seat?" Raoul

had always harbored ambition.

"That might explain his absence. I'll ask around and text you," Gerry promised.

Seth debated the wisdom of giving Gerry this number before deciding gathering information was sensible. Now, if he could fly, he could go on a spying mission while the pack was in turmoil. Admittedly, his wings didn't feel strong enough to fly long distances, but he could try tonight. His mind turned to Malikah. Would she be up for a nighttime adventure?

"Thanks for the info, Gerry. Appreciate it. Don't put yourself in the path of trouble, but if you trip across anything interesting, I'd welcome a heads-up."

"I'll do it," Gerry said. "You've always shared your knowledge with me. Unlike the other scientists, you've never treated me like an idiot."

Seth blinked, surprised by her words. "Thank you. Please stay safe."

"You too," she said. "I mentally applauded you for taking your work and leaving. I don't like the way our research was heading."

"Me neither. Speak to you soon." Seth hung up because anxiety slithered across his skin. Any sensible wolf paid attention to their senses. His mind turned to Malikah again.

"Malikah? Are you busy? Can we talk?" No time like the present. He'd ask her now.

"Not right now." Her voice was strained, the tension reaching him even though he was likely miles away.

"What is it?" His nape prickled afresh. Was it Malikah?

Her distress? *"Can I help with anything? Did your meeting with Sam not go well?"*

"Still with him. Need to focus. Oh, hell."

"Malikah, what is it?" But she went silent on her end.

Seth shoved his phone in his pocket and used his instincts to locate Malikah. It was easy since she was in the city. He hesitated when he reached an expensive office block foyer.

When he approached the gargoyle leader, he wanted it to be from a position of knowledge and confidence. His gut told him that now wasn't the right time to confront—no, present himself to this Sam character. Also, he disliked the way the gargoyle treated Malikah and her people. She mightn't have mentioned all the details, but Seth could read between the lines.

Seth retreated to a nearby sandwich bar. If he sat near the window, he'd see Malikah leave.

Not long after he'd walked into the sandwich bar, a tall and striking woman left the building. She was stunning, with her curvy figure and high-fashion dress clinging faithfully to her form. A second woman trailed behind her, as attractive but less imposing. Also, she wasn't in a towering temper like the first. This poked at Seth's curiosity as he wondered what had upset her.

Malikah emerged ten minutes later, harried with slumped shoulders. Her meeting with Sam had not gone well.

"Malikah?" Seth watched her through the window.

Malikah jolted and whirled, her arms raised as if she intended to strike.

"It's me. Seth," he said quickly. *"Sending you a head-to-head message."*

Man, he was slipping into those stalkerish tendencies again. It wasn't the tenor he wanted to send. He liked her. A lot, and his instincts propelled him to stay close. It was the strangest thing. August had seemed delighted when he spouted his mates explanation, yet the scientist in Seth remained dubious.

"Sorry, you startled me. Where are you?"

"See the sandwich bar across the street? I'm in there waiting for you."

"Why?"

"Tell me what sandwich you'd like, and I'll order it before I explain in person."

"All right, but I can't be long. I need to check on the kids. I'm worried and not sure what to do next." Malikah walked in the door, scanned the interior, and beelined to him. "Cheese, ham, and salad, please."

Seth placed the order and took a moment to study her. His pulse thrummed, and the temptation to grasp her shoulders and kiss her senseless was almost too much. Her lips were redder than usual, probably because she'd chewed them. A stress tell for her. "What's wrong?"

She caught her plump bottom lip between her teeth. Finally, she sighed. "Sam was his normal self, propositioning me. He'd just told me he'd help if I spent the weekend with him when his wife walked in with her friend. Oh, she was her usual lovely self—very gracious and welcoming—but I had to make up a bullshit story about being upset and crying on Sam. She thinks I'm interested in her husband, and that's bullshit. He makes my feathers ruffle, and it's an uncomfortable sensation."

"Tell him you have a boyfriend," Seth said, every muscle in his body tense at the thought of Sam pressuring Malikah.

"That would be a lie," she replied with a frown.

"We've had breakfast together, and now we're having lunch. We've talked, and soon, I intend to kiss you because you're a beautiful woman. It wouldn't be a lie."

"I don't have time for romance."

It was Seth's turn to scowl. "I don't expect you to drop everything for me. I understand you have responsibilities."

"You're an attractive, intelligent man. Why would you want me?"

"I can't believe you said that," Seth snapped. "I'm on the run because I stole a formula from my lab. Despite my admirable reasons, theft is never right. Because I'm in hiding, I stay in a crappy apartment. I've recently discovered I'm half-gargoyle and half-wolf. The wolves are hunting me, and Sam and his colony will consider me inferior because I'm a half-breed. I'm no one's catch. I forgot to add I'm experiencing this weird stalking thing with you. August thinks you're my mate, although I'm not sure what to do with that," he blurted. *Oh, man. Shoot me now. I've turned into a chatty Kathy.*

"My mate?" Her tone came close to a shriek. "And you only thought to tell me this now?"

10

MALIKAH BREATHED HARD, PANIC roaring through her while her chest heaved. Amid all her life chaos—from Sam's antics to her colony and the strange sickness plaguing the children—she hadn't considered how her body responded to Seth. But now that he'd mentioned the word mate, everything clicked into place.

Thankfully, she'd already slid into a chair because her knees turned to jelly. "You didn't think to mention this earlier?"

Seth frowned and started to speak, but the guy behind the counter hollered a number. "That's our order," Seth said. "Let's grab it and head back to your place to talk privately."

"That's a bad idea." Malikah wanted to wrap her head around the *mate* topic before the adults added their comments and insults.

"We could go to my place, but I promised to check on

your sick youngsters. Remember?"

Malikah hesitated between screaming and wanting to help her people. Her colony won. "All right, but promise when we discuss this, you'll whisper because gargoyles have excellent hearing."

"Are you ashamed of me?"

"More shocked."

"I can speak telepathically. They won't overhear a thing."

"Thank you." She spared him an apologetic glance. "I would fly, but we'll do that another time."

Seth collected the sandwiches and held the door open for her. Malikah set a brisk pace on the twenty-minute walk to the warehouse she called home.

"Malikah, what's the hurry?" Seth asked, his long strides helping him to catch her.

"I don't know. No, that's not true. I have this vague sense of unease, and it has hovered all morning. I thought it was stress—finding work and settling in this unfamiliar place."

"The feeling isn't retreating?"

His words rumbled inside her skull, and she replied with a thought rather than verbally. *"It's becoming worse."*

"Could it be coming from the other gargoyle colony? Or from within your colony?"

Malikah pulled a face. *"My world—any sense of control I had before the massacre is slipping away through my fingers. The adults in my group resent me, but we have no plan B. It's almost as if they're angry because they're alive. They haven't told me, but I guess they hate this place and want to leave."*

"*So speak with them. Not confrontational but lay out the facts and the burdens you're bearing for them. Ask if they want to return home or do something else.*"

"*But they're my people.*"

A wash of sympathy blasted from him, and heat burned her cheeks.

"*Malikah, you are a few gargoyles. Survivors. This country is one of opportunity where we can ignore the old traditions. Instead of deciding for your group, ask them what they want to do.*"

"*But they might leave me.*"

"*Would you rather their unwillingness to stay in an unfamiliar place caused them to hate you? If there is one thing I've learned since discovering I was part gargoyle, it is that family can come in many guises. My foster parents loved me. I don't know why they hid my gargoyle blood, but they helped me become the man I am today. My best friend is a werewolf, and rumor says he's consorting with dragons. I'm trying to say that maybe you should let your people choose their fate instead of ordering them to acquiesce.*"

Hurt rolled through her at his words. "I don't order anyone," she snapped aloud.

"Are you certain about that?" Seth asked. "I don't mean to imply you're a bad person, merely that you're resorting to what you know. You're continuing the same path your parents traveled when maybe you should embrace the advantages of a different country."

Malikah sucked in a quick breath to cool her anger. Anger at Seth. Anger at her people. But most of all, anger at herself because Seth was right, dammit. She had treated her people similarly and ridden roughshod over their opinions. Even worse, she hated what Seth had made her see. "What should I do?"

"Ask your people what they want. Offer them options. Give them the ability or confidence to strike out independently."

"But they know nothing of the world."

"Malikah, protecting them by keeping them ignorant is silly. You'll make them resent you more. Now is the perfect time for paranormals to embrace change. Give your people a chance to evolve with everyone else."

The more Seth spoke, the more she realized he was right. The old ways didn't work. She had to allow her people autonomy. Shortly before the attack, her parents had quelled a rebellion of gargoyles who wanted independence. Malikah had heard dissatisfied whispers, but her parents had refused to entertain alternatives.

In hindsight, she saw rights and wrongs. Her parents and the courtiers had been wrong, but so had their subjects' methods of settling their grievances. No one had won.

She turned the corner and strode halfway along the street, halting in front of an empty warehouse. "This is home," she said. "Sam helped us to find it."

Seth followed, and she saw him taking in the dilapidated building. She forced away her embarrassment. This was nothing like the manor house where she'd grown up. Hopefully, now that she had a job, she and the others could save and pay for better lodgings.

"Maybe something in the building is the problem."

"None of the adults are sick. That's what makes this so strange. If we'd brought disease with us, wouldn't we all get sick? The children were flying and healthy once we emerged from stasis on our arrival. This trip was a big adventure."

Seth frowned. "How did you end up in New Zealand?"

Malikah scowled and lowered her voice as they approached what he thought might be the kitchen, given the tempting smells wafting from the walled-off area. "We learned this after we arrived, and it was my fault. I was secretly meeting a human man called Alfred. I thought he loved me, but it turned out otherwise. Our group hid, and the attacking clan pushed us into stasis with a magical flare. While unconscious, Alfred found us and thought he'd make a quick buck. He sold us as garden statues, and that's how we ended up here."

"Wow."

Malikah snorted. "We awakened and escaped once we felt the air and sunshine on our bodies."

"Did anyone see you?"

"No. Even the children understood humans were around. It's the first lesson we teach our youngsters. No doubt the wolves trained you to keep your otherness from humans."

"Yes."

"Who is this?" Tamaini asked in a strident voice. "I thought we were lying low."

Malikah bit back a sigh. Now that she'd talked to Seth, she understood she hadn't handled this situation correctly. "This is Seth. He's a friend. I met him at the guardian's sanctuary."

Tamaini's expression turned sharp and inquisitive. If Malikah didn't know better, she'd say there was jealousy, too.

"Where are the others?" Malikah asked.

"They've gone for a walk to get fresh air. We're not prisoners."

Malikah tried to conceal her irritation and feared she'd failed. They'd be dead if she hadn't warned them of the attack.

"All right," Malikah said. "I wondered if we could have a meeting this evening. There are a few things I'd like to discuss."

"Yes, Your Majesty." Tamaini curtsied and flounced away.

Malikah never knew where she was with the woman. She was an annoyance and acted like a bitch. But what Seth had told her bore thinking about. He was right. The old rules no longer applied.

"Where do you want to eat our sandwiches?" Seth asked.

"I'd like to check on the children first. We have a rooftop with a magnificent view. The sun isn't too intense today, and I'd like the fresh air to cleanse myself after speaking with Sam."

Seth squeezed her biceps, his lips curving in a faint smile of approval. "Don't worry. You'll work things out."

Malikah led the way to the children's room. When the first two children had become sick, she'd organized another room for the healthy children. They'd moved them in case whatever the children had was contagious.

She pushed open the door and entered the stuffy room. The children appeared about the same, and her heart sank. "Could they have caught a local disease we didn't have in England?"

"Tell me what a healthy child looks like." Seth crouched before the boy. "Is it all right for me to touch him?"

"I think so. I mean, I have, and nothing has happened to me. A normal child should have pale gray-blue skin when in gargoyle form. I'll show you what I mean. When I go into stasis, my skin turns a pale gray with blue undertones." Malikah stepped back. She closed her eyes and allowed her mind to empty and completely relax. The stone slowly crept from the place above her heart and covered her skin until she could no longer freely move. She fell into deep relaxation, a state she hadn't allowed herself for too long. Malikah set her inner wake-up clock for ten minutes and allowed herself to drift off and rest.

Wow! Seth stared at Malikah. Her clothing and footwear had merged with her stone. He recognized the tilt of her head and flowing hair, but the stone covering her body was a faint gray-blue, as she'd said. Her skin differed from the children's—their loss of color was clear when compared to her.

He ran his hand over the boy's shoulder. "What is wrong with you?" He rounded the boy and noted his grimace. He checked the girl, and her expression held a similar twist of the lips. Intrigued, he strode over to Malikah. Her face appeared serene.

Seth frowned at the two children. He placed his hand on the girl's thin shoulder, the coolness of her stone seeping into his fingers. *Oh, little one. What is wrong with you?*

"S-sore t-tummy."

His head jerked when the tortured words popped into his mind. Excitement filled him on realizing it was the girl he was touching. *"Did you eat something?"* He sent the words back and waited anxiously for her reply.

It was slow in coming. So slow, he wondered if he'd imagined the words.

"L-lollies."

Seth sagged in relief. He wasn't imagining things. *"It's all right, little one. We're trying to help. Hang tight while we find a medicine for you."*

His mind raced. If he'd heard her right and she'd eaten sweets, could this be a type of allergy or poison? He and Malikah hadn't considered this an explanation for the children's illness. Seth sent a mental question to the boy.

"My name is Seth. Do you have a sore tummy?"

Seth waited yet received no reply. No, wait. He'd touched the girl before he sent his question. He crouched before the boy and repeated the mental query.

Once again, the reply took long seconds.

"Yes." The whisper in his mind was faint, and he frowned, wondering if the boy was sicker.

"Did you eat sweets too?"

"Yes."

"We're trying to help you. Hang tight, kid." Seth stood and strode to Malikah. *"Malikah, are you awake?"* She didn't reply, and he realized he hadn't touched her.

Something to do with the stasis meant he needed to touch the gargoyle to communicate with them. He curled his fingers around her wrist and tried to send his message. *"Malikah, can you wake? I need information."*

"Seth?" Malikah sounded sleepy.

"Yes, I need you to wake. I have questions." Unable to help himself, he stroked her cheek. The stone was cool while the metallic scent of gravel wafted around her.

"Can't. Set my internal clock for ten minutes. Once that is done, I can't change back in a hurry. I wanted a rest," she added, sounding sheepish.

Seth tsked. *"You forgot about our lunch date."*

"Never," she said. *"You have a wonderful power. Communication with others during stasis is a valuable commodity. You need to experiment to learn the extent of your powers. August will instruct you."* She made a sound resembling a yawn, yet her mouth and face remained set.

"Interesting," Seth murmured as he pulled back.

Since Malikah was out of action, he searched for others in Malikah's colony. He found the grumpy woman they'd spoken with before, but this time, a smile wreathed her face, taking her from plain to pretty. She carried a basket over the crook of her right arm, and she halted abruptly on seeing him.

"Where is the princess?"

"With the children. We've had a bit of a breakthrough. It sounds as if something they ate has caused their illness. I'm not sure whether it is an allergy or a poison. Can you recall what the children were eating before they became ill?"

The woman's brow creased, and her lips pursed before

stretching into a scowl. "Are you accusing me of poisoning my grandchildren?"

"No! I'm trying to help."

"Who are you?" she demanded.

"I'm Malikah's friend. We told you that earlier." Seth changed tack. "Are there other sick children?"

"We have another sick girl," she said, her reply sounding grudging. "They're in the room over there to the right of our kitchen."

"You don't have to stay with Malikah if there is somewhere you'd rather be," Seth said coolly. While he knew Malikah had little money, she'd found a job and did her best to provide for the gargoyles who'd traveled with her.

The woman's mouth dropped open. "What?" she asked once she'd recovered from her surprise.

"You and the others don't need to stay with Malikah if you'd prefer to go elsewhere. You could join the local group of gargoyles or go out alone. Get a job. Find different housing. If you don't like the city, perhaps you'd prefer to find a place in the country. There are plenty of farmers who are looking for employees and who will provide accommodation along with a wage."

"Malikah won't let us go."

Seth's brows lifted. "Have you asked her?" He strode away before he said something he shouldn't. He'd hate for Malikah to think he was poking his nose where he wasn't wanted.

The woman trailed him. "You don't know the princess like we do. She wants to keep us under her control."

"That's not true." Malikah's cool voice cut across the open space between her and them. "If you wouldn't mind, call everyone together tonight. We'll discuss this, and you can tell me what's on your mind instead of sniping at me or gossiping behind my back. Life is different in New Zealand. There is no reason to keep old traditions alive. No rules to say we must. Truly, if you and the others want to leave, no one is keeping you here. Seth, this way."

Malikah strode past him, waves of irritation radiating off her as she stalked into a cubicle.

The child in this room was older but with the same pale colored skin instead of the blue-gray Malikah's skin had taken on in stasis. Seth hurried to the girl and touched her cool shoulder. He studied her pained grimace, and his stomach churned with trepidation. Surely, if it were food poisoning or an allergy, more of the colony would suffer the same problem. Both children he'd spoken to had complained of a stomachache and had contorted expressions, as did this one.

"Hi there," he thought. *"My name is Seth, and I'm trying to help Malikah find a cure to assist you to get better. Did you eat something strange?"*

"You're talking to me." Surprise, along with pain, carried through to his mind.

"Yes, it is my gift. What food did you have before you became sick?"

"Soup and bread. For dessert, we had a lemon pie. There was only one, so only us children ate it."

"Do you have a sore stomach?"

"Very sore. Pain there is forcing its way outward. When

it got terrible, I went numb and into stasis."

"All right, sweetheart. I need to talk to Malikah now."
Seth removed his hand and turned to Malikah and the other woman. "She says the children ate a lemon pie."

11

MALIKAH FROWNED, THINKING BACK. "But everyone ate pie."

"The two young'uns were already sick." Less agitated now, Tamaini buttoned down her resentment, her worry for the kids taking precedence.

Malikah nodded. "Tamaini is right. The two younger children were already in stasis. Silver became sick after that."

"Right," Seth said. "The first two children told me they ate sweets. Where did the lemon pie come from? The sweets?"

Malikah shrugged and turned to Tamaini. "Where did they come from?"

"You can't be blaming this on me."

"We're not," Seth said, "but it would help if we could narrow down the food's origin."

Tamaini stared at the wall before speaking. "Women

from the local colony brought a basket of food. Another food basket arrived today." Her frown deepened, the lines on her broad forehead becoming more prominent. "Are you trying to tell me the food contains poison?"

"I don't know," Seth said. "You say you've eaten the same food?"

"I gave the children sweets. I watched them take a handful each. Their sharing impressed me." Tamaini pulled a wry face. "I doubt my siblings would've been as equitable at the same age."

"Can we see the basket of food that came today?" Seth asked.

"Yes, I placed it in the kitchen on the table," Tamaini said.

She led the way to the kitchen and abruptly halted in the doorway. Flint was busy stuffing his face with a piece of cake while he held a chicken leg in his other hand.

"Stop!" Malikah sprang and jumped him, her speed taking them by surprise. She knocked the remaining cake from his hand, and the treat sailed through the air and landed with a splat on the floor. The pale pink frosting separated from the cake and skidded across the faded linoleum.

"What did you do that for?" Temper was a storm marching across Flint's craggy features. "I've worked a long shift and was hungry."

"Are you responsible for pilfering from the pantry?" Tamaini demanded. "When I mentioned the missing food, you told me it was the princess."

"I haven't taken any food other than the soup and bread

we've had for our meals," Malikah snapped. "I did without so the children wouldn't go hungry."

"I can't believe you let me blame the princess." Tamaini turned, regret in her sharp features. "I'm sorry. This is the reason I've been so short with you."

"Never mind that," Seth said with impatience. "Let's check the food more closely. We need to determine if anyone has tampered with it or if it's more of an allergy."

"I didn't do anything," Flint objected, blue-gray circles filling his pale cheeks and temper in his words. "But I was starving, so I helped myself. I know it was wrong, but I can't hunt here."

Tamaini poked her finger at Flint's massive chest. His size didn't deter her from giving a sharp rebuke.

Malikah ignored their bickering to unpack the battered cane basket. She laid each of the items on the table. There was more soup—a container of chicken and one of pumpkin—and two loaves of fresh bread, still warm from the oven.

The delicious scent had her belly rumbling, and she realized they hadn't eaten the sandwiches yet. They were probably still in the children's room.

Along with the soup and bread, there was a block of cheese, a bottle of milk, a cake of some type, and a large packet of wrapped sweets. Malikah turned to Seth. "What do you think? Is there any way we can test the food to learn if there is anything suspicious added?"

"All the food is homemade. It would be easy to add poison if someone wanted to badly enough."

Malikah squeezed her hands together, tension bleeding

into her arms. "But why? Why would someone want to hurt young children?"

Seth scowled, unable to supply answers. "Do you know the identities of the women who brought the food?"

"I told you," Tamaini said. "Two women from the gargoyle colony. We haven't visited the group because the leader won't allow it, but they told me their names. Garnet and Pearl." She glowered at Malikah as if the lack of mingling was her fault. "The food was a welcome gift."

"Are they the same women who delivered the first lot of food?" Seth asked.

"No. The last time two different women came," Tamaini said. "I can give you descriptions and names, but how do I know they even gave me their true names or that they weren't wearing a disguise? Poison is a nasty business. They knew we had children because they saw them and mentioned the sweets in the basket. I don't get it." Her shoulders slumped. "Who would want to hurt an innocent child?"

"I have a contact," Seth said. "If I ask her, she might test the foods for known poisons."

She? Malikah's breath hitched, and her mind stalled at the mention. Her stomach burned, and the itchy ache rose to her chest. She rubbed her breastbone and breathed through the unaccustomed turmoil. She was a princess and could have any man she wanted. A sharp pain in her jaw made her realize she was clenching her teeth. She consciously relaxed, plastered on a smile, and tried to order her ruffled thoughts. All along, she'd tried to push Seth away. Part of the reason was her training and constant reinforcement of her station. Royals did not marry commoners. Yet Seth had stalked into her thoughts often, and now he was actively helping her.

"Malikah? Is something wrong?" Seth's teasing words sprang into her mind, making her start. *"You have this weird expression and have fisted your hands."*

"Sorry, I'd jumped into the past, which wasn't a happy place." She glanced from Tamaini to Flint. "What do you think?" she asked them because everything Seth said was right. The traditional ways were outdated. For true happiness, they had to embrace the future. "Should we confront Sam's colony? Or should we do as Seth suggests and get the food tested?"

Tamaini and Flint appeared startled by her questions, and shame filled her. Stone fire! She'd behaved like a haughty princess and ignored their opinions. This changed now.

"The poison might be something else," Tamaini said after a long pause. She glanced at Seth. "We should get your friend to test the food, or..." She shot a sly look in Flint's direction. "We could get Flint to act as our food taster. He's been doing the job, anyway."

"No!" Flint burst out, dropping the chicken drumstick he still grasped.

Malikah laughed, and that surprised everyone.

"What?" she asked, staring at each of them.

"You don't laugh often." Seth cocked his head, a smile curling his sensual lips.

His mouth grabbed her attention, and she ogled until she realized his smile was growing impossibly wide, the joke at her expense.

"You like me," he teased, the words gentle in her mind.

"I do," she agreed. Then she spoke aloud. "How about this for a plan? We'll ask Seth's friend to test the food for poison, then we'll comb the premises. Seth mentioned the children ate sweets before they became sick, so that's our best clue. But we'll check the warehouse. Why don't we meet after dinner, including the children who are still well? They might've observed something to help us solve this puzzle. I'd still feel better if we could find a medic to look at the kids."

"We could approach another paranormal group," Seth suggested.

"Would they help us?" Malikah asked. It had never occurred to her to ask for aid from others.

"I'll call my friend. Once I've spoken to her, I'll ring around. We can try the felines, the dragons, and the fae. The wolves—while they might help, I'd prefer to stay out of their sights."

"Why?" Malikah asked.

Seth hesitated and spoke to her mind to mind. *"I stole a formula I developed using the wolves' facilities and research dollars. I didn't like how they might use my invention."*

"How much danger are you in?"

"Not sure, which is why I'm keeping a low profile. I haven't seen any wolves for a few days. It's best if I keep my distance."

"Are you talking to each other?" Tamaini asked, a hint of intrigue in her expression. "You're staring, but it doesn't seem sexual."

"Oh, it has a sexual element," Seth said to Malikah. *"I'm just taking things slowly."*

Sudden heat invaded Malikah's cheeks, and she wrenched her gaze from Seth's. His teasing tone and words didn't upset her. Instead, they'd made her wonder about kissing and touching. She'd heard rumors, or at least the legends, that stated once true mates began a physical relationship, their bond became tighter and impossible to break.

"Wow," Tamaini said, wonder evident in how she bounced on her toes. "That is the stuff of legends. Can you try speaking to me this way?"

Seth placed his hand on her arm.

"I've only tried speaking to the children and Malikah." He smiled when Tamaini's eyes grew impossibly wide. "It's good to know I can communicate with you."

Tamaini returned his smile, her eyes sparkling. "You have an amazing power. Mine is an affinity with herbs. I grow them and make them into medicines."

Seth's eyes narrowed as Malikah watched. "Have you touched the children to intuit what they need to heal?"

Malikah turned to Tamaini with excitement. "Have you tried that with the children?"

"Yes," Tamaini said, "I sensed nothing helpful, but your man is right. That's what I do when I cook or make a healing poultice. When I finger the ingredients, my instincts guide me. I'm ashamed to say I only tried it with my granddaughter. I didn't touch the other children because I feared catching the disease."

"Nothing happened to me or Seth," Malikah said.

"We've both had contact with the others."

Tamaini gave a decisive nod. "I'll do that first, then Flint and I will tell the others of our current plan."

"Thank you," Malikah said. "If you have other suggestions, please raise them tonight."

Tamaini appeared startled by Malikah's words, and Malikah kicked herself. She was making mistakes left, right, and center. Her royal blood shouldn't automatically make her the leader. This realization made her determined to try harder. From today on, each of them would contribute to their decision-making.

"A fine plan." Tamaini bustled from the kitchen, dragging Flint with her.

"I'll get started on my phone calls," Seth said. "If Maria agrees to help, I'll need to get the samples to her."

"Let's think positive. We have a starting point. I'll repack the food on the assumption it's okay." Malikah crossed to the table and regarded the food with wariness. It was possible for a poison to travel into the body via skin contact or consumption. She used a napkin from the basket interior to pick up each item and repack it.

Why would Sam order this poisoning?

No, this didn't seem like Sam. He was a physical male rather than a sly, sneaky one. She'd seen him knocking two gargoyles' heads together when they didn't perform to expectation during a training session. That had been her first introduction to Sam's colony. He'd smiled hello and taken her aside before introducing her to his wife and the more important colony members.

Everyone had seemed nice enough.

Sam had visited her later in the week, and he'd made his first sexual proposition. She'd politely declined. Not that her rejection had dampened Sam's enthusiasm. He hadn't stopped chasing her, twisting each situation to lever Malikah into accepting him as her lover.

What he didn't know was she'd never agree to his propositions.

Seth was a different story. His half-breed status didn't bother her. In the past, it might have, but no longer. This was a new world with different rules, as Seth kept reminding her. She could form her opinions since her parents and grandparents were no longer around to force her to follow traditions. In New Zealand, she could make her own rules.

And right now, she needed to hustle because once she started her job, she couldn't do private stuff during work hours.

She finished repacking the food, frowning when she lifted the bag of boiled sweets. A closer look revealed each item tightly sealed in cellophane. Someone could've unwrapped each sweet and repackaged it with no one noticing. Malikah eyed the other items. Why would anyone poison children's sweets?

Seth must've finished his calls because he returned to the kitchen. "I explained the situation, and Maria can start straight away. I'll take the food to the lab now."

Malikah shoved aside the flash of jealousy that slapped her over the face. "I need to ask the other children if they ate sweets." She swallowed hard. "I wish I could find a medic."

"That's next on my list." Seth crossed the two steps separating them and hauled her into his arms.

Her rapid inhalation dragged in his scent—a combination of musk and something earthy that had her burrowing closer. He buried his face in her hair, his strength reassuring her. Some of the responsibility she shouldered eased away in his embrace, and she felt lighter.

Seth pulled away too soon, and she felt the loss acutely.

"See you later." Seth hesitated.

She gazed up at him, startled, then mesmerized by his smile.

"I can't leave without kissing you."

Shock filled her instantly because no man would've dared to kiss her when she lived with her family. Royal protocol plus a servant would've tattled. This, being with Seth, and trying to find her way, made her ponder the things she'd missed in her isolation. Sure, she'd mixed with other high-born gargoyles, but never someone of such low standing. Not socially, apart from Alfred. They'd had servants, of course. All this flashed through her mind before Seth's lips touched hers, and her mind drained of everything except him.

Her heart seized before her pulse leaped into a racy beat. His mouth was soft on hers. Tentative, as if he was waiting for rejection. Her hands settled on his shoulders, and Seth brought his tongue into play. He traced the seam of her lips and, startled, she opened her mouth. He took advantage to deepen the kiss. Every part of her tingled, and her eyes closed to savor the sensations.

Then, the kiss was over, and Seth was pulling away.

A protest flew to her lips because she wanted to order him to kiss her again. Her mouth opened to issue that command, but luckily, she stopped her imperious words, or at least the ones that would've made her seem a demanding princess.

"I would like another kiss in the future," she whispered.

Seth's grin was full of approval. "I can arrange that."

Malikah willed the heat from her cheeks. "Everything is in the basket." She scuttled away, not understanding why she was so flustered. But the more time she spent with Seth, the more she realized that perhaps Seth's guardian wasn't wrong about them being mates.

12

SETH STRUTTED FROM THE kitchen with the basket in hand, elated by their kiss. Now that he'd kissed her, he hungered for more. He'd had girlfriends and lovers before, but his feelings for Malikah differed.

This felt right.

He let himself out of the warehouse and scanned his surroundings. He'd been lucky none of the pack had caught up with him. This coming out to humans had distracted the wolves, but he wished he could talk to Iain.

"Iain," he called, picturing his friend in his mind's eye. *"Iain."*

No one replied.

Seth continued to the lab where his friend Maria worked. She was a fae, and from what she'd told him when he called her, her appearance was different now. She'd giggled when she told him this, adding that it was freaking out the man in charge of the lab. He'd taken a personal day, which meant she could slip in the tests for Seth.

Was it only gargoyles he could communicate with using this new power? He slowed when he reached the end of the street and edged around the corner, again studying the surrounding people. He grinned and increased his speed. The humans were busy gawking at the fae and other like species who had forgone using glamor. The paranormals were the ones going about their business and not gaping open-mouthed. He didn't spot a single wolf. He tested the air. No wolves. Perfect.

The lab was near the suburb of Parnell. Here, fewer people were wandering the streets, but the traffic was heavier. He still needed to remain vigilant, but he felt safer since he could attempt to fly to a rooftop. None of the wolves would see that coming.

He tried to contact Maria using his new power. *"Maria?"* He pictured her as he'd seen her last. *"Maria, are you there?"*

"Who's talking in my head?" came a familiar and grumpy voice.

"It worked! It's Seth. Do you like my new trick?"

"You're a wolf," Maria said. *"You don't have freaky mind powers."*

"I'm almost at the lab. I have a lot to tell you."

"You think?" she shot back. *"I'll meet you at the side door."*

"Five minutes," he promised and increased his pace. Maria wasn't patient, but she was damn good at her job. If any of these foods contained poison, she'd find it.

He arrived and rapped on the door. *"Maria, I'm here."*

He sent the words, and no sooner had he thought them than the door opened.

He blinked. Maria had been a blue-eyed blonde with pale skin in the past, which fit since she spent a lot of time in the lab. Now, her skin was a delicate blue covered with tattooed whorls. Her hair was indigo, and she'd styled it in intricate braids. She grinned, and he noted her pointy ears.

"I can see why your boss needs a personal day," Seth said with a wry smile. "You're beautiful."

"Huh," Maria said, baring her teeth. They were *not* of the blunt human variety. "Where is this food you want me to test? You say that three children are sick?"

"Or those sharp teeth might frighten him," Seth teased.

"Huh." Maria's gaze turned sly when it slid in his direction. "You're a fine one to talk about sharp teeth since you've been hiding a fine set yourself. Why are you hanging around with the gargoyles?"

Seth gave her a partial truth. "I have a gargoyle mate, which means I have a vested interest in their health. It makes my lady happy."

Maria led the way into the lab, and Seth followed, familiar with the layout.

"All right. What should I test first?"

"The sweets. The children seem to have eaten them before becoming ill. If you don't find anything suspicious in the candy, then we'll test the lot."

"I'd better get to work then." Maria rapidly prepared the equipment she needed. "I sense you're not telling me everything about this gargoyle situation. Is this woman part of the gargoyle colony? Why aren't they helping?"

"Malikah and her people recently arrived from Northern England. Sam, the head of the resident colony, doesn't want them to join his group. He says it's because the youngsters are sick, and he's worried about spreading disease."

"Plausible," Maria agreed. "Are you going to stand there or help me?"

"I can stay for a short time, but I want to contact the other groups and ask if they're willing to have their medics check on the children. Malikah's people traveled in a cargo ship, which took many weeks. None of them look particularly well."

"The gargoyles won't even let their medic check the children?" Maria asked, disgusted, curling her top lip and giving him a clear view of her sharp teeth.

"No, risk of infection again, according to Sam."

"But they're children. That's harsh," Maria said.

"Since we're not sure why they're sick, it's understandable. The wolves wouldn't let their medic come, even if I asked," Seth said. "I'm not popular with the pack. I disapproved of their intentions for my research, so I left and took everything with me."

Maria's head jerked up. "You stole your research."

Seth winced, but that was precisely what he'd done, along with changing a few pertinent equations. "Yeah."

"You'll be in trouble when they catch up with you."

"The wolves are in upheaval. The details are sketchy, but I hope to contact my friend and learn more."

"What did you do with your research?"

"I destroyed it, although now that the paranormal

species have come out, my invention won't be as useful to the pack. My best guess—they were intending to use it to infiltrate other paranormal groups and cause havoc from within."

"Why?"

"To gain more power and control."

Her blue gaze was intent and powerful. "Apart from you, I've never met a wolf I liked."

"Thanks, I think."

Maria grinned, showing a flash of those teeth again. They were a pristine white, the points wickedly sharp, and Seth never wanted to get on her wrong side.

They worked together for almost an hour. A piece of machinery beeped, and Maria turned to study the results.

"That's interesting. The bag of sweets held two varieties, so I did the tests on both. One contains poison while the other one doesn't."

"Which one?"

"The one with the blue wrapper holds the poison."

Seth picked up the packet and inspected a blue-wrapped sweet. He held it up to the light. He set it aside and picked up another. "Both have a pinprick in the wrapper. It would be like playing Russian roulette. Some would get the contaminated sweets and others wouldn't. It's a matter of luck. Do you know the type of poison?"

"You said the youngsters were turning pale?"

"Yes, but they're not like humans. Their skin is a pale blue-gray in their natural state."

"In that case, I have a wild idea. An intake of silver in a human turns their skin blue, especially when they encounter sunlight. A gargoyle would have an affinity with metals, but it's possible they might have a similar reaction to silver."

"How long will it take until you identify the poison type?"

"Depends on how lucky we are. It might be a five-minute search or take twenty-four hours plus."

"If it is silver, what is the treatment?"

"The condition has no treatment in humans. They put up with the blue skin. It's recommended they use sunscreen to lessen their sun exposure, and of course, they should stop taking the silver. My best guess is that this poison is reacting this way because they are gargoyles."

"I'll try to find a medic and tell them our best guess. If we're right, the sickness won't spread because the silver needs to be ingested. Right?" He frowned. "I have drops. They're formulated for wolves and are untested, so I hesitate to give them to kids. Besides, they need to swallow the drops, which is a problem while they're in stasis."

"You're correct on both counts. It's better to wait rather than try untested treatments. I'll get back to you as soon as I have results."

"Thanks, Maria. Given the faint pinpricks in the wrappers, someone did this on purpose. Malikah and her people shouldn't accept food from others."

"Yep, the food donor is no gift horse."

Anger flashed through Seth. "The rations came from the resident gargoyle colony, so I'm thinking Malikah should find a new home far away from Sam and his people."

"Yeah," Maria said, her gaze cold and flinty. "With friends like that, who needs enemies?"

Seth left Maria to her work. Outside, he wondered how to approach the other paranormal species. He'd always kept his head down and worked, while Iain had done more socializing because of his job and his position within the pack. Not that Seth had ever envied his friend. Ewan McKenzie had expected a lot from his son and had forced him into brutal fights and challenges to prove his mettle.

Yeah, Seth didn't mourn Ewan McKenzie in the slightest.

Seth scanned the street and walked until he found an area with a three-sixty view of his surroundings. He checked for wolves before eyeing the roof of the nearby building and wished he had greater confidence in his flying.

Seth snorted. He was a terrible wolf, and his gargoyle skills weren't much better. Now he understood why he hadn't truly fit with the pack, but would he find a home with the gargoyles any easier? Something to consider.

He pulled out his mobile and turned on the data. Hesitating, he wondered which paranormal species to contact first. Felines, he decided. He searched for contact numbers or email addresses and found a website. No phone number, but he emailed a request through, explaining the situation and giving his phone number for them to call him. A longshot since the felines might not monitor the website.

Next, he tried the dragons. They had a phone number, which he dialed and waited anxiously for someone to answer. Two beats later, a cheerful voice answered.

"Dragon compound."

"My name is Seth." Seth explained who he was, what he wanted, and why.

"Someone is poisoning innocent children? That is terrible. Please hold." The phone clicked on the other end, and suddenly music blasted him. Seth jerked the phone from his ear and waited. He didn't wait long.

"Seth," came a familiar voice. "Is that you?"

"Iain?" Seth didn't have to pretend shock. "What are you doing with the dragons?"

"Long story. Man, so much has happened since I last saw you. Where are you? Where are the sick kids?"

"They're living in an empty warehouse close to the central city," Seth said, giving directions. Excitement pulsed in him at Iain's calm acceptance. "Can the dragons help us?"

"Yes, we'll help. We're about an hour away," Iain said. "A group of us will come. I can't wait to see you. It feels as if a lifetime has passed, and my life has changed so much."

"Mine, too," Seth said in an understatement. "Um, I've developed this new power. I'll call you before you arrive, and you'll see what I mean."

"What new power?" Iain asked.

"Later." Seth hung up, elated at this easy offer of aid. Of course, Iain's presence with the dragons had helped.

Iain arrived around an hour later. Seth had expected him to arrive via a vehicle. He stepped outside just as two black dragons landed in the street outside the warehouse. Even more shocking, Iain clambered down from one dragon before it shifted to its human form. A woman, Seth noted as Iain handed over clothes. Tall with light brown hair, she held herself with confidence. The second dragon shifted to an older woman with dark blonde hair styled in a blunt, jaw-level cut.

Iain turned and spotted Seth. He spoke a few words to the women before striding over to Seth, a broad grin on his face. He was more relaxed, his expression happier than Seth had seen in months.

The pair embraced, and emotion rose in Seth as they clasped each other. He hadn't realized how much he'd missed Iain. They used each other as sounding boards and went out together socially as well as sharing the apartment. Since Seth had scarpered with his research almost three weeks ago, he'd lost touch with the rest of the pack. It'd be good to know the depths of the trouble he'd landed in for doing a runner.

"Hi, I know you," a feminine voice said from behind Seth. "Where are your glasses?"

Seth spun around and turned back to grin at Iain. *"Ah-ha!"*

Iain drew the woman against his side. "Seth, meet my mate Elspeth Murray. Elspeth, this guy has been my best friend since our schooldays."

"I'm pleased to meet you properly, Seth. Iain has mentioned you, but we've had a busy couple of weeks. Now, tell me why you were wearing glasses in the nightclub. I thought it was strange after I realized you were wolves."

Seth laughed, delighted with her intelligence. "Come

inside." He opened the door and ushered Iain and Elspeth inside. The other dragon, an older woman who carried a bag of supplies, followed.

"This is Elspeth's mother, Fiona," Iain said. "She offered to look at your little ones."

"I was in the lab earlier. My friend Maria's tests showed the sweets contained something we suspect might be silver. Too much silver turns a human's skin blue. If this is silver poisoning, the poison has bleached the gargoyle kids' skin pale and sent them into stasis. I can communicate with them, but we're not sure how to treat them."

"You communicated with them?" Fiona asked. "How?

Seth shot a glance at Iain and Elspeth. He trusted Iain, so he turned back to Fiona. *"Because I have discovered I can speak directly to one person at a time, mind to mind,"* he said in his thoughts, directing his reply to Fiona.

"Wow," Fiona said aloud. "That is impressive. Can you speak to the others?"

"Of course," Seth said and sent separate thoughts to Iain and then to Elspeth.

"How are you doing that?" Iain demanded. "You couldn't do that before, or if you could, you never told me."

Seth's mouth twisted. "Iain, you know how my shift to wolf has always been slower than everyone else's and how the trainers gave me grief about my pace?"

"Yeah." Iain was watchful, his gaze on Seth's face.

"Well, it turns out I'm half-wolf. The other half of me is gargoyle, which is why I'm with Malikah."

"Malikah?" Iain asked.

"That's me," Malikah said, entering the room from behind them. She strolled over to Seth and stood shoulder-to-shoulder with him. Seth went one better and slid his arm around her waist. For an instant, she tensed. Just when he thought she might make him look stupid, she softened and leaned into him. Her scent of flowers and the faintest tinge of metal seeped deep into his lungs, making him wish they were alone.

"This is Malikah. She is the leader of this gargoyle colony," Seth said.

"You still haven't explained your glasses," Elspeth said.

Seth laughed. "After doing hours of lab work, my eyes became sensitive to the light. My bosses saw me as inferior because I wore them." His mouth twisted with wry amusement. "Werewolves never have poor eyesight."

"And now?" Elspeth asked.

"My eyes seem better now, but my hypothesis is the bright lights were the problem. Gargoyle youngsters don't do well with direct sunlight and must build up an immunity."

"Never mind that," Fiona said, bustling forward. "Let me see your sick children."

"Of course," Malikah said. "This way, please."

Everyone trailed Malikah and entered the small room where the two gargoyle children stood in stasis.

"You poor things," Fiona cooed, crouching in front of the first. She smoothed her hand over the child's head before turning to Seth and Malikah. "You say they're alive." She pulled a face. "Sorry, I don't want to sound insensitive, but it isn't obvious."

"I can communicate with the children," Seth said.

"Normally, I'd test temperature and ask the patient about their symptoms. You're convinced this is poisoning?"

"Yes," Seth said.

"Who did this?" Iain asked. "They're kids. Who goes around poisoning food they know children will eat?"

"We're fairly certain the food came from the other gargoyle colony, but I don't know the women who delivered the food," Malikah explained. "I intend to visit Sam and question him."

The steely note in her tone told Seth she wouldn't shy from challenging Sam, even though it might cause trouble.

Fiona checked the other child and stood. "I'm afraid I'm not going to be much help, but I have a suggestion. How many of you are living here?"

"Fifteen, including the children," Malikah said.

"We have plenty of room at the farm," Fiona said. "We're closer to the witches there, and I believe it is they who might be your best bet."

"But there are fifteen of us," Malikah said instantly.

Seth squeezed her wrist, intent on sending her a silent message. She shot him a glance, frowned, and seemed to understand his point.

"What I mean is I need to consult with the other adults in my group, and I will do that this evening when we're all together."

"You have our contact number," Fiona said. "We'd be happy to have you as our guests while we try to discover a cure for the youngsters." She shook her head. "I can't believe someone would treat a child so."

"Thank you," Malikah said. "I appreciate your help. Where I come from, the species don't support each other."

"That is not our way." Fiona Murray stood tall and proud.

"I'll call you this evening, no matter which way we decide," Malikah said.

Fiona dipped her head in a decisive nod, the ends of her blonde hair swinging against her jaw. "We'd like to help. It is good for the paranormal species to work together. In fact, I believe it is imperative."

13

Iain drew Seth aside, his blue gaze intense. "How can you be half-gargoyle and half-wolf? That doesn't seem right."

"My birth parents weren't the same species. I've always had trouble with my shift. It's much slower than yours and our packmates. Our trainers called me lazy—the reason they shunted me into science rather than security. I didn't understand until recently, and it's been a steep learning curve."

"Can you trace your real family?" Iain asked with interest.

"August, my gargoyle guardian, says neither of my parents had siblings. Since their parents didn't approve of the relationship, I doubt that bodes well for me," Seth said drily. "August agreed that contacting relations might be problematic. I figure that's something to consider later."

"You could research them without meeting them."

"True." Seth glanced at Iain, then let his gaze drift to Elspeth. "Your parents wanted you to marry Janet. And what the hell is up with the wolves? Are the rumors right?" Seth swallowed, knowing this was tactless, but they were friends. "I-is your father dead?"

"Elspeth is my mate. She was the one my wolf wanted. I took her to Ohakune with me to check on my aunt, and things went from there. My aunt told Ewan, and he was...unhappy. He sent wolves to attack Elspeth. When I confronted him, I learned Finn and I aren't his natural sons."

"What? How?" Seth's mind whirled. "How did your father die?"

"Told you it was a long story," Iain said. "The short version is I confronted Ewan and learned the truth when he and my mother spilled the beans. Then, my mother—I'm calling her my mother, but she isn't truly—"

"What do you mean?"

"She carried James and me and birthed us, but she isn't related to us."

Seth's mind worked and came up with an answer. A surrogate, but none of this made sense. "Why?"

"Ewan purchased fertilized super wolf eggs because he wanted to build a superior army. That's the reason he pushed me hard and had his men go psycho on my arse. He was testing me to learn if his investment was paying off. He wanted to breed more wolves using me and Finn as..." His mouth twisted, and pain crossed his expression before he locked down his emotions. "Ewan intended to use us as studs."

Horror flooded Seth—anguish on Iain's behalf. "I wondered how you healed so fast. Quicker than anyone else. Your injuries were life-threatening, and most people would've died if they'd suffered half the trauma. You accepted the treatment, so I didn't like to interfere, not that anyone would've taken notice."

"I didn't understand either," Iain said, his tone bleak.

Elspeth had been listening to their conversation and joined them. "His plan was to build a superior army and take over." Her lips curled in disgust. "He'd used all the fertilized eggs he'd purchased. His next step was to marry Iain off and produce super babies."

Seth grimaced. "If that was his plan, how did you leave the pack? How did you and Elspeth get together? I presume that was why Ewan was pushing your marriage to Janet."

"For the first time, I disobeyed him." Iain's face remained expressionless. Even though they were close friends, Seth had difficulty reading his genuine reaction.

"How?" Seth demanded.

"Ewan called me to a family dinner, determined to force me to take Janet as my mate. I confronted him in his office. Alana arrived and shot him," Iain said. "Once that happened, something about my genes and Finn's called the pack. By this time, Elspeth and I were mates. The witches gifted us a few nights at a hotel in the city. The wolves congregated near the hotel, which was when the rest of the paranormal species took advantage and came out to the humans. Finn and I didn't want anything to do with the wolves, and since Elspeth and I were together, our natural place is with the dragons."

"So if Malikah and her people went to them, they'd be safe?" Seth asked. His friend wouldn't lie to him. Since childhood, they'd been constant companions, despite Iain's father's wishes otherwise.

"I give you my word they'd be safe."

"You mentioned witches?" Seth asked.

"Yes, they bound Elspeth and I together," Iain said. "Everything happened fast. The witches told us we'd have a few days of safety at the fae-owned hotel. At first, we thought the wolves were massing to cause trouble for us. I mean, the council had plans for me that didn't include mating with a dragon. But it turned out my behavior had compelled their wolves to mass. Enough about me. When did you realize you were half gargoyle? And that you have a mate?"

Seth swallowed hard, glad that Malikah wasn't present, even though he'd been open with her. "I didn't know what was wrong with me. I was dreaming weird shit about flying. Then, I'd zone out, and I'd have this weird covering on my skin. Shocked the hell out of me. One night I went into stasis and had this peculiar dream where I visited this mountain monastery. I met an enormous gargoyle there. I knew little about gargoyles at that stage. Once I got over my shock, August helped me. Turns out some gargoyles have guardians. No, that's the wrong word. They're more like teachers and advisors."

"What about Malikah?"

"I'd met her earlier. I spotted her in the city and couldn't figure out my compulsion to monitor her."

"You're mates," Iain said, the gleam of understanding in his eyes helping Seth's inner tension to subside.

"Yeah. I guess that's why you returned to the dragon club to meet Elspeth."

Iain's entire face softened. "She is amazing. I'm lucky to have such a wonderful woman standing at my side. She's studying science and wants to go into the food industry."

Seth pulled a face. "My future is debatable. I stole my research and destroyed most of it. No company will hire me. Once the council sorts themselves out, how likely is it they'll force me to replicate my work?"

"Given the pack disarray, it'd surprise me if they came after you. William and the council are squabbling, fighting for pack alpha privileges. It will take time for everything to shake out and return to normal."

"What should I do?" Seth asked. "I can't keep hiding when I want to spend time with Malikah."

"Persuade the gargoyles to accept Fiona's offer," Iain said. "Then we can make a plan to help you."

Seth nodded, grateful to his friend. "How far is it? My flying skill is like my shifting speed. Also, we'd need transport for the sick youngsters."

"We have a truck," Elspeth said, standing close to Iain.

His friend slipped his arm around her shoulders and continued their discussion. Iain was so happy. It radiated from him. Seth had known Iain and Ewan argued frequently. Ewan's constant refrain during Iain's younger years was to toughen up and fight back. Images of the brutal training, the weeks of scarce food, and the medical tests came back to Seth. Now everything made sense.

"Iain, I need your help to do something else," Seth said, using his new power to communicate with his friend.

"Anything," Iain said, his reply instant.

"Once Malikah and the others are safe, I want to visit the gargoyle colony and ask questions. Someone there placed poison in those sweets. I mean, that makes the most sense. Everyone I've spoken to is clear as to the food source," Seth stated. *"Lacing food with poison is disgusting enough, but to harm children is beyond despicable."*

"I'm in. Elspeth and I will do anything we can to help. Have you met the gargoyles? I don't know them. Elspeth might. Wait, I'll ask her." Iain stood without moving for long seconds before nodding.

"Right. She has met Sam, and she didn't like him. He hit on her even though he is married, and his wife was present."

"He hit on Malikah too. She asked for shelter, and he told her no, but he wanted her. Her refusal hasn't stopped him from repeating his offer. You communicate telepathically with Elspeth?"

"Yeah, cool, huh? I made the right choice when I returned to the club to ask her out. Elspeth is an amazing woman. My amazing woman,*"* he added with pride. He grew serious again, his brow furrowing. *"How desperate are Malikah and her group?"*

"They've been surviving by scavenging and charity from the food bank and the gargoyle colony. Three of them have jobs, and Malikah starts her job tonight."

"How certain are you that the sweets came from the gargoyles? Can we ask the kids that are still well? The adults?"

"Malikah promised she'd speak with the adults. There's tension within the group." Seth hesitated since this wasn't his secret to tell. No, Iain needed this information. *"This is confidential, okay? Malikah is a princess, but everyone in the Shadowclaw clan, apart from those with her, died in a massacre. From what I've learned, the royals were arrogant. They didn't care about those who worked hard around them. That caused resentment. Malikah survived, but she is still finding her way."*

"Have you checked her story?" Iain asked.

"This is my mate you're doubting here."

"Seth, think. She might be your mate, but you know nothing about her—only what she has told you."

"I believe her. August, my trainer, confirmed part of her story."

Iain held up a hand. *"I'm not trying to cast doubt. It's my background in security talking. I'm naturally suspicious."*

"You don't know her." Seth clenched his fists and fought the sudden anger that engulfed him at Iain's insinuations. Malikah hadn't poisoned the children. She was worried about them and genuinely trying to help the group.

"Seth, I'm sorry," Iain said. *"You're right. I don't know Malikah. You do."* His friend's sincerity came through clearly. *"If you vouch for her, that's enough. But we should pretend we distrust her and go to Sam at the gargoyle colony. Ask for information about her background and her purpose here. Tell him she has gone to the wolves and the dragons, and we're security checking her. This should lower his guard, and we might learn more. This plan is better than asking questions or accusing the gargoyles of placing poison in the*

sweets."

"It's a smart plan," Seth said, shoveling aside his grudging resentment because Iain was right. This was a clever way to bring them closer to the truth.

"What are you and Iain discussing?" Malikah asked.

Seth jolted while Iain's grin was sheepish. "How could you tell?"

"It's the body language," Elspeth said. "You're unmoving and zoned out."

Malikah focused on Seth. "Care to share?"

"We thought we'd visit the gargoyle colony. Pretend we're investigating you."

"I'm coming with you," Malikah said, straightening her shoulders.

"We want to catch them off guard. If you're not there, hopefully, they'll speak with frankness," Iain said.

"I can see that might work," Malikah said. "But I am still coming with you."

Seth scowled at her. "Don't you want to learn who is doing this?"

"Yes." Her shoulders slumped as commonsense prevailed. Seth could see the tick-tick of her thoughts as she regrouped and attempted to fashion an alternative plan. "How about if I come with you but wait outside the colony? I'll be close enough to communicate or answer questions."

Seth silently debated the matter, considering pluses and minuses.

"She has a point," Elspeth said. "How would you feel if we left you behind in similar circumstances?"

"Won't they have guards?" Iain asked.

"Yes, but they're not efficient," Malikah said. "When we first arrived, I sneaked close enough to eavesdrop and get a sense of how they might react to new arrivals. No one saw me because I'm excellent at blending. Superpower, remember? These are my people, and we're under attack. I'm going."

"All right," Seth said. "But I won't be happy if you make a sudden appearance. Our plan won't work with you present."

14

MALIKAH SCANNED THE GARGOYLES' faces. The faint curl of their lips and set expressions told her they didn't hold her in high regard. They still considered her an arrogant princess and thought she'd spout hot air and platitudes. Untrue. Landing unexpectedly in Auckland, trying to find a job, and the lingering shock at the annihilation of her family and home had stomped the arrogance from her. Oh, she still had her pride, but she understood that success in this world meant working in a team. Accepting and giving help, taking that hand offering aid when it meant the rest of her small colony would receive a better chance to thrive.

Even meeting Seth had changed her for the better.

She smiled, and immediately, grumbles resonated within the large room. The ill will killed her happiness. *Back to the present.*

"I understand you don't trust me. You resent me

because of my royal blood." She gathered her strength. This was harder than she'd predicted. She sucked in a breath and did what Seth had recommended. Hit them with truth. "We can't stay close to Sam's colony when it's obvious one of their residents wishes us harm. Someone gave our children poisoned sweets, and we can't afford for anyone else in our group to suffer."

"What options do we have?" Cameo demanded, her mouth twisted in a sneer.

"The dragons have offered us sanctuary at their country estate. I told them we'd make a group decision and contact them tomorrow. Their suggestion was for us to stay with them. Fiona Murray says they have cottages we can use for as long as we need them. Their place is north of the city, and she says the local farmers and horticulturists desperately require workers. We'd have access to jobs, and we'd be nearer the witch enclave. It's possible they could fashion a spell to draw the poison from the children. The dragons are contacting the coven and asking on our behalf. I didn't think you'd mind if it means the children can break from stasis." Malikah took a breath to ease the ache in her chest. "I've covered the main points. If you have questions, fire away."

"Let me get this straight," Cameo said. "You're giving us the right to say yes or no."

"My royal blood is of no consequence here. I'm not important. My vote is to go with the dragons. It makes sense to travel to an area with plentiful jobs. Second, it'd be better for the children to have fresh air and the freedom to run and play. The dragons have a school, and the children are welcome to attend. But my main reason is this would ensure the safety of our group. Someone means us harm. One last reason—it'd be amazing to fly over the countryside and the sea. I believe we could be happy there. Now, do you have any further questions? No? All right. I'd appreciate it if you'd let me know of your decision in the morning."

"Where are you going?" Cameo asked, suspicion filling her features.

Malikah bit back her instinctive retort, which had been that she didn't have to answer to them. *Wrong.* She needed to share. "Seth, Iain, and Elspeth suggested they go to Sam's colony to ask around and see what they might learn. We have a few details from the children, and hopefully, our arrival will stir up a reaction to help us learn more."

"We should come too," Cameo said, leaping to her feet.

"Seth and the others thought they might learn more without me. I protested, but they insisted. My task is to hide outside the colony and blend with the background so I'm close enough to answer questions."

"That makes sense." Tamaini's statement sounded grudging even as she accepted the edict to stay away from Sam's territory.

"They're worried one of us might lose our temper and allow the culprit to escape punishment. Frankly, if I get my hands on whoever is doing this, I'll throttle them."

"I want to toss them down a dark hole and bury them for eternity," Talon growled.

"We should live with the dragons," Rosslyn said. "This warehouse is horrid, and I don't feel safe."

145

"Okay," Malikah said. "Seth is ready to leave. If you're awake when we return, I'll let you know what happened."

THEY DIDN'T FLY ACROSS the city. They took a taxi and alighted a block away from the gargoyle colony. Like dragons, gargoyles had other properties, but since Sam had based himself here for most of the week, this was the best place to start their search.

Seth turned to her, his gaze lingering on her face, before he pulled her into his arms and tenderly kissed her. His sudden embrace caught her off guard, but she couldn't deny the spark it ignited. The intense kiss held passion and sweet uncertainty, leaving her craving more.

A cough sounded behind them, and she jumped. Seth's hands fell away, leaving her aching and bereft.

"Stay safe," Seth said, his gaze shimmering with promise. "Don't put yourself in danger because I'd like to kiss you again. In privacy next time."

She gripped his forearms, making certain of his attention. "Will you let me know what is happening?"

His expression softened, and her pulse gave a brief blip. "As much as I can."

Good enough. "Please be careful. We don't know the reasons behind the poisoning. This could be a random psycho or something else."

"Shush." Seth placed warm fingers over her mouth. "We'll discover what is happening and why."

Malikah hugged Seth before stepping back. "Be

careful." Her gaze wandered to Iain and Elspeth. "All of you." She strode to the parking building entrance and slipped inside. *Please let them learn the identity of this person who was harming their children.*

"What's our approach?" Elspeth asked.

Seth ripped his gaze off Malikah to focus on Iain and his mate. "Do you still have your security identification? Tell the gargoyles Malikah has hired us to investigate the poisoning. Tell Sam we've discovered the poison came in the sweets, and we wondered where they'd bought them. After that, play it by ear."

"Are you okay with Elspeth and I taking the lead?"

"Yeah. I haven't met Sam yet and want to stay in the background and observe. Tell them I'm a scientist and you're worried their people could be in danger. You might even insinuate the wolves are getting rid of other paranormals, so they control the entire Auckland area." Relief filled him when Iain didn't mention asking about Malikah's past. Seth trusted her and August had told him enough that he believed her story about the massacre.

"Sneaky." Elspeth's glance held approval. "If someone came to me with that story, I'd buy it."

Iain clapped Seth on the shoulder. "Yeah, the story contains enough truth to make it believable. Right, let's see what we can shake free."

The trio strode to the entrance and rang the bell. Seth had walked past this building many times, but he'd never spotted guards. To most passersby, the building resembled an office block. Since the paranormals had come out, the guards had made themselves visible and stood in a partial form, their curving horns and furled wings on display.

A group of human teens skateboarding down the street gawked in interest.

"You got the wrong place?" a skinny Māori kid called.

"Yeah, those there are gargoyles," his young, equally thin friend said with relish.

His mates nudged each other, their toothy grins telling Seth they thought this might be entertaining.

Elspeth chuckled. "Which one of you guys wants to give them a thrill?"

"If we didn't want to speak with this Sam, I'd do it. Give them dragon eyes," Iain said. "Ask them about strangers giving them sweets. Tell them about the poisoned children. If they're skating on this street a lot, they might have seen something to help our investigation."

Elspeth saluted Iain, and Seth grinned. He'd liked Elspeth when he'd met her earlier, and seeing them interact gave him confidence for his future with Malikah. "I like your mate. She makes you happy."

"Yes." Iain rang the bell again. "They're slow in answering. Are we sure they're here?"

A gargoyle landed on a ledge above them with a thump. "What do you want?"

His gravelly voice and abrupt arrival stopped Elspeth from conversing with the kids. The teenagers backed up while Elspeth stepped in front to offer protection. When nothing further happened, she spoke to the children and rejoined them.

"We're here to see Sam. If he's not here, we'd like to see

whoever is in charge."

"Why?" the gargoyle demanded.

"I'm a private investigator looking into a poisoning case. Several gargoyle children have had stasis forced on them, and they're slowly dying."

"Someone poisoned them? Are you sure? I heard kids from the other colony were sick, but we were told to keep away because the illness might spread to our young ones."

"Who are you?" Seth asked.

"I am the head guard. Graphite is my name."

"Might we come inside? We have discovered the identity of the poison and how someone administered it," Seth said.

"How?" Graphite demanded.

"The poison was in a packet of sweets. Some sweets contained poison, while others were edible. It was a case of playing Russian roulette with the children's lives," Iain added grimly.

"Where did the sweets come from?" Graphite asked.

"They were part of the contents of a food parcel given to the gargoyles by two women from your colony," Iain replied, not pulling his punches.

"The human children," Elspeth said, interrupting. "They told me they skateboard here most days. A woman approached them with a packet of sweets yesterday. They took them and thanked her but tossed them into a bin because their parents told them not to take sweets from strangers. I'm going to retrieve them now. Bet at least some contain poison."

"What has that got to do with us?" Graphite demanded,

his shrug of bulky shoulders dismissive.

"The woman came from your building. The kid I spoke with almost hit her last week, and they and the woman had a shouting match. She threatened them and told them to play somewhere else. Her friend gave them the bag of sweets," Elspeth said. "They gave me a description. All I need to do is find those sweets and test them. If they contain poison, we'll have an excellent case against this woman who logically is a member of your colony."

"Fuck," Graphite said.

"Exactly," Iain said. "Let us speak with Sam."

"He's not here. He took his wife away for the weekend."

"When will he return?" Seth asked.

"Tomorrow evening," Graphite said.

"Will you allow us to question your people?" Iain asked.

Graphite's wings flickered in agitation. "You don't think one of us will poison kids? That's...that's a despicable act."

"Yes, it is, which is why we wish to speak with your people. Do you have the authority to let us do this?" Iain asked.

Graphite's bulky shoulders heaved. "Yes, but I wish to witness the questioning. I'll need to report to the boss on his return."

"We have no objection to that," Iain said.

Graphite disappeared and seconds later, the door opened. He stood back to allow them entry. "Please excuse my curiosity, but why did the gargoyles hire two werewolves and a dragon as their investigators?"

"The leader of the small group wished to have a neutral

party run the investigation. Now that we've discovered the poisoned sweets came from your colony, she understands she's entering dangerous territory."

Graphite opened his mouth, but Iain continued speaking. "We're aware anyone might have added the sweets to the parcel. That is why we wish to question those who prepared the food and those who delivered it to Malikah's colony. We are not accusing anyone."

While Iain organized with Graphite the best way to interview the gargoyles, Seth contacted Malikah. *"They've agreed to let us question their people."*

"They offered no resistance?" Her anxiety throbbed through her question, her concern that this situation might detonate into trouble.

"Graphite seems reasonable, especially when he heard about the sick children."

"Please take care. You're vulnerable when you're in their territory."

"I might have a task for you. Just a sec." Seth turned to Elspeth and spoke in an undertone. "Should I ask Malikah to search the rubbish bins?"

"Good idea. I'd prefer to wait here and watch for trouble. The more eyes, the better."

"I'll ask Malikah to speak with the kids if they're still skateboarding. They can show her exactly where they tossed the sweets. We'll have to hope the city hasn't collected trash yet."

Elspeth's mouth firmed, and determination radiated from her. "We will catch the culprit and make sure he or she never repeats this horror story."

"Thank you," Seth replied.

"You're Iain's best friend. I'd help you in any way I can," Elspeth said.

Seth sent the information to Malikah.

"Thank you for giving me something to do. I was going crazy up here," Malikah said.

"It's not a straightforward task. The kids are smartarse and full of attitude. You'll need your A-game," Seth said, picturing the kids. Malikah wasn't used to dealing with commoners. Her people were equally tentative and hostile toward her. From the little Malikah had shared, he understood their reactions. Although it was clear to him, Malikah was trying to better her relationship with the other gargoyles.

"I can do this." Malikah interrupted his thoughts. *"This is important, so I must use my charm."*

Seth grinned at her more formal tone. *"I'll contact you soon."*

"Iain has organized the people to arrive one at a time. We're starting with the kitchen staff," Elspeth murmured to catch him up. "We should listen and observe. Make the gargoyles uncomfortable because ill-at-ease people blurt interesting information."

"Who is first?" Iain asked Graphite.

"The cook," Graphite replied. "She is our kitchen head and responsible for the meal plans and staff supervision."

The tall and voluptuous woman with short red hair glided into the room and took the seat Graphite gestured toward. She sat without a blink. She didn't seem astonished at the presence of non-gargoyles, so

Seth presumed Graphite had warned his people. He frowned, wishing they could've questioned the gargoyles without giving them a warning. Unfortunately, years of polite paranormal protocol between the species meant this would never happen.

Iain and Seth exchanged a glance, and Seth nodded for Iain to go ahead with the questioning.

"What can you tell us about the box of food prepared for the new gargoyle colony?" Iain asked.

The gargoyle observed him with a steady gaze, her eyes clear, her posture relaxed. "Sam directed his wife to organize the parcel. She came to me and suggested several items to send to the refugees. I checked our stores and packed the box myself."

"Did you place a packet of sweets in with the supplies?"

"Yes," the cook said without hesitation. "We'd made a fresh batch of boiled sweets and one of fudge. I added them to the food box. Gargoyles have a sweet tooth, and I knew the children would enjoy the treats."

"You packed the box yourself?"

"I did," the cook said, once again without hesitation and her expression open and honest.

"This woman didn't do it," Seth murmured to Iain.

"I agree." Iain turned his attention to the woman again. "What did you do with the box after you'd packed it?"

"I placed it on my office desk until Sam organized someone to deliver it."

"Does anyone apart from you have access to your office?"

"The door is closed but not locked when I'm away from

my office. It's visible from most of the kitchen, and it is unlikely anyone sneaked into my office and added poison to the sweets."

"But not impossible?"

"No."

"Do you have any suggestions as to how poisoned sweets might have made their way into the food box?" Iain asked.

The woman issued a harsh sigh. "I hate this. I oversaw the preparation of the sweets because I was teaching the youngsters the proper process." She paused, her brow crinkling as if she were deep in thought. Her head jerked upward. "What color were the sweets?"

15

MALIKAH PEEKED FROM HER rooftop perch to study the busy thoroughfare below. Buses chugged along the road, halting to disgorge passengers while other commuters sped to their destinations. Pedestrians carrying shopping bags hustled to the nearby car park building. She spotted the kids playing on their skateboards about a block away, which dragged her back to the matter at hand. Her sick kids. The not knowing had frustration bubbling through her, and she was finding it difficult to remain still. Even a gargoyle child could do better.

"Malikah?"

Every muscle in her body relaxed on hearing Seth's voice. It seeped into her mind, filled with warmth and caring. He was a decent man, and she was coming to rely on him for advice. In the past, she might've rejected his help, which showed how much she'd changed from that spoiled Northern England girl. She trusted him.

Not once had he failed to keep his promises or shown anything but genuine caring for her and her colony of misfits. The thought of her parents' disdain made her stomach churn. She could almost hear their mocking voices, calling him a half-breed.

While she mourned her parents' deaths, looking back, she understood why their people had resented them. In time, they might've rebelled. Instead, the clan from the south had taken advantage of their complacency and annihilated them in the surprise attack.

She couldn't help but feel fortunate to have survived and wanted to embrace everything this new world offered.

She refused to mess up this opportunity.

"Malikah, are you there?" Concern filled the warm voice.

"Sorry. You caught me daydreaming. Has something happened?"

"I need you to conduct a search and speak with human children." Seth explained what he wanted her to do and why.

"All right." Malikah was pleased to have a task, although she wasn't confident in her abilities. These human children would likely run a mile and refuse to speak with her, just like the gargoyle kids. Her understanding that blind power wasn't enough to win trust and loyalty made her wary and doubt her abilities in social interactions. It was actions and deeds that counted. *"I'll search for the sweets first and speak to the children if they're still around."*

"This will be a slow process," Seth warned. *"The questioning might take longer than we'd hoped. The staff is*

loyal and not giving us much."

"We're making progress. Go. Concentrate on the interviews," Malikah said.

Once Seth turned his focus back to the interviews, a stir of panic bubbled in her belly. For once, it wasn't acute hunger. Anxiety seeped into her, fear that she might mangle her task. Aware she was procrastinating, she stiffened her spine and flew to street level, her wings outstretched to maneuver on the breeze.

"Whoa!" someone blurted.

Malikah tucked in her wings and rotated slowly to face a wide-eyed human kid. He had skin a shade darker than Seth's, and his eyes were golden brown. He wore ripped jeans, a faded green T-shirt, and a decent serve of attitude.

Malikah batted down her fear. This was a human kid. Kids, she amended when she noted more joining the first. She'd dealt with humans before, and these pint-sized ones shouldn't present trouble.

"Who are you? What are you?" the kid demanded.

"I am Malikah." Looking more closely, she noted he wasn't a child but at that halfway stage between child and adult. The teens didn't seem scared. They didn't realize gargoyles could kill a human in seconds with their sharp talons and the blades on their wings. One punch from her solid fist would put this boy down, yet not one showed fear. They truly didn't understand her race.

"I am a gargoyle," she said.

"Can we touch your wings?" another child asked, awe in his voice.

"Yes, but you must do something for me."

"We don't do blowjobs or any of that shit," the tallest in the group spat.

"No!" Luckily, Malikah's horror emerged in the bark of her reply. "You spoke to my friends earlier. About the sweets two ladies gave you?"

The kids' bony shoulders dropped, and their hostility eased.

"Are they gargoyles too?" a short kid with long black hair clasped in a tail asked.

"One is a werewolf. One is a dragon, and my boyfriend is half werewolf and half gargoyle." It gave Malikah a thrill to acknowledge Seth as her boyfriend, even if it was a tepid description of what lay between them. *Mates.*

Now that she'd had time to consider the matter, it no longer scared her. She liked Seth, and possibilities stretched between them in a warm hum of energy.

"Is it true someone gave children poison in their sweets?" a kid asked.

"Yes," Malikah spoke honestly, so they understood how important it was for her to retrieve those sweets. She laughed inwardly, plainly hearing her mother's horrified words. Royals do not associate with commoners and not with humans. *Disgusting, dirty creatures. They have no morals.* Her mother and father had uttered many such orders, none of which had helped them to survive the massacre. She dragged her mind from the past. "Three of the children in our group have succumbed to stasis."

"What is stasis?" one boy asked, curiosity lighting his brown eyes.

"That is when a gargoyle goes to its stone form and

freezes in position," Malikah explained. "One of our gargoyles can speak with others telepathically. He spoke to each child, but their brains were confused, and they could only tell us they became sick after eating sweets."

"So they're alive but frozen and aware?" the boy, who appeared to be the leader, asked.

"Yes."

"Are they in pain?"

Malikah hesitated. "They're distressed."

"Can you cure them? Take them to a doctor?"

"The dragon medic has visited. We've transported the children to the dragon's compound, and they're consulting with the witch coven." Once again, she told the truth and didn't hedge because of their age.

The kids shared an uneasy glance, their eyes big and round.

"Witches? Like with big hats, pointy noses, and warts?" a boy with blond hair squeaked.

Malikah grinned. "I believe these witches are more attractive. From what I understand, you could pass them on the street and never know."

"The people who spoke to us earlier looked normal," a tow-head kid said.

"Elspeth told us someone from this building gave you sweets," Malikah said, wanting to get the conversation back on track. "Can you tell me about that?"

Once again, the kids shared a speaking glance.

The largest kid spoke. "We skateboard here after school and during the weekends. Few cars. Rad obstacles. We make noise." He shrugged his bony shoulder. "We're kids.

Ma says that's what kids do. Last month, a new boy—he's not here today—almost hit this lady when she came out of the building. An accident. He didn't mean to do it. I think she was grumpy when she stomped outside. Her face was all red. Mato said sorry. He apologized twice, but the lady was real bitchy. She swore at him before she got into a black sports car and drove away. Another time, she almost ran us over, driving on the wrong side of the road. She wobbled when she tried to walk." His lip curled in disgust. "And she smelled like my uncle when he comes home from the pub."

"Can you tell me what this lady looked like?"

"She tall and blonde. Pretty." His hands traced a curvy, feminine shape in the air, and one boy snickered. "She's here a lot. I've seen her with other ladies and a big blond man."

Not much to go on since many in Sam's colony had fair coloring. "What happened next?"

"We kept skating until five before we caught the train home. We saw the same lady with another one the next morning. Saturday. She glared at us and stomped inside. Not long after, the lady she was with came out with the sweets. She told us they were testing a new recipe and acted all disappointed when we didn't eat them straight away. It started raining, and I told her we had to go. When we were around the corner, I tossed the candy into a bin. Something 'bout her insistence... Didn't feel right, ya know? That's why I dumped them."

"You did the right thing," Malikah agreed. "Can you show me the bin?"

"Yeah, this way." He gestured and started walking. Malikah fell into step with him. The other kids followed, amusing Malikah. It made her think of the wizard who lured children away from their homes when the village failed to pay for services rendered. This gaggle of kids joked and teased and spoke loudly, bringing a smile to her face. To them, this was an unusual adventure to add excitement to their day.

The truth—if those sweets had contained poison, these kids were lucky to be alive.

They rounded the corner, and the kid's leader halted. "Charlie is searching the bin!"

Malikah spotted a shaggy man in a long black raincoat digging through the trash. "Stop!" she shouted and started running.

Charlie retreated, holding a bread roll and a packet of candy aloft. "Mine!" he cried. "They're mine."

"Charlie," the kid said, advancing slowly as if approaching a scared animal. "Those sweets are poison. They might kill you."

"They're mine," Charlie snapped, still backing away.

"He can't eat them," Malikah murmured to the children. "I'd hate anyone else to suffer like our kids." She thought furiously. "Give me the sweets, and I'll give you two new packets."

"You'll let me keep the roll?"

"Yes, that's yours."

Charlie ceased backing up, a shifty slyness catapulting across his features. "I want two packets of lollies and a chocolate bar."

Malikah spluttered a laugh. "You drive a hard bargain," she said, amused despite the seriousness of the situation. "Deal."

Charlie marched to the nearest brick wall and dropped onto the pavement, his back against the solid surface. He set the packet of candy beside him and pulled the roll farther from the paper bag. He surveyed it, brushed off what might have been a candy wrapper, and started to eat.

"Can I have the sweets?" Malikah approached him slowly in case she scared him into running.

"No," he said. "I want my chocolate bar first."

Frustration swept Malikah, and temptation whispered—for a brief second—to take the sweets by force. She could do it easily and wouldn't have hesitated in the past, but that wasn't the way to establish trust. She huffed out a breath while she tried to work out the best course of action.

"If you have money, I can send Max," the kid's leader suggested, gesturing at a kid.

"I don't have cash," Malikah said, scowling. And she had exactly five dollars in small change back at the warehouse, which wouldn't purchase sweets and chocolate. "Not a cent."

"You're lying," the towhead said. "All adult people have money."

"Check my pockets," Malikah said, her voice grim now because this lack of finances was embarrassing. She'd never had to worry before, and her parents had never stinted in providing her every need. That had been the first shock of many since she'd reached Auckland.

"You really have no money?" the blonde kid asked.

"No, I start a job soon. My friends might have money. They're in the gargoyle building."

"Call them," a kid prompted.

Malikah stared at him blankly. "How?"

The kid rolled his brown eyes. "Geez, don't you know anything? Use your phone."

"I don't have one."

The kid gaped at her. "Everyone has a phone."

"Not me. I lost everything before I came here."

"You a refugee?"

Yep, that applied to her.

"Don't you have some rinky-dinky powers you can use?" the kid's leader asked.

"Um, I can fly," Malikah said, wishing fervently that she didn't feel so useless.

"Malikah?" Seth's voice interrupted this embarrassing conversation regarding her shortcomings. *Thank goodness.*

"Just a minute," she said to the kids, raising her hand while she focused on Seth. *"Seth, I need enough money to purchase two packets of sweets and a bar of chocolate. I don't have any, and I won't get my hands on those sweets until I pay up."*

There was a pause. *"Someone holding those things for ransom?"*

"Yeah."

"Sounds like an interesting story," Seth said. Another pause. *"Iain will be out with cash in a few minutes."*

"Tell him we're around the corner, close to the end of the street."

"Don't worry. Iain will find you," Seth said.

Someone tugged hard on her sleeve. "You all right?"

"I was asking Seth for money," Malikah said to the head kid. "What's your name?"

"Levi." He sent her an odd look.

"Right, Levi. Iain will be here in a few minutes with money."

"You mind speak?"

"Not really. Seth is the one with the power to do that. I am good at camouflage."

"Cool." Levi's eyes shone with curiosity. She could see his questions spinning.

Luckily, Iain came into sight, loping toward them.

"You could take them from Charlie," Levi said.

"I could," Malikah said. "But that isn't fair to Charlie. A trade is fair."

"How much money do you need?" Iain asked.

"Enough for two packets of sweets, a chocolate bar, and something for the rest of us to eat while we wait," Malikah said.

"The fish and chip shop next to the dairy is good," Levi said.

Malikah grinned at him. "Enough for fish and chips for us and Charlie."

"Excellent plan. Things are slow in there, and I'm convinced a couple of them are lying through their teeth." Iain did a swift headcount and handed her several notes.

"Levi, could you get the food and the sweets and chocolate for me while I stay here to chat with Charlie?" Malikah asked after Iain disappeared around the corner.

"You'd trust me?"

Malikah nodded, restraining her amusement. "You could run off with the money and leave me in a mess. Plus, I'd end up hungry," she added. "I turn grumpy when I'm starving. I should point out that running would be a huge mistake on your part. *Huge.* Do you know why?"

Levi shook his head, and she noted the boys listening with close attention.

"Because I have wolves at my disposal. Dragons and gargoyles, too, but wolves are the scariest. Not only do they have sharp teeth and claws, but their tracking abilities? *The. Best.*" Malikah's lips quivered, the urgent and unroyal urge to giggle fighting hard for release.

The kids, however, took her seriously. Levi shared quick glances with the rest of his group, and as one, they nodded agreement.

"We can really buy fish and chips with the money?" Levi asked.

"You can," Malikah agreed. "I'll tell you a secret. I've never eaten fish and chips." Not a lie. Her mother classified it as a peasant dish, which meant it wasn't a meal they'd try.

"What sort of candy should I get?"

"Ask Charlie if he has any preferences," Malikah said. "I'm going to stay and watch those sweets like a hawk because if they contain poison, we might work out who is hurting the gargoyle children."

Levi nodded. "Do gargoyles skateboard?"

"I don't know. None of us has ventured far from our warehouse. I'll ask and let you know."

Levi hesitated. "If they haven't, we could teach them."

Malikah smiled. "The kids would love that. Are you okay with teaching girls?"

"I'd have to check with the others," Levi said.

"That's fair," Malikah agreed and handed over the money. "When you get back, I'll get you and the others to describe the lady again."

"She's here a lot," Levi said. "Might be easier to point her out to you."

"Excellent plan," Malikah said, renewed anger filling her. She was disgusted that a gargoyle woman would intentionally give kids poisoned sweets. She couldn't work out the why, and that bothered her most of all.

16

FRUSTRATION BUILT IN SETH as they interviewed everyone who served food in the colony kitchen or purchased supplies. Not a scrap of helpful information ensued. The facts: the sweets had held poison, and the item had come from this colony. Someone must know something. The last two people came and went, and Seth remained no wiser. He hadn't sensed lies, which made this situation even more difficult.

"We need to speak to whoever delivered the food," Iain said, having returned from giving Malikah money.

The head of security shrugged. "I'm afraid that won't be possible. Besides, I doubt Sam would want you to question his wife while he was absent."

Seth froze. "Sam's wife took the food."

"One time," the security guy said, his cavalier attitude suggesting they were overreacting and grasping at straws. "An act of kindness on her part. You can hardly blame her.

I mean, why would she poison kids she doesn't know?"

An excellent question and one Seth had no answer for, dammit. "Who went with Sam's wife to deliver the food?"

"Probably Fluffy. The pair are as thick as thieves." He scratched his chin. "From memory, that was the first delivery. The second time, Sam and his wife were out of town at a business conference in Rotorua. I believe the cook organized the food basket. Surely she told you that?"

She had, but the head of security hadn't been present, and Seth wanted to compare stories. Seth stretched out his hand. "Thank you for your time and for letting us question your people. We appreciate your cooperation."

The gargoyle shook Seth's hand but gave a faint eye roll, as if this was beyond him. He trailed them until they reached the courtyard. There, he handed over to a younger gargoyle and departed without a backward glance.

The guard followed them outside and planted himself on the top step. The gate clunked shut in dismissal.

Well. That had been helpful. Seth fell into step with Iain and Elspeth and decided he'd experiment and try to communicate with both at the same time. He focused and imagined splitting his question in half before sending the words forth as he'd done in the past. *"That was a bust. We didn't learn much more than we knew already."*

"I disagree," Iain said.

"Yep, I'm with Iain," Elspeth replied after a faint hesitation.

"You both heard me?" Seth asked aloud.

"It's weird. Your words sort of tickle my brain," Elspeth said. "It's different from when I mindspeak with Iain."

"That's the perfect way of describing the sensation," Iain agreed. "We should look more closely at Sam's wife. I've never met her. Have you?"

"I haven't met any gargoyles apart from the ones in Malikah's colony. I'm a half-breed and given my experiences with the wolves, I haven't pushed a meeting. My gargoyle advisor mentioned I'm an anomaly, although he wasn't speaking with malice."

"Think of it this way," Elspeth said. "You can shift into a wolf and into a gargoyle. You have wolf allies and, through me, the dragons. That makes you a major kick-arse dude."

Iain gave a half laugh, half snort while Seth shook his head and smiled. Elspeth was perfect for his friend, and it thrilled him to see Iain cheerful and relaxed. He hoped he found the same happiness with Malikah.

Just as he thought of Malikah, she strolled around the corner with a gaggle of kids who were talking loudly to snare her attention. She spotted them and grinned, lengthening her strides to reach them faster. Seth had never seen her so at ease. It was a good look for her.

"How did it go?" she asked, her gaze expectant.

"We're sure none of the kitchen staff committed the crime. My opinion—someone tampered with the food after it left the kitchen. They gave us the impression Esmerelda and Fluffy delivered the food basket immediately, but using an injector needle wouldn't have taken long. Or a few minutes if they'd doctored the sweet packet earlier and exchanged it with the one in the hamper," Seth said.

"This might help." Malikah held up a grease-streaked

brown paper bag, beaming. Her posture was erect, and she radiated confidence that hadn't been present earlier. "Charlie finally surrendered the sweets the boys tossed in the trash."

"What was the price?" Seth asked. That triumphant expression looked cute on her. Gods, he wanted to kiss her again. His need was an acute ache in his chest, but now wasn't the right time for romance. The wolf pack might be in disarray, but Raoul was a tenacious bastard who hated to lose. Seth had pricked his pride, and a wounded wolf was a dangerous one. He'd hate Malikah or her people to get caught in the crossfire.

Malikah's grin widened. "He was a tough negotiator. Charlie gave them up for two packets of candy, a bar of chocolate, and half of my fries."

Seth scanned the bunch of kids, who were paying close attention to the discussion. "Can you give us a description?"

Malikah gestured at a gangly preteen. "Levi volunteered to point her out tomorrow. He said she goes in and out of the building most days. He hasn't seen her today, which is unusual."

"We don't want her to spot you," Seth said, a wave of sudden fear taking him by surprise. "The kids need to find somewhere else to skateboard, even if it's only for a few weeks. Are you willing to do that?"

"We will on one condition," Levi said, instantly. "We want to meet your gargoyle children."

"Why?" Seth asked.

"We think it'd be cool to play with gargoyles."

"They're like regular kids," Iain said. "When I was growing up, I played with human kids. They never knew."

Elspeth grinned. "You're probably already playing with paranormals and don't know it."

The rapid glances left and right from each of the kids made Seth laugh. "No, we mean at school," he said. "They're normal kids who enjoy playing the same way you do." Hopefully, he was saying the right things, because from what he'd gleaned from Malikah, her kids had experienced a rough time of it.

"We're relocating to a place north of Auckland," Malikah said, "but I can bring the kids to visit you guys once we've made sure everyone is safe and well."

"All right," Levi said. "We'll skateboard at the other end of the street where we can see, but we're not too close. I'll call you when the lady arrives. Sometimes, she comes with a man, but mostly it is with her friend."

Seth glanced at Malikah, then spoke his thoughts aloud. "That sounds like Sam's wife, Esmerelda. No, it couldn't be," he said, frowning. "What reason would she have to hurt innocent children?"

"There's no point speculating. We'll get these checked for poison." Malikah smiled at Levi. "What time will you be here tomorrow? No, better. Call Seth when you leave school."

Levi jerked his chin in acknowledgment. "Later."

He and the rest of the kids trotted away and disappeared around the corner.

"Do you think they'll be safe playing here?" Malikah asked. "I don't like it. I feel twitchy."

"That's because someone is watching us," Iain said in a low voice.

Seth had sensed something off too, and it was weird experiencing this through wolf and gargoyle senses. "Anyone feel like food? I want to drop these sweets at the lab and get something to eat. I'm starving."

Malikah fell into step beside him. "When will we have lab results?"

"Depends on my friend's workload. She mostly crams this into her spare time. I'm hoping less than a week. She'll do her best."

"I don't like this." Iain spoke in a low voice. "There's more than one following us."

"I haven't spotted them," Elspeth said.

Iain scanned the street. "I haven't glimpsed anyone either, but I feel their presence. It's an itch in the middle of my back. They're good. Probably professionals."

"Wolves?" Seth asked, apprehension running up and down his spine.

"They're not above us," Elspeth said.

"No," Malikah said. "They're on the ground. If it was a gargoyle attack, they'd be up higher. We feel safer when we can look down and scope out our surroundings."

"We need to get off the street," Seth said. "Which is a problem for me. My shift to gargoyle is as slow as my shift to wolf. What about if I try to communicate with them? My voice in their head might shock them into telling us who they are or what they want."

"Can you do that?" Iain asked in surprise.

"No idea. You guys keep watch while I concentrate. I

find it difficult to multitask with gargoyle things."

"Wait until we get to the main street," Elspeth suggested. "It might not stop an attack, but there will be more people around."

"If that's what we're doing, we'd better move it," Iain warned.

Seth scowled and barely resisted a glance over his shoulder. "They're trying to cut us off. My bet is they don't want witnesses."

"You're enjoying this." Malikah glanced at Seth. "You are, too."

"A wolf thing," Iain said easily. "We like to hunt and evade. It's something we're taught and practice from pups."

They hustled, but seconds before they attempted to enter Queen Street, a black form slid in front of them.

"I don't recognize him," Iain said.

"Unfortunately, I do," Seth muttered.

17

Pissed but resigned. Those were the vibes Malikah caught from Seth. As if he'd expected this man and was powerless to prevent the meeting.

"Who's that?" she whispered.

Seth heaved a sigh. "That's Raoul, the head of the pack's science team and my ex-boss."

"You've led me a merry chase, Puny," Raoul called in a strong, no-nonsense voice. It was the confident tones of a man used to having his orders followed without question. "You promised you'd almost perfected the inhibitor. You gave me your word you'd complete the assignment."

Seth drew up sharply. He glowered at the bulky man wearing a black suit and shoes so shiny, Malikah thought she'd see her reflection if she dared to step closer.

"That was before I learned what you intended to do with *your* groundbreaking product. The product I worked on for years," Seth spat.

Iain, who'd remained silent until now, stepped up to Seth's side.

"You! You screwed up my timeline." Raoul's features darkened and his almost black eyes flashed with temper. "Take them down. All of them."

Six figures in black stepped from the shadows, snarls on their faces and weapons in their hands. Two more werewolves slunk from the dim passage in their wolf forms.

Malikah reacted instinctively, letting the transformation rip through her. Desperation made it a rapid shift, and seconds later, she seized Seth. Her massive wings beat hard, lifting them into the air. Seth was heavy, despite his lanky build, and after an initial surge, she plummeted.

Fear—crisp with an edge of steel—flooded her as her wings struggled to keep her aloft. No, she couldn't crumple, couldn't strike the ground. She'd already failed her people and now the children were sick. She refused to blunder again. Malikah grunted and redoubled her efforts, clutching Seth with her talons. Seth struggled, shouting words she couldn't hear because of the roaring in her ears.

Behind them, flames seared the air with heat, with power, with yelps.

Elspeth. Malikah couldn't afford to look, to help. She'd retreat and regroup with another plan later.

A weapon fired, the explosion ringing her ears. Seth grunted, the sound more wolfish than gargoyle. She spared a brief glance downward and saw she was clutching a reddish-brown wolf. In that brief second, she also spotted Raoul's frustration.

"Shoot them, damn it!" he roared, pulling a gun from

his pocket.

Malikah renewed her efforts to fly higher, over the rooftops and out of range. The lane was a narrow one, surrounded by tall brick buildings and signage. Malikah darted forward, flying low because of the obstructions. Bullets zinged, spitting dust and splinters of wood at them.

More flames lit the gloom, and a wolf howled in pain. Exhaustion filled her muscles, restricting her speed. Up ahead, a gap in the signage. Could she escape over the rooftops? She zigzagged in that direction, ignoring the surge of gunfire and fighting fatigue.

Where the devil were the human police?

Gunshots in the city streets weren't commonplace. Someone should've notified the cops by now.

Renewed shooting echoed in the narrow lane, then a second later, her leg burned so badly she almost dropped Seth. With a grunt, she forced herself higher and over the rooftops until she spotted a flat surface.

Below them, a light glowed. A man screamed, sending a shudder through Malikah.

Malikah's landing wasn't a thing of beauty. She thumped to the hard surface, groaning at the reverberation through her legs. Recalling Seth, she rolled and noted he was now in human form, his clothing rags.

Long moments later, she pushed up from her prone position and took stock. Her entire body throbbed, as if she'd forced it past capacity. Even her wings ached as she tucked them to her back.

"Seth. Seth?" Tentatively, she shook his shoulder and when he didn't react, panic reared in her. Malikah's throat tightened and tears blurred her vision.

He had to be all right. She forced herself to calm, sucking in several hoarse breaths before rolling Seth. Blood seeped from a wound on his hip and another on his leg.

"Seth. Seth. Seth," she muttered, groping to check his pulse.

The thready beat beneath her fingertips reassured her. None of his wounds seemed life threatening, but he wasn't cognizant and didn't look like regaining consciousness soon. She brushed Seth's unruly hair away from his face, stilling when blood coated her hand. Carefully, she explored his head wound. Either a bullet or another type of projectile had grazed him. It didn't appear deep but bled profusely. She shifted to her human form and ripped the hem of her blouse to make a pad. She pressed it against the injury.

The sounds of the attack had died down, and Malikah ran across the sloping rooftops, jumping without hesitation until she could see the lane. Several men sprawled on the street. She couldn't see Raoul but noted charred lumps and shuddered. Wolf remains.

"Iain? Elspeth?" Her breath caught. "Are you there?"

"Iain got shot," Elspeth called. "He's shifted to wolf to press the bullet out of his body. We think the bullet contains silver, and his healing is taking longer."

Elspeth's calm demeanor went a long way to soothing Malikah's angst.

"Seth has a head wound and a gash on his hip and leg."

"It's safe here now," Elspeth said. "Everyone who got too close burned, and Iain had a gun. They didn't expect him to return fire."

"What about Raoul?"

"He disappeared. Everything happened so fast I didn't see him leave. When he stopped issuing orders, we assumed we'd injured him. He isn't among the dead or wounded."

"I'm coming down. I don't like to leave Seth alone for too long, but he's safe," Malikah said, rapidly shifting.

It took every scrap of energy to glide to street level.

"Elspeth." *Great gargoyle heavens.* Iain looked worse than she'd envisioned. He shifted into his wolf and sent her a doggy grin. "Are you sure you're okay?"

"He will be," Elspeth said with confidence. "He's too stubborn to die, especially since I'm pregnant, and if he dies, I'll be furious at him." Her mouth twisted. "This seemed to help him decide to live."

Iain huffed. He shifted and hurriedly dressed, looking much better. "I'm fine."

"Congratulations," Malikah said.

Elspeth pulled a face. "It's not what either of us planned, but we're happy. It means changes for both of us. Instead of doctoring Seth on the roof, can you bring him down? The humans will arrive soon. If his cuts and wounds are minor, let them treat him."

"I'm not sure I have the strength to bring him down. Not without injuring him more." Wooziness had her blinking to focus, and without warning, her knees buckled. She hit the pavement with a grinding crack. Ouch! Tears stung her eyes, but she bit back the pain. Now was not the time to faint.

"You're injured," Elspeth said, concern flooding her

expression. "Wait there and watch Iain. Shout if you see anything suspicious."

Malikah nodded. "I'll guard him with my life." She meant it.

Elspeth retreated to the main street to shift. Soon, a black dragon gained altitude before hovering at roof height.

Malikah pushed to her feet, forcing her traitorous limbs to support her weight. A siren blared, and Malikah frowned. The vehicle was coming closer, as were the shopkeepers and pedestrians who'd fled the moment guns started firing.

Before she could decide what to do, Elspeth arrived with a still unconscious Seth, and the humans backed to the safety of the stores. The sirens kept coming closer, the constant wail reverberating through her head and pushing at her panic.

Elspeth shifted and hurriedly pulled a pair of black sweats from a pack Malikah hadn't seen until now.

"Don't worry," she said with a kind smile as she dressed. "Seth is conscious."

"Thank you," Malikah said, her attention split between Seth and the incoming police cars. Judging by the siren's wails, their arrival was imminent.

"Check on your mate," Elspeth said. "We'll have to deal with the police. Don't make any sudden moves. We don't want them to arrest us. Hopefully, the humans hiding in the store saw everything and will reassure the police officers we mean them no harm."

Malikah stumbled over to Seth. She kneeled beside him,

checking his wounds again. Blood still trickled from his head, and she discovered two other injuries. One was a long furrow, while the other appeared deeper.

She glanced up and found Seth watching her, his blue eyes holding pain.

"You're awake. Can you shift to wolf and back?" She stood and gave him space, silently praying that he could transform. Her breath eased out as his shift began.

A police car pulled up, and two officers climbed out. They glanced in their direction and did a double-take.

"You over there," a male voice shouted.

Malikah swallowed, fear flashing through her.

"Don't worry," Elspeth said. "Iain and I will deal with them. You help Seth."

Malikah nodded and breathed deeply to calm her racing heart. Seth's transformation was slow, and she winced because his grimace told her the morphing hurt like hell.

"Seth," she said once he finished his shift back. "How do you feel?"

"Like crap."

"Your friends are taking care of the police. Do you have the energy to shift back to your wolf?"

"No." The word was more grunt.

Malikah took in his naked body and glanced away, heat pinking her cheeks. The man was lean, yet her glance had taken in tempting muscle and... The warmth in her face turned up a notch to fiery. "You don't have clothes. Um...that might be a problem." An understatement.

The humans across the road had grown braver and lined the sidewalk, brazen in their attempts to gawk at the paranormal creatures. Some had whipped out phones to record the event. Others spoke excitedly, entertained by the encounter between two paranormal groups. Meanwhile, the two cops acted twitchy, and Malikah gave silent thanks New Zealand police officers didn't carry guns. Not yet. That might change, not that guns would aid much against magical beings.

Malikah helped Seth to sit upright.

"I like your gargoyle form. Your voice. It's lower. Husky." His gaze lowered to her lips and lingered. "Sexy."

"Enough of that," Iain said, breaking the seductive spell.

She whirled to face him. "I didn't... We weren't..." She trailed off as she took in his teasing grin.

"Stop ribbing my mate," Seth said, and Malikah turned back to him in concern.

"He needs medical care," she said. "Gunshot wounds and an enormous lump on his head. He's too tired to shift back to his wolf."

"We could take him to the gargoyle healers," Elspeth said.

Malikah sighed. "I doubt they'd help us. They'll worry about trouble following us to their compound." Whoa! Not that she was bitter, but she didn't understand why Sam had made her life so difficult.

"Do we have a spare set of clothes?" Iain crouched beside Seth and checked his wounds. "Why didn't you dodge the bullets?"

Seth's snort emerged and transformed into a groan. "Don't make me laugh."

Elspeth checked her pack and pulled out a pair of track

pants. She thrust them at Malikah. "Help Seth put these on. I'll ask the people for first aid supplies while Iain organizes transportation."

Iain beamed at his mate as she strode across the street, her shoulders back and full of confidence. "I love my bossy wife. I'll be back with transport. Won't be long."

Malikah stared after him and glanced at Elspeth, who was already speaking to the humans. She didn't show fear or anger or impatience, even though she was a dragon and capable of demanding. Malikah couldn't help comparing Seth, Iain, and Elspeth to those she'd called friends back in England. They wouldn't have helped her or those they considered inferior, and to her shame, she would've behaved similarly.

"Can you stand?" she asked Seth.

His eyes had closed, and his face had lost its color.

"I'll try," he croaked. "This wasn't how I wanted to get naked with you."

"Shush. We'll discuss that once you recover."

His eyes flicked open. "We're going to have sex?"

Malikah found herself blushing. "Yes." Seth was a decent man. It hadn't taken her long to discover his sincerity wasn't an act, and she liked the person she was when they spent time together. She helped Seth maneuver his legs into the stretchy pants.

Elspeth returned with a souvenir T-shirt, medical pads, and a roll of surgical tape to hold the pads in place. "I had to give him my watch and promise to go back with money, but this should help. Ah, here's Iain. Do you have any money?"

He handed over his wallet, and Elspeth trotted over to the store. She was back in minutes, clipping her gold watch into place.

A vehicle pulled up beside them. Iain spoke to the driver and opened the front door while Elspeth climbed inside the rear. Malikah helped Seth into the back before scrambling after him.

"We're heading to your warehouse," Iain said. "I thought that was best. We'll arrange for someone to pick us up from there."

"Thank you," Malikah said, turning her attention to Seth. Without his glasses, his eyes were more noticeable—a beautiful blue like the sea on a sunny day. Her thoughts drifted during the journey to the warehouse. She didn't need to worry about her group since she trusted Elspeth's mother to keep them safe.

"Right," Iain said. "While we're en route, tell us why Raoul is so determined to get his hands on you. What have you done that you haven't told me about?"

18

SETH SIGHED, AND EVEN that hurt. He ached everywhere, and the wounds throbbed insistently in perfect rhythm with his head. He suspected the bullets held silver. It was typical of Raoul to take control of everything he and the other scientists had ever invented. Luckily, he'd been smart enough to research antidotes for anything he'd created. Once he'd understood Raoul's motives, he'd missed recording every step of his experiments. He'd included enough to make the paperwork appear correct.

"Can we detour to my apartment?" Hell, he sounded as exhausted as he felt.

"Why?" Iain demanded.

"I need my first aid kit."

"We have one at the warehouse," Malikah said. "It's basic, but given your healing powers, it should be enough."

"No," Seth said, the word heavy on his lips.

"Why?" Iain demanded.

"Silver." Seth barely squeezed out the word. Wooziness filled his brain while his lips had turned numb and uncooperative.

Iain cursed and spoke rapidly to the driver.

"New apartment." Even to his ears, the words sounded garbled.

"That's not the right address," Malikah said.

"But that's the apartment we shared," Iain said.

"Seth has another apartment," Malikah said.

"Yes." Another unintelligible sound from him. He had trouble keeping his eyes open, but his hearing wasn't too bad. He tried sending a thought to Malikah. *My first aid kit is under my bed. I've labeled everything. Silver poisoning treatment. Should work if we hurry.*

Relief flooded him as Malikah urgently spoke to Iain. Tension leached from his shoulders as he slumped. Malikah—at least he thought it was his mate—picked up his hand and wove their fingers together. *Yes, Malikah.* Her light scent, rich with pine and the wild of nature, drifted from her. Elspeth sat on his other side; hers was an amber fragrance with tinges of the Orient and a faint charred undertone.

Seth focused on the scents and the physical touch of the hand holding his. An anchor. A weight that kept him from drifting away. And then came the moment when even that wasn't enough. Seth surrendered to the darkness.

"He's unconscious," Malikah said, fear writhing through her.

His hand sizzled with wet heat beneath her fingers. Seth

had taken that last bullet for her. Recalling the unselfish act underlined how much she'd changed. In the past, she would've taken his deed as her due. She was the royal; his duty was to save her from death, even in his injured state. A snort escaped, dark amusement at her past self. Good gods, she and her family had acted with arrogance. Never again. She smoothed Seth's sandy blond hair off his brow and silently willed him to live.

"How long?" Iain demanded the driver.

"Ten minutes if we don't hit traffic," the driver returned.

The vehicle's brakes shrieked when the driver pulled up beside an old building. Shops and small businesses, with sold or closed signs taped on the doors, took up the ground floor. Most of the windows on the next floor were in a broken state. Boards and cardboard covered some of the gaping holes.

She and Elspeth piled from the cab. After paying, Iain helped with an unconscious Seth, picking him up in a fireman's carry.

"Which way?" he asked.

Malikah hesitated, racking her brain for everything Seth had told her about his flat. Foremost was the memory of his shame. She understood because the area was squalid, with the buildings crammed together higgledy-piggledy. Even she—a newcomer—had heard about this street. At the far end, two men watched them with interest.

"The flat entrance is at the rear of the building," she said, praying her memory wasn't playing her false. But logically, the door must be at the back.

"This way," Elspeth said.

Malikah spotted the men following them. "We have trouble on our heels."

"Doesn't matter," Iain said. "You're coming home with us once we've doctored Seth's wounds. One, it's safer, and two, Seth needs to tell me more about Raoul's plans."

Malikah hesitated. "I'm starting my job tonight. It's taken me ages to find employment, and we need the money." She trusted Seth's friends, telling them the truth without hesitation, even though her pride smarted at the confession.

"You can still work but return with us this afternoon, or does the sun bother you?" Elspeth asked.

"I can handle a bright summer day."

"We're settled then," Elspeth said simply. "Iain will rest easier if Seth is safe." She pulled a face. "We have wolfish news to share. You would've heard the kerfuffle with the paranormal species coming out to humans. Read the stories in the paper—the ones the blogger Sarah Johnson wrote."

Iain glanced at the two determined men heading their way. "Malikah, you take care of Seth, and Elspeth and I will stop those men from causing a nuisance."

Malikah crossed to Iain.

"Can you manage him?" he asked.

"I can walk." Seth's eyes remained closed, and his face was the color of parchment.

"Right," Malikah said briskly, glad he'd regained consciousness. "You walk, and I'll guide you."

"Up the stairs. Second door on the right," Seth

mumbled, his words barely audible.

Malikah took Seth's weight and nodded at Iain's silent query. She could manage, and the quicker, the better. Trusting Iain and Elspeth to deal with their followers, she maneuvered Seth up a flight of stairs. Their footsteps thudded against the metal treads, echoing in the open stairwell.

Malikah reached Seth's floor and staggered. She dragged Seth halfway along the corridor before pausing to breathe. Maybe she should leave him here and run for the first-aid supplies. *Yeah, that would work.* She tried to ease Seth down, but he dropped like a heavy stone, and she winced.

"Sorry." Malikah strode to Seth's apartment. She dragged in a breath and tested the scent. While her sense of smell wasn't as good as a werewolf's, she caught Seth's musk and a stranger's. She reached for the doorknob, expecting it to be locked. It wasn't.

She cautiously opened the door and scanned the one-room apartment. Someone lay on the bed. Seth's bed. Malikah made a quick decision. She could always shift to gargoyle if she needed a surge of strength. The man—it was a man because his long ginger and gray beard looped over his arm. He also smelled human, but he stunk. If anyone needed a bath, it was this man.

He'd made free with Seth's food and drink since a can of baked beans and an empty beer can littered the water-damaged counter. Malikah spotted other signs of the man's nosiness, but it was obvious Seth didn't spend much time in the sparsely furnished room. The one chair bore numerous scratches and a patched cushion. The bed was the only other piece of furniture.

Aware of the ticking clock and Seth's injuries, she edged closer. The man truly reeked—an odor she couldn't describe if she tried. In self-defense, she dropped to the ground to peer under the bed. Relief filled her as she spied Seth's bag. This interloper hadn't made a thorough search of the apartment. *Yet.*

Malikah wriggled nearer, her hand closing over the bag's strap. She dragged it toward her before a startled grunt had her freezing. She jerked back, yanking the bag with her.

"Who the fuck are you?" a rough voice demanded.

Malikah pulled the pack to her stomach in case the man made a grab for it. "Shouldn't that be my question? This isn't your apartment."

The man sat up, revealing his dirty white T-shirt. It bore two suspicious blotches—baked bean sauce, if she were to guess. And were those toast crumbs in his beard? She shuddered and edged away. Someone should hose down this man.

"It's not your apartment either," the man snapped.

"It belongs to my boyfriend."

"Yeah?" The man lifted his chin and narrowed his gaze when he saw Malikah holding the bag. "What are you doing with my pack?"

Malikah sprang to her feet. "It belongs to Seth."

He was going to make trouble. She could practically see his mind working. He wanted the bag and thought he could take her.

Dammit. She didn't have time for this.

The man leaped off the bed before she reached the door.

He grabbed the pack, but Malikah held tight.

"Give me the bag, and you can have the apartment." An excellent deal in his favor, but the man was stupid. Malikah called up her gargoyle form, gripping the bag with all her strength.

The man fell back with a shocked curse. "What the fuck?"

"Let me leave with the pack," Malikah repeated. "You can have everything else." Hopefully, there was nothing here that Seth valued.

"Hand over the bag." The man's eyes glinted with crafty craziness. He still thought he'd emerge the victor in a physical fight.

A loud thump sounded outside, and a fiery light rose above the street window. Dragon fire? Gunfire sounded, and urgency pressed against her chest. *Hurry! Hurry!*

"Give me the fucking bag."

"No," Malikah said. "I don't want to hurt you, but I will if necessary."

The man sneered, his scoffing jeer displaying his opinion. His gaze darted left and right before he sprang.

Instinct took over. Malikah plowed her fist into his fleshy belly. The air exploded from his mouth in one fetid blast, and he dropped to his knees, wheezing. He bowed his head and continued gasping for breath. After two raspy huffs, he curled into a ball.

Nightly stars! She hadn't hurt him that badly. She gaped at the stinky man, willing him to breathe. No, he was still living. Malikah jerked the pack from his hand, and with one last glance and a silent request for forgiveness, fled, taking the bag with her.

She found Seth where she'd left him, his face pale and his breathing as raspy as the man she'd punched moments earlier. She cast a guilty glance over her shoulder, then jumped as a blast of flames seared her vision. *Hurry. Right.* She rifled through the pack, giving silent thanks Seth had labeled everything. She found the small plastic bottle he'd mentioned.

"Seth. Seth!" She grasped his shoulder and shook him.

He didn't react, his head lolling and striking the wall. She winced. *Think, Malikah.* She glanced at the bottle in her hand. It contained a liquid, and it had a pointy top. Perhaps she could squirt it down his throat. Assuming she could get him to swallow the medicine.

"Malikah!" Elspeth shouted. "Did you get it?"

"Yes, but Seth is barely conscious. I'm not sure how to get the treatment into him."

Footsteps clattered on the stairs. A shirtless Iain, his expression fierce. "Elspeth is grabbing another cab. We'll force the stuff down his throat."

Malikah nodded, hearing Iain's worry—the same anxiety that crowded her chest and throat. "Right."

"I'll open his mouth. You squirt the medicine. Seth, mate. Wake up." He grasped Seth's shoulders and hauled him upright with brute strength. "Get ready."

Iain opened Seth's mouth. Seth moaned but didn't struggle.

Not unconscious. A good sign.

"Seth, swallow," Malikah said, her voice urgent. She paused a beat, then squirted the liquid toward the back of his throat.

"Swallow," Iain ordered.

To Malikah's immense relief, Seth obeyed. She waited before repeating the action.

"How much should we give him?" she asked.

Iain frowned. "Maybe one more lot, then we'll see how much he recovers. We can always repeat the dose if he doesn't improve."

"Makes sense," Malikah said, so thankful Iain and Elspeth were with her. She hated thinking of how she and Seth might've fared alone. "Thank you for helping us." She squirted three more drops into Seth's mouth before stoppering the bottle and replacing it in the bag.

"Seth is my best friend," Iain said, hauling a grumbling Seth upright. "If it hadn't been for his friendship, I doubt I would've turned out as well as I have. He suggested moving away from home to gain more independence from my father." His expression turned somber. "I'd do anything for Seth."

It was what he didn't say that brought out envy in Malikah. She'd never had a friend like that. Her so-called friends had been after connections and privilege rather than companionship.

"I'm glad Seth has a friend like you," she said, meaning it. Given Seth's half-breed status, he would've had a rough childhood. He mightn't have known he was half-gargoyle, but his wolf part had been weaker, which would've led to abuse.

"Taxi has arrived," Elspeth called.

"Coming," Iain shouted back. He grinned at Malikah.

"She took care of the two men who thought us easy pickings."

"Were they Raoul's men?"

"Nope. Opportunists after easy money," Iain said. "Was there anything else Seth needed from his apartment while we're here?"

"A man has taken over his room. I...ah...punched him in the stomach."

"I wondered why you'd turned more gargoyle." Iain hauled Seth upright.

"The man was sleeping in Seth's bed when I arrived." She paused, thinking. "It didn't look as if Seth kept much there. I grabbed the pack, and the man woke. He wanted it, which led to a disagreement. I punched him."

"Sounds as if he deserved it." Elspeth winked at Malikah. "You'd better shift, or you won't fit in the cab. I've called my father, but he is picking us up from your warehouse. I believe a few more items require transporting to the farm."

Five minutes later, they left. Malikah kept a close eye on Seth, willing him to become more aware. When he remained still and uncommunicative, worry seeped into her. "Do we need to give Seth more of the medicine?"

Iain turned in the front seat to study his friend, his lips pursed. "We don't want to overdose him when we don't know the potential side effects. Let's wait until we reach the warehouse."

Malikah turned her attention back to Seth. He sat slumped over, and every time she looked at him, panic unfurled in her. Finally, she picked up his hand and curled their fingers together. The physical contact helped to drive away her unease. She'd just found Seth, and the man had crept past her prickliness. She'd come to like him. It didn't seem fair that she should lose the one thing—person—who made her feel good about herself, made her want to be a better gargoyle. She liked who she was when she was with Seth, and she didn't think she was acting selfish to want their relationship to continue. Malikah clasped Seth's hand tighter and puffed out a startled breath.

Seth's eyes were open, and he was watching her.

"Seth," she said. "You're awake."

He frowned at her, his confusion clear. "Who are you?"

19

SETH'S HEAD THUMPED—AN INEXPERIENCED musician playing drums inside his skull. His side throbbed, and his mouth was so dry he didn't think he could force out a single groan, let alone more words. A woman held his hand, her expression full of concern. He got the sense she knew him. He didn't recognize her.

Another woman sat on his other side. She was familiar, but no. Not a name came to mind. He dragged in a breath. She smelled smoky and mysterious.

"Seth," a voice came from the front seat. "Good to see you've joined the land of the living. We were worried about you."

Seth rifled through his memories and came up empty. Frowning, he stared through the window at the scenery. They were in a vehicle and traveling through the city. He swallowed, trying to produce saliva. It didn't work. That throbbing in his head increased with each move.

"Seth, Dad is picking us up from the warehouse. Hopefully, we won't run into further trouble," the more familiar woman said.

"What warehouse?" His voice emerged like a croaky frog, and he swallowed again.

"Do you recognize any of us?" The man studied him closely and shared a concerned look with the vehicle's other occupants.

Seth hesitated and shook his head.

"You've scrambled your brain. Never mind. We'll check your wounds at the warehouse and get you to a healer. They'll fix you."

The man spoke with confidence, and the tension in Seth's chest lessened. For some unknown reason, he believed him. Seth slumped back and closed his eyes because the bright sunshine hurt. He had wounds? Yes, his side smarted, and his arm. His leg.

Had he lost blood? Because his mind moved at a snaillike pace. A geriatric snail. He attempted to piece together his last hours, his last day, and...

Nothing.

It was like staring into an endless gaping void.

When the vehicle halted, Seth cautiously opened his eyes. The shadowed street stopped the direct blaze of the sun, and he blinked to focus. The old warehouse had seen better days, and the gate bore a prominent closed sign. Broken windows and missing timbers showed the owner's neglect. The sooner someone leveled the building and redeveloped the site, the better.

"Why are we here?" he asked.

"Wait until we pay the driver," the more familiar woman said, placing a hand on his arm.

Seth obeyed, buttoning his lips and waiting. He wasn't confident in his ability to exit the vehicle under his own steam. Not with legs that trembled like jelly and a stomach that swirled and bucked. He couldn't recall eating, but the contents of his belly churned warningly. Seth closed his eyes, intensifying the sensations assailing his flesh. He wasn't usually weak. Was he?

The women exited the vehicle, but Seth remained seated.

"Seth, mate," the man said. "Let's get you out so the driver can leave."

Seth nodded and regretted the move. Little men with bongo drums had taken up residence, and pain arced behind his eyes. Gentle hands grasped his shoulders and tugged him. Seth tried to assist, but his legs did their jelly thing and caught on the seat. He grimaced and cried out. Knees shouldn't bend in that direction.

But eventually, he exited the taxi. He took half a step and wavered.

"Hell," the man said.

Iain. The man's name popped into his brain. They were friends. *Yes.*

"Who are the women?" he asked Iain.

"You don't recognize them?" Iain slung his arm around Seth's shoulders. "Think you need a steady hand. Whatever Raoul and his goons shot into you has side effects. Either that or your potion."

"Sore," Seth said.

His friend shot him a worried glance. "Maybe we should dose you again. Ah, here's Dougal. Fiona, too. She can look at you before we head off."

A woman with kind eyes surveyed his wounds. She made him swallow several drops of medicine. He must've slept because he woke in a bed, shirtless, each of his wounds covered with pads and tape. He had no bloody idea of his location, but a sense of safety assailed him. Peace. He assessed his pain levels. Better than earlier.

"Seth, you're awake."

"Malikah, where am I?"

Relief poured into her violet eyes. "You remember me."

"Of course I do. What happened? No wait. Raoul shot me. The bullets held silver."

"Yeah, you were out of it for a while. The healer says your gargoyle side saved you from severe poisoning. That and the cure you told us to administer before you lost consciousness. We're at Elspeth's parents' house, north of Auckland. Seth, you should see their land. It's beautiful, and my people are so happy. And best of all, the healers think they've found a cure for the kids. They started treatment this morning."

"That's good because, as a last resort, we could've tried the anti-silver drops I invented. I wasn't sure they'd even work because they hadn't been tested properly. Has my friend called?" Seth asked, unable to take his gaze from Malikah. Her features were sharp, but they fit her face and proud bearing. She wore her regal air like a cloak. Some might call her snobby, but he could see it was a cover for her insecurity. His gaze landed on her lips and lingered. He wanted to kiss her. "Come and lie down. Tell me what has happened since Raoul shot me."

She drew close enough for him to seize her hand. "We haven't heard from your friend, but wouldn't she have called you?"

"I gave her Iain's number. Aren't you supposed to be working at your new job?"

"I accepted an offer of farm work. It meant I was closer to my people and the sick children. I worked yesterday and will work later this afternoon."

Surprise filled him since he seemed to have time gaps. "How long was I asleep?"

"Since yesterday. The healer told us not to worry—that restoring rest was what you needed."

"Oh." He thought for a moment. "Raoul isn't going to give up."

"He seemed determined." Malikah scanned his face, her brow crinkling. "Exactly what is he after?"

Seth hesitated before sighing. "I developed a drug the wolf hierarchy wanted to use to take over other paranormal groups. At least, that's my assumption. Along the way, I accidentally discovered a version of my drug temporarily stopped a werewolf's shift." He shrugged, irritation showing in the sharp jolt of his shoulder. A mistake because it set off a chain reaction of hurt. He winced and breathed through the discomfort.

"Seth?" Worry sounded in her voice, and he took ease from this. She liked him.

"When will I be able to kiss you again?"

A faint pink crept into her cheeks, the effect charming.

She was so pretty.

"You can kiss me any time you want." She met his gaze and didn't flinch when he grinned.

It was more of a leer, so her calm acceptance surprised him. He hesitated before pushing harder. "I like you a lot, Malikah. What if I want more?"

"I'd like that." Her blush intensified, but she didn't shy from him or break their heated gaze. "But you need to heal properly before you exert yourself."

"Party pooper."

A slow grin crept across her lips, her violet eyes sparkling with amusement, heat, and caring. That she felt something for him in return was the best incentive to recover. Malikah was interested in him, even with his half-breed status, and that meant everything to him.

"I'm glad you're working here rather than in the city. Raoul is smart. Crafty. He's ambitious, which makes him dangerous. Watch for him and perhaps warn your people about him. I don't want them caught in the middle of my drama."

"What does Raoul want to do with your drugs?"

"No idea. The man is a decent scientist, so I falsified the formula. My gut told me something was off. I hate to think what else he has stolen. Now that Ewan McKenzie is dead, it leaves a gap in the chain of command. Raoul is taking advantage."

"I read an Auckland member of parliament fought Iain and publicly took werewolf leadership."

"So I hear, but Iain is stronger. He could've beaten William without breaking a sweat. I think Iain was sick of werewolf politics and wanted out."

"That's exactly what Iain decided," Iain said cheerfully. "The wolves are broken. William might think he can haul them together, but it'll be a mammoth task. First, he'll have to get them to follow his orders. The younger, stronger werewolves will balk. The older wolves would've tested my patience if I'd taken over. They would've objected to Elspeth and expected me to take a werewolf mate. We're better off staying far away. We can create our own pack and be better for it."

Elspeth arrived, a smile on her face. "You're awake. How are you feeling?"

"Sore."

"Your friend called," Iain said, and Seth glimpsed anger in his expression, his clenched hands. "The bag of sweets from the street person contained poison. Someone tampered with about half."

Fury raced through Seth. The signs pointed to someone in Sam's enclave. Was it Sam's wife, or was she an innocent used to deliver the means of death? "Do we know the exact poison?"

Iain rattled off a scientific name familiar to Seth.

"We'll be able to treat the kids. I don't know if they'll recover fully, but at least we have a fighting chance."

"They're improving. They're still in stasis, but their skin appears more natural," Malikah said.

Relief flooded Seth. "Are the healers optimistic?"

"Yes," Iain said. "I spoke to the head healer after I received the call. She is changing their treatment and giving them a shot as we speak. She's confident they'll emerge from stasis soon. All we need to do is catch the son-of-a-bitch who hurt innocent kids."

20

SETH RESTED FOR ANOTHER day, his legs quivering like a newborn calf's every time he tried to leave the bed. Silver poisoning shouldn't affect him this badly. Frustration filled him because he needed to safeguard against Raoul. The man wasn't stupid, and he'd discover Seth's whereabouts soon enough. Then there was the kids' poisoning. If Sam's wife was the culprit, she deserved punishment. Proving it was another story.

Seth scowled, his body aching. Sitting around drove him batty when he'd prefer to seduce his beautiful Malikah. Right now, she was at work, and he missed her.

A knock came, and the door burst open. Iain strode into the bedroom, more relaxed and happier than Seth could remember. Iain hadn't even worn that easygoing expression as a child, thanks to his father constantly forcing him to prove himself.

"We need to take action on the poisoned sweets," Iain

said.

"I'd start today, but I'm likely to fall flat on my face."

Iain snorted. "Stop acting like a wimp and get out of that bed."

Indignation blasted through Seth. "How would you like to discover everything you thought about yourself was untrue?"

Iain didn't flinch. "Since I met Elspeth, I've learned everything about my life was a lie."

Seth groaned. "Ah, hell. I was feeling sorry for myself and forgot. Ewan had big plans."

"He lusted after power," Iain said bluntly. "My best guess is he wanted to drive out the other paranormal species until only the wolves remained. That's why he was adamant we shouldn't come out to humans. That made his task harder."

Seth dragged his hand through his hair, trying to think. "Do you have other family? Other siblings? Relations?"

"Elspeth, Finn, and I have done research, and it looks as if we have siblings in a Canadian pack. One of Elspeth's friends—a photographer—is checking for us. We don't want people learning about our existence because that might put us in danger with other packs."

"Crap, Iain. That must've been tough to learn."

Iain's face twisted. "Alana took great pleasure in telling Finn and me we were abominations and that Ewan had forced her to carry us. He treated her like a broodmare, and she lost several babies that would've been our full siblings."

"What about your sisters?" Seth asked.

"Unrelated to Finn and me. That's why Alana was

always cold and never showed affection. Your parents treated me more like a son than Alana and Ewan did."

"Yeah, but I don't know much about my background either," Seth said. "I got the impression my parents' deaths were unexpected. At least now, I understand why my wolf is so weak. My gargoyle half is equally ineffective. I can't even fly properly."

"Research your background," Iain said impatiently. "We might have secrets in our pasts, but we're strong. I've told you this before, but it bears repeating. Your wolf might not be the toughest, but you have a super-sized brain. Use it instead of feeling sorry for yourself."

Seth grinned, not irritated at his friend's blunt words. Iain was right. He'd received opportunities and made the most of them. He needed to continue in that vein instead of letting others' thoughts color his perceptions. Starting with Malikah. "What are you doing this afternoon?"

"Elspeth and I might check on the gargoyle children before driving into the city to see if those kids have spotted the lady again. Fiona wants to pick up supermarket supplies. Why don't you come? Wear a hat and sunglasses."

"When does Malikah finish work?" Seth asked.

"Around six. We should be back by then."

An idea occurred. "Could you help me with something?"

"Sure," Iain said without hesitation.

Fatigue clawed Seth, but he felt better. He needed to work in a lab to strengthen his silver vaccine. Iain might need it one day. He couldn't use his old lab, but maybe he could rent space or use a friend's workspace. Seth decided to ask around.

He told Iain what he wanted. "Where is the best place to set this up?"

"Elspeth will know. Let's find her."

Iain led the way out of the bedroom.

"Malikah will love that," Elspeth said after listening to his request. "I have the perfect place for you. It's private but romantic. I doubt it will rain tonight, but a gazebo shelters this spot." She sent an impish grin in Iain's direction while absently rubbing her belly.

"Thanks," Seth said. "If you're tired, Iain can show me."

"I'm pregnant, not ill," Elspeth snapped. She grimaced immediately. "Sorry. I am tired, but the rose arbor isn't far, and it's one of my favorite places. Besides, I want to help. I like Malikah."

Seth liked how Iain smiled more these days. It was easy to see their excitement about their coming child.

"Show me this special place so I can proceed with Plan Seduction."

Iain rolled his eyes while Elspeth giggled, but they led the way into the garden. Elspeth was right. It was a beautiful, romantic spot with the heady scent of roses filling the air. The guttural chortle of a tui came from a sizeable puriri tree. There must be a fountain nearby because the faint tinkle of water added to the background melody.

Elspeth came to a halt by a wrought-iron table with two matching chairs. "We have cushions for the chairs, and Mum will have a tablecloth and candles. You'll need an ice bucket for the champagne, and I can help prepare the food."

"Thanks," Seth said, "but you need to rest. I'm a reasonable cook, and canapes and snacks aren't challenging."

"I can help Seth," Iain said in a stern voice.

"But I want to see the finished result," Elspeth said, sounding peeved *and* tired now.

"I'll take a photo before and during the event," Seth promised. "Plus a selfie of me and Malikah tucked away in private solitude."

"Let's get you inside for a rest. I promised your mother I'd help her with the bulk supplies," Iain said. "How about I bring you a snack after that? That will give you time to have a nap."

Elspeth sighed. "If I must."

With Fiona's help, Seth made the private nook comfortable before preparing food. Iain arrived in the kitchen soon after Seth started making a dip.

"Thanks for shoving me out of my funk. I feel better now that I'm taking action."

Iain clapped him over the back. "It's what friends do. The healer mentioned your wounds will leave scars. Is that a side effect of the silver?"

"Yeah, wolves have problems pushing silver out of our bodies, and even the antidote couldn't negate every scrap." He hesitated. "I'm not sure how to handle Raoul. Now that your father isn't supervising him, Raoul is out of control. He doesn't care if anyone gets hurt. His greed is blinding him."

"I saw his determination. He won't kill you because

he needs your expertise, but that won't stop him from hurting you to get what he wants."

"The man has always been driven." Seth sighed, feeling every one of his wounds kick with pain. Iain was right. Raoul's tunnel vision stopped him from seeing the harm he caused. If Raoul could use his friends or Malikah as a lever to get Seth to cooperate, he'd do it. That was the problem.

"You're safe in the dragons' territory, but if you leave, he'll find you."

"Tell me something I don't know. I wish the kids had identified the woman," Seth said, changing the subject. "We're lucky none of the gargoyle kids have died."

Iain ran his hand through his hair, leaving it ruffled. "That's what Fiona said. What the hell is wrong with people?"

Seth pulled several packets and jars from the fridge and grabbed two small tins from the pantry. He pulled a platter from a cupboard and assembled his antipasto collection. The slices of cold meat, pickles, nuts, vegetable batons, and smoked mussels smelled enticing, and satisfaction roiled through him. Next, he unwrapped a wedge of brie, a round of smoked cheese, and a hunk of strong cheddar.

"I feel as if I should take notes or at least snap a photo to witness this unusual event," Iain said.

"Piss off." Seth's rude retort merely earned him delighted chuckles instead of driving his friend away.

"You never went to this effort when it was your turn to cook."

"You're not Malikah," Seth said without heat. "Tell me

you don't wait on your mate and grant her every wish."

Iain's laughter faded, but amusement stamped into his mouth and cheeks and created crinkles at the corners of his eyes. "We've both changed and found ourselves strong women."

"I haven't caught mine yet," Seth reminded Iain. He didn't add he was worried Malikah might spurn him, given his half-breed status. But he told himself this was a brave new world in which creatures with paranormal blood stood alongside humans without fear of rejection or harm. "Do you think the laws the government is pushing through will stem the humans' panic?"

Iain sobered. "I don't know. At least the unease hasn't boiled over into violence yet. It helps that paranormals hold authority positions. Our prime minister is a feline. At least half of the sitting parliament comprises paranormals. They've always worked alongside humans and run the country. Our prime minister's policies have increased growth and decreased lawlessness. The vocal human groups can't refute facts. Paranormal folk might resemble monsters, but we're capable of restraint."

"Which is more than some humans can say," Seth said, thinking of the human who'd attacked innocent diners at a crowded restaurant with an ax only last month. He set a packet of crackers out and sliced a granary loaf. "What do you think?"

"Nailed it," Iain said. "Malikah will be home soon. Will you whisk her off to your romantic hideaway immediately?"

"No. I'll give her time to shower and change and ask her

to dine with me. I want to do this right. Besides, even in my limited experience, females like to tidy up before a date."

"Sounds like a plan." He gripped Seth in a quick man-hug. "Good luck. Malikah is lucky to have you in her life. You're a good man and a catch. Don't forget that."

"A DATE?" MALIKAH ASKED in surprise. Fatigue pulled at her, and she wanted nothing more than to jump into a shower and relax. She opened her mouth to say no, but something stopped her. A sense it'd be a huge mistake if she refused this offer.

"I'd like to spend an hour or two alone with you. We're not going far, and I can have you home early."

He didn't beg. He didn't try to blame her and twist everything, so it appeared she was being demanding, like Alfred. Her thoughts of Alfred and the vast difference between the two men changed her mind. Seth didn't have a selfish bone in his body.

She smiled and didn't have to force the action. It was a genuine and happy smile. "As long as you promise we won't be home too late. What do I need to wear?"

"Comfortable clothes. Jeans and runners," he said, his relief clear.

He'd thought she'd reject him. *Never.* Without a second thought, she closed the distance between them and softly kissed his lips before stepping back.

"I smell like the barnyard," she said.

He grinned. "You do. I didn't like to say. Can you meet

me here in an hour?"

"One hour," she said and retreated to the stairs leading to the upper floor of the Murrays' home. Once she reached her bedroom, she stripped and padded into the en suite. Soon, hot water pummeled her aching shoulders, relaxing tense muscles. Her mind drifted to Seth. She enjoyed his kisses, his caresses, and she wanted more.

Seth was genuine and had helped her and her ragtag group without hesitation.

She dried off and dressed in a borrowed pair of jeans, a pretty blouse bearing little purple flowers, and the denim jacket Elspeth had given her. She left her hair loose, spritzed on a little of the citrus scent she'd found in the en suite, and called herself ready.

The shower had refreshed her, and now she looked forward to her date.

About three-quarters of an hour later, Malikah hustled down the stairs. She found Seth loitering at the bottom, his expression stressed. When he spotted her, his face creased with a smile of happiness. He held out his right hand, and she took it, her heart leaping in anticipation.

"You look beautiful," he said, producing a lilac rosebud behind his back. "This is for you."

Her heart melted, so glad she'd agreed to this outing.

"Where are we going?" Seth had dressed similarly to her.

"Not far," he said, tugging her hand.

"What about my rose? Shouldn't I put it in water?"

"Bring it with you," Seth said. "Let's go." He threaded his fingers through hers and drew her closer until they walked hip-to-hip.

She breathed in his scent. A hint of aftershave with citrus undertones—a liking for the fresh, crisp fragrance something they had in common. Beneath the smell of oranges and lime, she detected his wolf's muskiness and the metallic hint of his gargoyle. She breathed in deeper and frowned.

"Something wrong?" He wasn't wearing his glasses now that the sun had dipped to the horizon.

"When we first met, your wolf overpowered your gargoyle. Now, I sense both."

"I've been working on fitness. Iain has been helping me with August's exercises," Seth said as he led her around the front of the house and through a side gate she hadn't noticed.

"Where are we going?" She'd assumed they'd need to drive to their destination.

"I wanted you to myself."

He seemed uncertain, and that doubt made her hesitation settle. While she was tired, she'd wanted to hang out with Seth. Until now, they'd been surrounded by her people and their problems, and now they were staying with Elspeth's parents. A quiet house it was not. It'd be fun to spend time with Seth, and the instant she acknowledged that, her anticipation grew. What had Seth planned for her?

Seth led her past a rose garden, most of the blooms finished for the season. Bright red rosehips adorned the plants in pops of color. Elsewhere, the garden was a sea of green, although Malikah didn't recognize many plants. Her parents had owned a lovely garden, but they'd employed gardeners to produce the showpiece displays.

"This way," Seth said as they passed a rosebush with flowers the same color as the one she still held.

Seth led her deeper into the garden and out of the wind. Despite the growing gloom, a bird sang. On the horizon, the sky turned vivid pink, with orange and yellow banners intersecting the deep midnight blue.

Seth tugged her around a tall formal hedge into a candlelit area with a table and two chairs. It was a private oasis, and as she took in the minor details, her throat tightened with emotion.

"You did this for me?" she whispered, her heart so full her voice wobbled.

"I wanted to do something special," Seth said. "Woo you."

"You're an excellent wooer." Her smile was tremulous. "Thank you, Seth. This is the nicest thing anyone has ever done for me."

"Sit. Let me put your rose in water."

Malikah handed over her rose and watched Seth place it in a crystal bud vase and set it in the middle of the table.

"Would you like a drink?"

"Thank you," Malikah said.

Seth pulled a bottle of champagne from an ice bucket and expertly popped the top. Seconds later, he handed her a glass and poured one for himself.

"A toast," he said. "To us."

Malikah had no qualms drinking to that. "To us. To you. This is the nicest surprise."

He studied her intently before speaking again. "August

believes we're mates, and it's true that I care for you. Deeply. But I don't want to force myself on you, so if you don't feel the same way, tell me. The last thing I want to do is cause a nuisance of myself."

Bubbles of panic flooded her stomach. No! She hadn't meant to scare him away.

21

"I want this. I want you," she blurted. Her words rushed out uncensored, but she wasn't sorry. Life was too short for hesitation. "Seth, August is right. I've been stubborn, refusing to admit this to myself, but I'm happier when I'm with you. I feel a sense of contentment that isn't present when we're apart." She paused then led with her heart. "Also, I keep thinking about kissing you, and...and...I wonder what you look like without your clothes."

Seth laughed, but it wasn't cruel. The corners of his bright blue eyes crinkled with what she suspected was happiness. "I'd enjoy that, but let's eat. Tell me about your job and how your people are getting on."

Malikah smiled and lifted her glass in a silent toast. A promise. She could work with that.

He gestured at the platters of food on the table and picked up a side plate and tongs. "What takes your fancy?"

"I'll take some of everything." Her stomach chose that moment to rumble, and heat raced to her cheeks.

"I'm hungry, too. Let's feed the beast." Before handing her the plate, he expertly piled on cheese, sliced meats, bread, olives, and other things she couldn't identify.

He filled another plate for himself and sat close to her. "Are you warm enough? Fiona gave me blankets, but we're protected from the breeze."

Malikah placed her hand on his arm, then leaned closer and kissed his mouth. A quick kiss, but an intimate one. When she drew away, he was watching her with a soft smile curving his lips.

"What was that for?"

"A thank you and a promise."

Seth cocked his head to the right, the action wolflike and familiar. "What sort of promise?"

"We should start sharing a room instead of dancing around each other."

"Do you mean it?"

"Seth, you're the first person I think of when I wake in the morning and the last before I drop into stasis. I've fought August's pronouncement but can't keep battling my heart. You've become a friend and more to me."

"Yes," he said and set his plate on the table. He took her plate, too, and placed it out of the way before scooping her off her chair and settling her on his knee. "My hunger can wait. I'd rather kiss you—a proper one that sends all the right messages."

His mouth met hers, and Malikah relaxed. Their kiss went from soft to hot and heavy in seconds flat. Her breasts prickled against her bra, her clothes cumbersome and in the way. She wriggled until she faced him and straddled his legs. Once situated to her satisfaction, she raised her hands and thrust her fingers into his hair. Seth groaned against her mouth, and the ridge of his erection pressed enticingly against her. Gah! Clothes were such a nuisance. She pressed closer, allowing her breasts to slide against the planes of his chest. Malikah knew the man had muscles beneath his lean form, but now she was doubly aware and eager to touch every one.

Seth traced her lips before twirling his tongue with hers. So much better than Alfred's kisses. Seth demonstrated patience and expertise, and she knew from experience he would do anything to help those in need. He cupped the back of her head and escalated the assault on her mouth, their kiss going from sweet to demanding.

When their lips finally parted, he grinned at her, and she'd swear her heart turned a somersault. His breath caressed her face, his gaze keen as he studied her. Whatever he saw seemed to reassure him.

"My room or yours?" he asked, that tiny smile still quivering around the edge of his sensual mouth.

"I don't care." Her stomach grumbled.

"Perhaps I *do* need to feed you. Eat, woman. The last thing I want is for you to collapse from lack of food."

She laughed. "You'd better let me off your knee then, 'cause I won't be able to concentrate on this bounty of food with you distracting me."

She loved the roguish twinkle that entered his eyes and how he lifted her easily as if she weighed nothing. Soon, she sat on a chair with a rug over her lap, drinking champagne and nibbling the assorted treats.

Once they'd filled their bellies, she looked up through the arbor and stared in wonder at the night sky. Funny, but she'd never taken the time to do something as simple as study the stars. She'd always been in a hurry to grasp whatever greedy pleasures she could before her parents arranged her marriage.

"I hated it here at first. The other gargoyles in my group despised me and what I stood for with my wealthy parents. They made no secret they blamed me for ending up at the bottom of the world. And when the kids started getting sick, that was my responsibility, too. They thought Sam would take us in and blamed me for his refusal." Malikah sighed. "Now that we're at the farm, they're visibly happier, although they haven't mentioned a thing."

"They're feeling guilty. Deep down, they understand you weren't at fault, but the huge upheaval in their lives and the deaths of their loved ones made them direct their anger and fear at you. From what you've told me, you've struggled to keep them safe. It isn't your fault someone poisoned the children. Now that their lives have improved and the prognosis for the kids is positive, they'll come around. Who knows? Sam might change his mind and let them join his colony."

"I don't trust Sam. No matter how often I tell him no, he keeps pushing."

Seth's gaze narrowed. "Bastard. Does his wife know?"

"No idea, but I suspect he's got something going with his secretary. It makes me wonder who else he's messing around with."

"And if his wife knows," Seth said.

"They're away on a holiday together," Malikah said. "That makes me think she's aware and doesn't care or that she's a wronged wife and one day she's gonna find a world of pain. Enough about Sam and Esmerelda. My group is happier. Fiona and Dougal enjoy having staff to help in the vineyard and with the cattle. It's better to keep to ourselves, especially if someone in Sam's clan means to harm our children."

"Would you like to dance?" Seth asked, the question taking her by surprise.

"Here?"

"I have music and the yearning to slow dance with you under the stars."

"You're a romantic," she said with wonder.

"Maybe. You should enjoy it while you can. Sometimes when doing lab work, I'm forgetful and absentminded. Most women get sick of me forgetting dates."

"When I was younger, I painted and sketched. My mother insisted it wasn't ladylike to wander around in paint-stained gowns or have ink beneath my fingernails. She ordered the servants to take my supplies. I resented my parents and their plans for me. I rebelled, which saved my life. If I hadn't sneaked out to see Alfred, the human I was meeting, I would've died with everyone who attended my parents' party."

"This Alfred. Did you love him?"

"I thought I did, but that night I learned he had another woman. He was using me."

"Did you confront him?"

"I was too angry and ashamed for trusting him. In hindsight, fate was with me. It was his fault we ended up in New Zealand. I learned he found us in the abandoned shed and thought we were garden statues. He saw a way to make a quick profit."

"But your gargoyle features aren't that different from your usual form," Seth commented in surprise.

"I have no idea if he noticed. Anyway, he collected money, and we ended up shipped to New Zealand."

"And you escaped."

"Luckily. We emerged from stasis in a warehouse near the Auckland port. The colony that attacked our home used something to force everyone into stasis, which made killing the survivors easier. We were lucky we were hiding, and Alfred found us rather than the enemy. The stasis lasted for the entire sea voyage to New Zealand."

Seth grinned. "The shipping agent must have been furious when his shipment disappeared. I would've paid to see his expression when he discovered an empty warehouse."

Malikah grimaced. "As angry as Tamaini and the others were, it was lucky no one discovered us before we escaped. I'm also lucky to be in one piece. It was only because Talon, Tamaini's son, had witnessed the attacks and the atrocities the enemy committed. He talked the others down. He told them it was thanks to me they escaped with their lives, and it wasn't my fault my boyfriend was a money-hungry moron."

Seth's gaze narrowed, apparently reading what she

hadn't said and how she'd had to make promises to survive. Somehow, she'd kept those promises, but it was more by luck than anything else. Ironically, Sam's refusal to offer help had benefited her. She didn't trust Sam. He hadn't cared about the sick children. There would be a showdown between them. However, she didn't want to fight him, so she needed diplomacy. Not exactly her forte.

Seth reached over and placed his fingertips against her forehead. "Stop with the weighty thoughts. They'll give you wrinkles."

Malikah batted his hand away. "I'd like another glass of champagne. Another thing from my past I never appreciated." She wrinkled her nose. "I doubt my family would recognize me now. Life here is different. It's informal. Honest. And I've made friends. I enjoy working alongside the dragons. At home, we only associated with gargoyles and humans if necessary."

Seth topped up their glasses. "Have you had enough to eat?"

"Yes, thank you."

"No room for dessert?"

"You've hit my weak spot. I have a weakness for sweets." She sobered. "It could've been me stuck in stasis. I had one of those candies."

Seth grasped her hand. "This isn't your fault. We're lucky the entire packet didn't contain poison. The healers have expressed their satisfaction with the children's progress."

She opened her mouth to ask how he knew this, but he anticipated her question.

"The kids told me their stomachs no longer ached. We chatted this morning when I visited. I look forward to the day they can play with the other kids. When they go to school."

Malikah drew in a sharp breath. "They'll be able to go to school?"

"Yes, of course. The local school accepts children of other species. Several teachers are dragons, and I believe one is fae. It will be good for them to have the company of different kids, different species."

"For the kids to improve and have a chance of a normal life is everything." She winked at him. "You promised me dessert?"

"I did. What do you think about chocolate?"

"Anything featuring sugar gets me excited."

"Fiona Murray told me about a local market stallholder selling handmade chocolates, so I took myself there this morning. I tasted one or two. I think you'll like them."

He whisked the cover off to reveal a colorful display of chocolates. Some resembled butterflies and strawberries, while others bore decorative flower motifs on top. A few were plain but no less beautiful with their different colors and glossy surfaces.

"Which would you like to try first?" Seth asked. "I have a flavor chart."

"Surprise me," Malikah said, anticipation growing. Such gorgeous chocolates. Seth had organized a delicious meal. She tried to imagine Alfred doing this and failed. Hindsight told her Alfred had been interested in one thing. *Sex.* No, two things. He'd wanted to wheedle money out of her.

"Try this one." He held a round chocolate topped with a purple flower to her lips.

Malikah opened her mouth, and he popped the chocolate inside. She bit down, and her tastebuds lit up with the bitterness of the dark chocolate and the soft center with a definite kick of alcohol. She closed her eyes as she swallowed to savor the bitter, sweet, and sour mixture.

"What do you think?" He traced the outline of her mouth with his forefinger, and a sharp sensation shot through her. It darted to her breasts, and a tiny croak escaped her.

Seth grinned and kissed her parted lips. Malikah bit back her groan of enjoyment this time, but it was a close thing.

"Would you like another chocolate?"

"Does a gargoyle have wings?"

Seth's smile widened, delight shining in his blue eyes. He turned to survey the plate and chose a white chocolate shaped like a scallop shell. The top was blue. "This one is coconut and Malibu."

The coconut and white chocolate combination was delicious, and she sighed happily.

"A third?" Seth asked, his lips curved in a pleased smile.

"You should have one," Malikah said. Greedy was not a good look.

Seth picked up a strawberry-colored chocolate. "This one looks like a strawberry, so I assume it will taste like strawberries."

"Hand it over," she said, making her voice stern. Her stomach clenched, and her nerves sizzled like the bubbles in her champagne. She wasn't good at flirting. Experience had shown her that, but she wanted to try with Seth. She wanted so badly for nothing to go wrong between them, and that told her everything. The feelings and emotions, the friendship...the kinship she felt, and the sense of belonging and rightness whenever she was with Seth made her want to do her best. She wanted to return his affection.

"Why?" Seth cocked his head, curiosity and intrigue filling his familiar face. A face she could get used to seeing over the breakfast table every morning. That made her smile. He popped the chocolate into his mouth and bit down, his low hum and visual pleasure at the taste doing things to her insides.

"Because I want to offer it to you." A thought occurred that made her belly quiver because she'd be laying her feelings bare. Her knee bounced. Once. Twice. Three times. Malikah cleared her throat. "My grandmother, when she was alive, was a superb storyteller. All her tales were about the gargoyles of old. She told me a story about a royal prince and a servant girl. Back in those times, it was a custom for courting couples to offer food to each other. They took this tradition seriously, and for one to offer another food meant they had feelings for the other. They were offering themselves and wished to live with the other for the rest of their lives."

"I offered you the chocolate and gave you the other food."

"It's the feeding by hand," Malikah said, her throat tight. A surge of vulnerability scoured her. It made her understand if she'd continued with Alfred, she would've ruined her life. Her parents had been right, although their reasons had more to do with snobbery and their disdain for humans.

"I fed you by hand." Seth's blue eyes glowed with glints of gold, his wolf peeking at her.

"Yes," she whispered. She swallowed the lump in her throat, yet she had no reservations about what she intended to do next.

"At the start, I didn't think you liked me much."

"Your intensity frightened me. I had the others to consider, and I was worried about keeping them safe. They resented me enough as it was without me adding to the problem. Once I met you in the gargoyle dreamland, my advisor reassured me. Understanding that you possessed gargoyle blood helped." The longer this took, the more she bounced her knee.

Her gaze went to the plate of chocolates, and without giving herself time to think, she plucked one from the plate at random. While she had no doubts, she worried about Seth's reaction. Would he reject her? He'd made the first move, following her around the city like a stalker. He'd shown determination in his pursuit, yet he'd never crossed the line that had made her feel threatened. Alfred had...no!

She couldn't believe that of Seth.

Malikah offered him the chocolate. Their gazes met, and the intensity she saw in his blue eyes had her fingers trembling. Her breath caught. Anxiety had heated her body, and the chocolate smeared her shaking fingers. Seth's warm hands touched hers as he closed his mouth around the treat and her fingertips. A frisson of pleasure stole her breath. Seth drew her fingers from his mouth, his gaze on her the entire time as he savored the chocolate. With slow, languid licks, he cleaned each digit.

Malikah gaped at him, her heart racing at the intimacy of this act.

"Delicious," he said, and she shivered.

"Are you cold?"

She gulped, heat racing to her cheeks. Her gaze shot to the table, picked a point and hovered out of the way of danger. Out of the way of more embarrassment.

There was a beat of silence before Seth said, "Are you still hungry?"

"No, thank you." So polite. Her mother would be proud.

"It's such a lovely night. Why don't we take a stroll through the garden before we go inside?"

"What about packing up the leftover food?"

"It will take mere moments," Seth said. With competence that told her he was no stranger to the kitchen, he soon had everything packed away. Next, he tugged the blanket from her grasp and neatly folded it before tucking it on top of the picnic basket. "There you go. It didn't take long. Now, how about that walk?"

When she hesitated, mainly because she wasn't certain she could stop herself from grabbing his butt or doing something equally naughty.

"I'm trustworthy, you know." His grin held pure sin. "What do you think might happen out there in the dark?"

"It's not you I distrust," she said in a low voice.

His gaze grew interested, his smile slightly impish.

"Oh?"

"I want to kiss you again," she blurted.

All the human left his face, replaced by stark need. Heat. Passion. He stepped closer. "That is spectacular news."

For an instant, she thought he might leap at her, and her pulse galloped. Instead, he held out his hand and waited for her to make the next move.

She stared at him, uncertain. Oh, she wanted him, but her mother's voice kept echoing through her mind. Which was plain stupid. Her parents were dead and had no say what she did with her future.

The world was changing, as were the rules.

She took his hand and puffed out a hard breath, hopefully her nerves with it. She couldn't understand why she was suddenly behaving so weirdly, and then it came to her. All along, at least since she'd discovered Alfred's perfidy, she'd been reacting instead of consciously making decisions. Seth was asking her to trust him, giving her a choice, and this was throwing her.

Heck, what sort of leader was she?

"Thank you for tonight," she said, and the second the words left her mouth, inner calmness descended on her. "I've had such a lovely time. I've never been on an outing like this with a man."

"Never?" Seth picked up the picnic basket in his free hand.

"No."

Seth subtly guided her deeper into the shadows. Gradually, her eyesight adjusted to allow her to better see their surroundings. Fiona was a keen gardener, and the gardens must be a blaze of color during the height of summer. Even now, the plants grew vigorously, and she made a mental note to visit during the day.

"Can you hear the stream running into the pond? Fiona got Dougal to divert it, so she could make a goldfish pond. We'll head in that direction since it's on our way."

"Are you enticing me farther away from the house?" Malikah held back her giggle with difficulty. She never giggled because, according to her mother, it was undignified. Funny, but only now did she realize how her mother's constant rules had stomped the joy out of life.

"I'd never do that. I thought we'd take the longer route and enjoy the starlight."

Pleasure flared in Malikah. "In that case, I'm wholly on board with your evening walk."

The house was no longer visible, hidden by more mature trees. Without the interference of manmade light, the stars spread across the sky in a twinkling blanket. Seth clasped her hand and together, they savored the spectacle.

The abrupt crunch of a stick startled Malikah, but before either of them could react, three men in black launched an attack.

22

SETH SENSED NOTHING UNTIL he heard the crack of a stick. Before he could thrust Malikah behind him, the men jumped them.

Despite his inferior status in the wolf pack, he wasn't helpless. Iain had trained with him and shown Seth how to defend himself against someone stronger.

Seth reached for that experience now. Two men rushed him while the third stalked Malikah, swagger in his attitude. Seth met blow for blow, punch for punch, and Malikah fought at his side, not making it easy for the lone man trying to subdue her.

A punch clipped Seth's jaw, sending him flying backward. He hit his head and saw stars.

Get up. Get up now.

Seth forced his legs to push him upright.

"Seth," Iain called from a distance. "Are you out there? The alarms have gone off."

Malikah screamed, and Seth struggled upright. One man grabbed his forearm and attempted to drag him away. Seth let the man tug him a few steps and used the forward momentum to his advantage. He aimed a fist at the man's chin, putting wolf and gargoyle power behind the punch. The man toppled.

Malikah screamed again, and Seth whirled, desperate to help her. Iain appeared from the trees in wolf form. He growled a vicious warning, but two men had Malikah now, one with a gun aimed at her temple.

"Come any closer, and she dies," the man spat.

Seth froze, and Iain skidded to a halt beside him. Elspeth arrived with her father, both still in their human forms.

"Stay right where you are," the man with the gun said, and his hand was steady as his friend dragged Malikah into the trees.

Elspeth and her father retreated silently, and Seth prayed they were circling to approach these thugs from the other direction.

A third man tried to clamber away, and Iain released a warning growl. The man stilled, his gaze wary.

The roar of a starting vehicle and, seconds later, screeching tires told Seth the worst.

"Who do you work for?" he demanded, his temper spiking as he stalked closer to the man Iain was guarding.

"I don't have to tell you nuffink," the man spat.

Iain seized the man's arm in his mouth and bit down before the man could react.

Excellent strategy. Seth repeated his question. "Who hired you?"

"I... Dammit, tell him to stop," the man ordered. He tried to wrestle free from Iain but only succeeded in losing his beanie.

Seth frowned at the man's pointy ears for two seconds before repeating his question for a third time.

"Sorry," Elspeth said, puffing slightly. "They got away. Dad shifted and followed them. He'll let us know where they take Malikah."

Iain must've bitten down harder because the elf cursed. At least, Seth assumed he was an elf, given his height and those ears.

"Who hired you?" Seth gritted out.

"Dude called Raoul," the elf said. "Tell him to let me go."

Raoul. Seth cursed. He'd caused this mess because he wanted to do the right thing.

Iain released the elf and backed up. The man surveyed his arm and swore, muttering about rabid dogs and shots. He scrambled to his feet and ducked into the trees. Seth didn't bother chasing since he had his answers.

Raoul wanted him so badly he'd use those Seth cared for.

"Were the others elves or something else?" Seth asked.

Iain shifted. "I didn't get any scent from them. Raoul must've dosed them to suppress it."

"Will he hurt Malikah?" Seth asked, his chest aching along with his throbbing chin. That guy who'd hit him hadn't held back.

Iain shrugged. "She'll be safe enough. He'll use her as a lever, so you follow orders."

"I can't—not in good conscience. Raoul wants these

drugs to either gain power, or he has a buyer."

"Given his insistence, I'd bet on the second option," Elspeth said. "Don't worry. We'll get her back. We'll mount a rescue as soon as Dad lets us know where they're holding her."

Seth nodded, but his heart didn't cease its racing, nor did his panic lessen. A lot could happen between now and when they rescued Malikah. He'd thought their presence with Elspeth's family would protect them. They should've been safe in the garden.

Somehow, Raoul had tracked them here. He must've ordered them followed. Seth hadn't suspected or sensed anyone watching them, but they must've to know they were walking outside.

He cursed silently. If they hurt Malikah, he'd never forgive himself.

His phone rang, and he plucked it from his pocket. He swore when he saw the caller and Elspeth and Iain moved closer.

"Raoul," Seth said in a hard voice.

Iain placed his hand on Seth's forearm. "Don't let on you know his men have her and don't let him rattle you into saying something you shouldn't. Deny she's your girlfriend."

"She is my mate."

"Telling Raoul that gives him a greater lever. We need to stall, give ourselves time to plan," Elspeth said, sympathy in her voice. "You're important to Raoul's schemes."

Seth clenched his fists, beads of sweat forming on his forehead as he thought of Malikah in Raoul's hands. The wolf was increasingly desperate to capture Seth. And Seth couldn't trust Raoul to release him if he did whatever lab work his ex-boss deemed urgent.

The phone rang again, and Seth made a mental note to change his ringtone when he had a spare moment. "Yes?"

"I have your girlfriend."

Even though he'd known this, Seth's stomach clenched.

"What girlfriend?" Seth asked, playing it cool while everything inside him rebelled. She was his love. He ached each time they parted, only feeling right when he was in her company.

"Stop fooling around. I have the woman, and if you don't arrive at my lab within the hour, I'll deliver her back to you in pieces." He paused as if considering. "Her right hand first."

"Malikah has nothing to do with this. Let her go. She's an acquaintance, that's all."

"You kiss your acquaintances?" His silky voice made Seth's skin prickle. *The bastard.*

"What do you want?" Seth asked in a flat voice. He suspected what the wolf wanted—to make money off Seth's hard work and to screw with other paranormal races.

"Come to my lab and work on the formula. I need it perfected."

"Not unless you release the woman," Seth said, keeping all emotion from his voice.

"I'll let her go afterward. Give you an incentive to focus. Oh, and tell that dragon following us that we know he's there. Tell him not to do anything stupid because I will not hesitate to kill the girl." He hung up, leaving Seth frustrated and angry and wishing he were in the same room. He'd enjoy knocking Raoul around and thought he could do it these days.

"Cocky arsehole didn't even tell you the location of his lab," Iain said.

"Do you think he'll hurt Malikah? Make good on his threats?" Elspeth asked.

"Yes," Seth said.

"Yes," Iain said almost simultaneously. "Ewan liked him because he focused and got results. They were two peas in a pod."

"But Ewan didn't see through the man's character," Seth said. "If he had, we wouldn't be in this mess."

"Right," Elspeth said. "We need to contact Dad and ask about the lab's location."

Seth saw sense in this suggestion, even though his first urge was to leap into a vehicle and hare off to Malikah. "I can mindspeak with Malikah," he said. *Idiot.* How had he forgotten that? "Once I get closer to her location."

Iain gave a thumbs up gesture. "Excellent. She can tell us where she's being held and how many men Raoul has at his lab."

"Plan," Elspeth said. "Once we speak with Mum, we'll drive to Auckland."

Before they reached the house, Fiona bustled outside. "Dougal wants to speak with you."

"Go," Elspeth said. "I'll explain the rest to Mum."

"Dad, it's Iain. Where did they take Malikah?"

"To wolf headquarters. Rumor says they have labs here.

Is that correct?" Dougal asked.

"William is having trouble holding the pack together. At least that's what I've heard," Iain said. "I didn't think anyone was working at the main offices."

Seth growled, the expulsion of sound rattling from his throat. "Which is why Raoul feels secure in using wolf premises to do his double-dealing. At least I'm familiar with the lab and the building. That might be an advantage."

"Dad, we're heading your way and will try to devise a rescue plan. Anything else we should know?"

"Not yet but bring me clothes. It's damn drafty on the roof."

Iain laughed, and Seth managed a smile.

"Will do," Iain said. "We're driving."

Dougal grumbled, but Iain disconnected the call. "Let's move."

They jumped into Iain's vehicle and were soon on their way to Auckland.

Seth didn't talk, slipping into his mind. He didn't trust Raoul to keep his word. He'd hurt Malikah to get back at Seth for daring to go against him. The man was a bully. A devious one with an agenda. He appeared to have a timeline, and that made him lethal.

Iain shot him a sideways glance.

"What will you do?" Iain asked.

"I don't have options," Seth said. "I can't see a way to grab Malikah without her getting hurt. Raoul will do anything, say anything to get his way."

"Why can't he do the work himself?" Iain asked. "That

would be the obvious path for him to take."

Seth made a scoffing grunt. "He might have the paper qualifications, but he has coasted through his career on others' work. He took credit for my lab results. It took me a while to tweak to his game. I applied for other positions to advance my career, and he consistently blocked me."

"You never said. I knew you hated him, but you seemed happy working in the lab."

"I was until the skullduggery and secret work came to light." Seth's mouth twisted. "Once I understood, I tweaked formulas and recorded results that didn't happen. My best guess is Raoul tried to replicate my results and couldn't. He wouldn't understand why, and it would never occur to him I'd falsify the results."

"What exactly were you working on?"

"The suppression drug and another to stop a wolf shifting. I assumed your father intended to wage war on the other packs and take them over. It was the wrong direction for our pack, which was why I left."

"Not my father," Iain said, his tone mild.

But Seth spotted the distaste in his friend. The disgust, and he shared it. Ewan McGregor had been a monster. A wolf greedy for power. He hadn't cared who he destroyed while making the control grab.

"The drugs and the rush for their success will be why Ewan didn't want to come out to the humans. If he'd lived, he'd be furious at the other species taking advantage and making a public announcement."

"But it's obvious Raoul has plans for the drugs," Seth said. "He has a buyer lined up. Maybe he has had this plot in mind for some time."

"The paranormal species overseas haven't made themselves known." Iain signaled a right turn and drove onto the street where the wolves had their headquarters and labs.

Seth cast out his thoughts, hoping to connect with Malikah. The silence in his head pushed at his foreboding. If Raoul hurt Malikah, Seth would make his fury known. While he was a peaceful man at heart—a problem according to the pack trainers—he was part wolf, and that half thirsted for revenge and payback. His gargoyle half was but a step behind.

"What's the plan?" Iain asked.

"I don't see we have any option," Seth said. "I'll have to do the lab work."

"But Raoul won't keep his word."

"I know. My best option is to cooperate and watch for an opening to kick his arse. He thinks I'm weak. I might've acted that way in the past because I wanted to keep out of trouble. But he's kidnapped Malikah, and I can't contact her mentally, which means she's unconscious. Raoul isn't aware I've changed, grown stronger. This is the last time he'll underestimate me."

Instead of offering an argument or advice, Iain nodded. "What should I do?"

"What about if I tell Raoul I need a lab assistant?"

"Won't he offer so he can watch you?" Iain asked in surprise.

Seth scoffed, the harshness of the sound abrading his throat. "The man has coasted along on the shirttails of others. He can't do half of the stuff in the lab, and he'll refuse to take my orders. It's a pride thing for him—he's puffed up like a bullfrog."

"I don't know the first thing about lab work," Iain protested.

"You excelled at science during our school days and enjoyed it. Besides, you're my friend, and you're smart. You'll be more useful to me than Raoul."

"If anything happens to me, Elspeth will gut you. She likes me exactly the way I am."

"I'll take that under advisement," Seth said drily.

"Right." Iain pulled up in front of the Wolf Headquarters, which was strangely silent. Typically, there'd be a doorman on guard at the entrance. People, both wolves and humans, would come and go, deals and business meetings occuring around the clock.

"Is William really in charge?" Seth said, watching the quiet building with trepidation.

"He's trying to take control, but several others on the council crave the prestigious alpha position. There will be more loss of life before they settle this."

Seth opened his door and climbed from the vehicle. Iain joined him on the sidewalk. "It's good you and Finn are out of the mess. You're safer with the dragons."

"Yeah. I let William beat me in a fight. Did you hear that?"

Seth studied his friend's face. "Why?"

"It was the only way to get the wolves to disperse from the inner city. There would've been more bloodshed because they were frenzied and out of control. Before

Alana shot him, Ewan told me it was my fault. Something about my blood and breeding called to them. That's why the wolves massed in the city—to get close to me."

Seth studied the building's main entrance, once again wondering why they couldn't see anyone. The businesses across the road were open, although none had visible customers. "Ewan didn't respect you, Iain. Everything he did showed that. He might've told the truth, but he might've lied because it suited his purposes."

"True. I told you Elspeth, Finn, and I have been researching our background and true parents."

"I'll help any way I can," Seth said. "All you need to do is ask."

"Thanks." Iain straightened his shoulders, gazing at the large man who'd appeared in the doorway. "Looks like our escort has arrived."

"Let's do this." Seth sucked in a quick breath and strode forward. Iain fell into step beside him.

"What's he doing here?" Raoul demanded.

"I need someone to help in the lab, and Iain has worked with me before. I want to see Malikah first."

"I'm calling the shots," Raoul spat.

"You need me," Seth said, his tone impassive while inside, he writhed with anger. The smug bastard. Seth forced himself to push past his fury. To think clearly. "I need Iain to help, so first, show me Malikah."

Raoul swore under his breath but gestured them inside. "Any funny business and the girl won't survive."

Seth ignored him as they headed to the labs on the basement floor. Already, his mind raced ahead. Could he stall? Make the drugs do something other than their initial purpose? No, that probably wouldn't work. Raoul would expect a test—probably using one of them as a guinea pig. He'd have to do the work right because Raoul wasn't stupid.

Seth was still undecided about what to do when Raoul pushed open the lab door and held it for them to enter. Seth's back itched until they were through the door and out of Raoul's reach. He didn't trust the man one bit.

"You should find everything you need at the number two workstation. I've left the notes and formulas from the previous sessions, plus the final product and the ingredients we used. How long will it take?"

"Three to four hours for the entire process," Seth said without hesitation.

"Work fast," Raoul said and turned to leave.

"Aren't you forgetting something?" Seth said.

"Right." Raoul plucked his phone from his pocket and pushed a button. When someone picked up the other end, he said, "Walsh wants proof that the woman is alive and unharmed. Point the video at her." He waited before gesturing at Seth. "Here's your proof."

23

MALIKAH WAS ALIVE AND moving, but tape covered her mouth.

"Your woman is fine," Raoul said with disinterest. "Get to work." He spoke into the phone, low words that sounded like orders before hanging up.

Malikah was okay, but he'd spotted the bruise on her cheek. He'd noted the militant sparkle in her eyes. Pissed anger pulsed beneath the surface. *Attitude.* His mate wanted to punch something. Someone.

"Don't try Raoul's patience too much, sweetheart. Iain and I are here." He didn't receive a reply but pushed aside his concern.

Seth scanned the formula and, feeling the weight of a gaze, looked up to find Raoul sneering in distaste.

"Why couldn't you follow the formula and make the product?"

Raoul's facial muscles tightened, and a tic kicked into

life at his temple. Ah! Seth understood now. He'd tried to make the drug but thought he'd mucked it up, so he needed Seth's help. The stupid man didn't even realize the formula was incorrect.

"Enough chatter. Get to it."

Seth shrugged and reached for the scales. He arranged the chemicals in order and nodded at Iain. "Glove up and weigh the chemicals as I call them out."

Raoul rumbled out a satisfied hum before exiting the lab. Seth heard the lock scrape home.

"Seems as if we're locked in until we produce his product," Iain said.

"He didn't lock the windows," Seth said with great smugness. "An exit point."

Iain's lips twisted. "You might have wings, but I don't."

"Ah, but you have dragon contacts." Seth perused his notes, written a lifetime ago. "Besides, flying isn't as easy as they make it look. It's a good job gargoyles are built tough."

Iain cracked a smile. "Fell on your head a few times, did you?"

"Head. Arse. The entire experience left a mass of bruises. August enjoyed the spectacle." At Iain's snort of amusement, he said, "Better get working."

"Have you decided what to do?"

"I'll make his damn drugs, but I hadn't finished tests and all the checks and balances, so who knows how it will turn out."

"What would you like me to do?" Iain asked.

Seth measured lumps of white chippings onto a scale

before tipping them into a stone mortar. He picked up a matching pestle and handed them to Iain. "Grind that to a fine powder while I weigh the other ingredients." Seth busied himself and tried to focus, but his mind drifted to Malikah. Ironic. Their romantic relationship was moving like syrup on a wintry day. While he was enjoying learning about his woman, he ached to hold her and show the depths of his feelings. Every part of him—mind, heart, and soul—hungered for deeper intimacy because their connection hadn't cemented into a mate bond. And he should be focusing on the present and saving her instead of daydreaming.

"I'm envious of you and Elspeth," Seth said, breaking the silence.

Iain ceased his grinding to nail Seth with a sharp glance. "You have a mate. It's obvious you and Malikah care for each other."

"I'd feel better if we could get to the sex part," Seth said bluntly. "Aw, crap. Forget I said that. Malikah is...I'm worried Raoul will hurt her, and my mind is splitting in dozens of directions, some of which are not important or relevant at the present."

"Understandable." There was a moment of silence before Iain said, "Once we retrieve Malikah, why don't you take her somewhere romantic for time alone? That's as important as looking after her people."

Seth considered this and gave a decisive nod. "Sounds like a plan. Finish the grinding for me, then check out the window and any ledges we can use. See if you can spot Dougal. This won't take me long."

"You implied it was a complicated process," Iain said with a frown.

"Raoul is a terrible scientist. I've told you that."

"Oh," Iain said. "Okay."

"Malikah, where are you?"

"Seth?"

Seth was so startled, he fumbled with the instrument he was using. He lurched forward and only just caught the expensive piece.

Iain, who'd been leaning outside, jerked back and closed the window with a dull thud. He whirled to face Seth, his arms raised and his mouth open in a snarl. He only relaxed once he saw they were alone.

"Malikah answered me," Seth said. "She didn't before."

"Where is she?"

"Haven't asked yet. I was so startled by her reply I almost dropped this." He placed the expensive piece on the counter and stepped away.

"Well, hurry because the sun is rising, and we'll have less cover."

"Just a sec." Seth closed his eyes and focused, but the door flew open to reveal Raoul. An armed guard stood to the side, his weapon trained on Seth and Iain.

"How are you getting on?" he asked, his tone smarmy and condescending.

"We'd move faster if you didn't interrupt," Seth snapped.

Raoul backhanded Seth, the power behind the blow sending Seth flying against the stainless steel workbench.

"Oh, very mature," Seth snapped, wiping blood from a

cut on his cheek. "Injure the scientist so he can't work."

Raoul advanced on Seth, his intent clear.

"Raoul." Alpha power sizzled in Iain's voice, and his blue eyes turned golden. "Let us work. The job will go faster if you stop micromanaging. Go."

Raoul took two steps before skidding to a halt. He glowered at Iain, then turned his temper on Seth. "Your ability to make the drugs is keeping your woman alive. Remember that." He stalked from the lab, making a production of locking the door.

Seth grimaced at the chemicals in his mixing bowl, read his notes, and reached for another ingredient. He read the label and added two spoonfuls of the mustard-colored powder. "Let me put it into the machine. It will spit out the pills. Is Raoul gone?"

"Yeah. He thinks he has the upper hand."

"Not likely," Seth said. "Any luck with the window before I try to contact Malikah again?"

"The ledge is nonexistent, but we could get out with a dragon's help or if you flew."

"Let me speak with Malikah first, then I'll try to contact Dougal."

"You can do that?"

"If they're close enough, I can initiate conversation, but they can't start the communication. Not sure how it works, but that's the limitation."

"Pity you didn't have that power when we were kids. We could've gotten into a lot of mischief."

"Yeah. See if you can sight Dougal."

"Better check if we still have a guard." Iain sidled over to the door to listen. "Nope, he's gone. Raoul places a lot of trust in a lock."

Seth didn't reply, focused inwardly on Malikah. *"Malikah, are you okay?"*

"Seth, where are you?"

"In the lab with Iain, making Raoul's drugs for him."

"How many labs are in the building where you used to work?"

"Five," Seth said. *"They're all next to each other. Go to the window, open it, and look for Iain. Wait, do you have any guards?"*

"No. The door is locked, but I can't see anyone."

"Right, then look out the window. If you can see Iain, that would be a plus for us."

"That's locked, too."

"Can you break the lock or smash the window without drawing attention?"

"They've tied my hands behind my back, and I can't break the binding. I've tried." Frustration sounded in her voice. Irritation.

"All right. Keep trying to free yourself because I think we're close. We'll work out a plan this end, and I'll keep you informed." Seth glanced at the door before hustling to the window to peer outside. "Would anyone notice if Dougal did a fly past and peered into the lab windows?"

Iain snorted. "He's hard to miss. One of us needs to go outside and peer through the windows."

"It's a long way down."

"If you contact Dougal, he might stand by and catch us if we fall," Iain suggested.

Seth brightened. "Plan."

"I have a better head for heights." Iain headed for the window.

"No," Seth said, halting Iain mid-stride. "One, you have a child on the way, which means you must keep safe. And two, it's my mate and my fault we're in this position. I want to get us out of this mess."

"That doesn't mean your friends can't help," Iain said.

"I couldn't help with your father," Seth said. "You didn't tell me what was going on with you."

"Because we were youngsters and didn't have options. He would've had you killed if you'd interfered. Hell, he was testing me, pushing to assess my capabilities. Besides, you helped me more than you know. It was your idea to move away from the pack, and your suggestion to open bank accounts the pack couldn't touch. Both things helped me to get from under my father's influence. The money and our investments have helped Elspeth and me immensely."

Seth crossed to his friend and hugged him. Hard and with great feeling.

When they finally parted, Seth said, "Okay. Let me try to contact Dougal before you go out. I'm not sure if it will work." He called up the man's human and dragon images and shifted his thoughts toward Dougal.

"Dougal?"

"Who is this?" came a grumpy retort.

"It's Seth. Iain and I are in a lab." He spoke to Iain. "Iain, can you go to the window and stick out your head?" Once his friend had done that, Seth continued his mental

conversation. *"Can you see Iain?"*

"Just a moment," Dougal said. *"No. Can you describe where you are in relation to the front of the office block?"*

Seth told Dougal.

"I'll pretend I'm flying away but will reposition myself."

"Don't put yourself in danger."

"I positioned myself opposite Raoul's office to make certain he saw me. Let him think I'm giving up and leaving. Give me five minutes, and I'll circle to the rear of the building."

Dougal broke the mental contact, and Seth told Iain what was happening.

"What if a guard spots Dougal's return?"

"We'll have to risk it. It's time to make our move."

Iain stuck his head out of the window. "I see him." He pulled himself through the window with effortless grace to balance on the ledge.

Seth took half a step toward the window before the door flew open. Raoul. He took in the situation with one glance and leaped at Seth, his shift speeding over him, converting him to a sleek fighting weapon. Sharp teeth snapped, missing Seth's arm by millimeters.

Seth might've panicked in the past, but Malikah was in danger. He refused to back down or run. He reached for his gargoyle magic—something Raoul wouldn't expect. His shift was slow, but it toughened his hide and increased his body mass. And a side perk, it kept him clothed, his clothes magically adjusting to his larger body.

By the time Raoul whirled, his shift was almost done. Raoul released a growl. Seth didn't hesitate. He pounced, throwing his body at Raoul and attacking, claws extended, horns down.

He speared Raoul's flank, slowing the powerful wolf. Raoul's pained growl brought satisfaction. Seth had never stood up to Raoul before and with the training he'd been doing with Iain, he was stronger and quicker. Now, he had Malikah to fight for.

Raoul went for his throat. Seth nimbly danced out of his way, learning—to his astonishment—that Raoul wasn't that fast. He relied on his size rather than agility to repel others. Using this knowledge, Seth taunted Raoul. With his clawed hands, he grasped the wolf's tail and gave it a sharp tug.

"Seth, we've located Malikah," Iain called from the open window.

Raoul growled, the snarl holding fury, and Seth wanted to laugh.

He pulled back his fist and punched, sending Raoul flying against a workbench. Raoul yelped and was slow to rise. Seth dashed the contents of his lab work off the counter. Test tubes smashed against the tile floor and the pills spilled and jumped in all directions. The expensive microscope crashed against the workbench and toppled. That gave Seth pause, but he brushed aside his disquiet and continued to destroy his work.

Raoul picked himself up, slow to understand Seth's actions. Seth ground several of the pills beneath his broad, booted feet.

Belatedly, Raoul came to his senses, his snarl vicious. He lurched forward, throwing himself at Seth. His sharp teeth gripped Seth's arm. Seth kicked him in the ribs, but Raoul refused to let go. He bit down harder, and Seth flung him against a workbench. Raoul's teeth ripped free of Seth's arm, and pain tore through him. A chunk of bloody skin dropped to the ground, and Seth grimaced. He balanced on the balls of his feet, his gaze on Raoul, but the bigger man didn't move.

Seth hesitated before he approached the fallen wolf. He checked for a pulse, even as he avoided looking at the damage he'd inflicted. Raoul remained unresponsive. Seth wasn't sure the man's wolf could heal him. He grabbed the formula Raoul had given him. Raoul probably had copies, but he couldn't worry about that now. It was more important for him to get Malikah and leave. He could worry about Raoul later—if the wolf survived.

Seth shoved the papers inside his shirt before stalking to the open window and sticking out his head. Dougal perched on the opposite building with Iain standing at his side. Seth pulled himself out and onto the ledge. While he had the strength to get himself out there, finding the power and confidence to fly was another matter entirely.

The wind whistled past him, the chill a shock against his gargoyle-warm body. A wrenching crack followed by breaking glass to his left had him jerking his gaze in that direction.

Malikah.

Seth didn't think twice. With an agility he didn't know he possessed, he darted along the ledge and helped Malikah to clear the glass. He wrenched on the frame, uncaring of the noise. Raoul was unconscious for the moment.

"What the hell?" a masculine voice shouted.

Seth yanked on the window frame, ignoring the glass gouging his granite-hard hands.

A gun fired, shoving panic into Seth. *"Malikah!"* he called telepathically.

"I'm all right," she replied instantly, but she sounded breathless.

Seth didn't believe her because his wolf half smelled the copper tang of fresh blood. A blast of rage took him by surprise, but he went with it and sprang through the open window.

The wolf holding the gun fired but missed. Before he could try again, Seth was on him. He punched the man in his gut, and while the wolf struggled for breath, Seth socked him in the jaw. The wolf groaned, his legs going from under him.

"Go," Seth snapped at Malikah. Long, rapid steps took him to the door. He opened it and peered outside. Two wolves, still in human form, hustled toward him. One fired, the bullet coming damn close to his face. Seth jerked back and searched for a way to bar their entrance. Unfortunately, the lock was on the outside.

"Go," he growled at Malikah when she hesitated. She clambered through the open window, took a moment to center herself, and shift. His breath eased out the second he saw her take flight.

She was safe.

Voices sounded outside, and Seth hurriedly shoved a desk against the door. It wouldn't keep the shifters out for long. Hell, did they know he'd downed Raoul? Would they bail? Who the hell was paying their wages now?

Seth sprinted for the door. He'd made it halfway when the desk went flying in an explosion of screeching wood and gunfire. Seth didn't stop. He crossed the few final feet in a dive. Broken glass crunched under his boots and a splinter lodged in his finger when he reached for the broken window frame. A gun fired and seconds later, his leg burned. Adrenaline kept Seth moving. He clambered through the window, upper body strength helping him through. The ledge was so narrow his boot slipped, greasy from blood. His vision wavered in and out on seeing how far down it was.

"Fly, Seth!"

Malikah's screamed words reached him from where she stood on a nearby rooftop.

He'd only partially shifted, and now he tried to slow his racing heartbeat to focus on a full shift. As always, his body responded slowly. *Too slowly.* He edged along the ledge, hopefully far enough away that he wouldn't get shot.

"Where did he go?"

Raoul's voice. Seth cursed under his breath. What did he need to do to stop this wolf? And how the hell had he recovered so fast?

"Get him. I want him alive."

Seth inched farther along the ledge. Could he climb up? That might work because if he tried flying, he'd likely kill himself. A wolf stuck his head out the window, looked left. Right. And spotted Seth. He pulled out a gun and fired.

His shift completed, and Seth prayed his harder hide protected him from bullets. It didn't. Pain seared his hip. A window on his other side opened, and another wolf looked out, this one with a grin.

"Why don't you come inside?" he drawled, pointing his weapon at Seth.

Seth wasn't dumb. He understood if Raoul got him, things wouldn't go well. Without giving it much thought, he used the remaining strength in his legs and pushed off the ledge.

24

Seth sank like a stone. Adrenaline shot through him as air rushed through his hair. Every flying hint Malikah and August had offered disappeared. His mind turned blank—so blank that every scrap of limited experience vanished.

He sailed past the second floor before the thought of undulating his wings came to him. The compulsive heave of his shoulders slowed his descent. Encouraged by this miracle, he frantically flapped again, and thankfully, he ceased falling, hovering somewhat unsteadily, but he'd take the win.

"Seth," Iain shouted from above.

Seth glanced up to see Iain, Dougal, and Malikah eying him anxiously. He wobbled and overcorrected, intending to go upward, but a gust of wind caught him. He swept sideways and smacked into the side of the wolf pack's headquarters. The air exited his lungs in a whoosh, and he was falling again. Dazed, he was again slow to react.

"Move your wings!" Malikah hollered.

Thankfully, her panicked instruction got through, and he made a feeble up-and-down motion. He slowed a fraction, but not enough. His collision with the ground tore the air from his lungs. Pain followed swiftly on the heels of his crash.

Steaming piles of horse crap!

He couldn't do anything right. He was a weak wolf with pathetic strength and a failure as a gargoyle. Even the kids flew better. He'd seen them flitting around the orchard while their parents picked fruit.

He hoarsely gasped for breath, even as he ran a mental catalog of his damage. Huh! Everywhere hurt, and he'd swear cartoon birds circled his head.

"Hey, mister! You okay?"

Seth dragged in a painful breath and rolled. He flopped onto his back like a fish out of water, opened his eyes, and blinked against the bright light. He'd lost his glasses somewhere. With a pained groan, he lifted his hand to block the sun's glare.

"Mister!"

A body obstructed the brightness, and Seth breathed silent thanks. He blinked several times, then counted the aches and pains pummeling him. They hadn't magically disappeared, nor had his wolf or gargoyle sides healed him. If anything, his two beasts seemed to silently battle each other.

"Mister?"

"Is he dead?" a boyish voice asked.

"Not dead," Seth croaked. "Winded."

"Ya got wings. Why didn't ya flap 'em?" another boyish voice commented.

Seth focused enough to see four boys surrounding him, curiosity emblazoned on their features.

"Seth! Seth?"

"Malikah," he croaked, his cheeks heating because, dammit, he was a poor excuse for a gargoyle. Why would a woman like Malikah take an interest in him?

The kids parted to allow Malikah into their circle, and Seth's mind kicked into gear enough to spot Iain and Dougal still in his dragon form.

"Whoa!" a kid said. "That's a big arse dragon."

"He's with us," Malikah said.

"Your man flies like a stone," a blond kid with a missing front tooth commented.

"Thanks," Seth croaked, embarrassed because the kid spoke the truth. He could hardly deny his ineptness.

The purr of a vehicle came from nearby. Seth registered the noise but didn't worry too much since he lay on the pavement. A more metallic scent had him pushing to a seated position despite his protesting muscles. Nothing seemed broken, but man, he hurt.

"I told you not to loiter around our building," a haughty feminine voice snapped.

Ah. He'd landed near the gargoyle colony. Luckily, he hadn't slammed into the middle of their courtyard. They might've attacked first and asked questions later.

Seth struggled to rise, wincing at his tender muscles. He bit back a groan and hauled his protesting body upright.

Immediately, he hunched to ease his pain, and he doubted the woman noticed him. She hadn't spotted Malikah either.

"Leave before I send the guards to deal with you," the woman said, her tone unpleasant. She meant every word, but her vitriol wasn't directed at him.

She was snarling at the kids.

"That's her," a skinny kid said in an undertone. He hitched up his jeans, trying to look cool, but Seth sensed his unease. The kid edged closer to Malikah. "That's the lady that gave us the bag of sweets."

"Is that Sam's wife?" Seth murmured.

Disgust curled across Malikah's expression. "That's Esmerelda Ironwing."

"Esmerelda." A less grumpy and more timid voice broke the silence.

The kids shifted uneasily, and Seth glimpsed a woman with blonde hair that puffed around her head in wisps of frizz. Ah! Fluffy, Esmerelda's sidekick.

"What?" Esmerelda snapped, not taking her gaze off the kids. "Call the guards. I want this trash out of my sight."

"Esmerelda." Fluffy tugged at her friend's silk sleeve.

The statuesque beauty turned to her friend with a snarl. "What do you want?"

Instead of answering, Fluffy jerked her head in Dougal's direction. Iain was standing beside his father-in-law, both men wearing impassive expressions.

"Oh." Esmerelda blinked, her demeanor changing. "Have you come to see Sam? We've just returned from a brief vacation, so he's catching up. Business and colony matters, you understand." Her gaze lit on the kids, and her mouth tightened. "Wait while I get the guards. Scruffy children hanging around our entrance is not the impression we wish to give our visitors."

Seth caught Malikah's silent signal to the kids.

"We're goin', lady," the kid's leader said. At his subtle gesture, they wandered past Esmerelda and Fluffy, insolent sneers on their youthful faces.

Seth would've laughed if he'd had the energy. Every inch of his body smarted, along with his pride. His clothing hadn't emerged unscathed, either. He'd ripped his shirt sleeve and had a huge bloodstain on the front. With hunched shoulders and unkempt clothing, he resembled a homeless man. Once again, his otherness stopped him from fitting in.

"You!" Esmerelda snapped, her glare back in force and aimed at Malikah. "What do you want?"

Malikah lifted her chin, and Seth almost smiled because she hadn't lost her upper-class arrogance. "We need a healer, but since Sam is here, we'd like to speak to him."

"Sam is busy," Esmerelda said. "I've told you we were away, and there is much to catch up on after our vacation."

Iain strolled closer, and Dougal matched him step for step, his black scales shining in the scant sun.

"Why don't you send someone to ask him if he will see us," Iain said. "We have an important matter to discuss."

Esmerelda puffed up, her chin rising, her patently fake smile holding superiority. "I am Sam's wife. Tell me, and I'll communicate with him."

"I think not," Iain said, his voice easy.

Dougal responded with a flare of flames from his great maw. He followed this with a testy rumble that vibrated through every pore of Seth's aching body.

Esmerelda took a step back before she could halt the tell.

"Please tell Sam we're here to see him," Malikah said.

Fluffy swallowed hard. When Esmerelda didn't grant them entrance, Fluffy gave a strained laugh. "I'll go," she said and beat a hasty retreat. A gargoyle guard appeared, and Fluffy spoke to him hurriedly, gesturing at Seth and his party. The guard nodded and disappeared.

"Seth, how are you?" Malikah murmured. "Do you need the healer, or can you wait until we return to the farm?"

Seth hesitated because, if he was truthful, he could do with painkillers—something to take the edge off the throbbing in his head and arm. Concentrating hurt, and right now, he needed to focus. "Let's see how receptive Sam is to our news."

"The bitch is lucky I'm not attacking her," Malikah gritted out.

"We feel the same way," Iain said.

The guard returned and spoke to a hovering Fluffy. She sent a swift glance in Esmerelda's direction.

Malikah stepped forward. "Will Samarak see us?" Despite their unexpected arrival, she used the gargoyle's formal name, silently signifying an official request.

"What happened to Raoul?" Iain murmured.

Seth blinked, his arm throbbing where Raoul had bitten him. "We fought. I was terrified he'd hurt Malikah. He's still alive. Should I have killed him?"

"No," Iain said. "Our beasts don't rule us. Fighting to stay alive or against an attack is one thing, but cold-blooded murder is a step too far."

Relief swamped Seth because he'd wondered if he was making a mistake, leaving Raoul. The other wolves had been coming, and he'd worried about Malikah.

Iain patted his back as Fluffy gestured for them to enter the gargoyle's stronghold. Seth tried to hold back his wince and failed.

"Sorry," Iain said. "That was one impressive dismount from the window ledge."

Seth shot Iain a piercing glance of suspicion. Yep, that was a sly dig. "I knocked out Raoul," Seth said in a mild voice as he limped after Malikah. His mate sailed forth with fury in her sails. This was one meeting he didn't intend to avoid.

Malikah halted without warning and whirled to face Esmerelda and Fluffy. "I would like you to come with us," she said, not explaining or saying anything else, merely resuming her march toward the gates.

"Your lady is scary," Iain whispered.

Seth grinned. "Yeah. Isn't she magnificent?"

This meeting with Samarak Ironwing might go pear-shaped, but the anger simmering inside Malikah and firing her belly had to escape somewhere. This gargoyle must recognize the cruel streak in his mate. How could he not? If she stooped to poisoning kids, she could commit other crimes. How many other people had she injured? Killed?

Malikah stomped through the gates and found Sam waiting in the courtyard. Interestingly, he bore his human form, but two heavily weaponized gargoyle guards flanked him.

"Malikah," he said, his gaze flitting over her companions. "You bring a dragon to my territory? Is this a declaration of war?" His mouth quirked, but the smile never reached his eyes.

"Right now, all I want is a friendly chat." But she was here to attack his wife.

Sam studied her for a beat longer, and Malikah struggled to maintain her patience, her temper. She wanted to plow her fist into Esmerelda's nose and work off the burning in her chest in the manner her guardian gargoyle had trained her. She'd yank the woman's hair from its sophisticated updo and give her a taste of the suffering she'd inflicted on those innocent kids.

Seth stepped up beside her and wove their fingers together. He was wearing a half form between man and gargoyle, which should've been impossible for him. She was learning to expect the incredible from Seth. The man was a miracle, and he'd come to save her.

Seth was in pain and exhausted—she could feel the fatigue radiating off him—but he was standing at her side, prepared to take whatever was coming. Warmth suffused her at the silent support.

She loved him.

Malikah lightly squeezed Seth's hand in deference to his injuries and confidently pushed forward.

After a brief word with his guards, Sam inclined his head

and gestured for them to follow.

Dougal retreated and took to the wing. He perched on the side of a neighboring building.

Sam's jaw hardened, but he said nothing and walked into a reception room for guests. "Can I get you something to drink?"

Not likely! She refused to eat or drink anything in this nest of vipers.

"No, thank you," Malikah said with a polite smile.

Esmerelda and Fluffy turned in the opposite direction. No, that wouldn't do. She wanted to watch Esmerelda's expression when she outed her. That thought halted her steps, and Seth sent her a quizzical look. But flying bats, what if Esmerelda had acted with Sam's permission? Was a trap about to spring on their heads?

No, Dougal was present, and Iain was no pushover.

"Esmerelda," she said, pushing sweetness into her voice. "Do you have time for me to speak to you and Sam?"

"What do you want?" the woman snapped.

Sam scowled. "Esmerelda, why don't you take ten minutes to sit with us? I know you're busy, but ten minutes won't make much difference."

"If I must," Esmerelda said with a long-suffering sigh. "Fluffy, you come too."

Fluffy hesitated but followed after Esmerelda cast an impatient glower over her shoulder.

Okay, all the pieces were in play. Now it was up to her to call checkmate.

Malikah strode into the room, wincing when she heard Seth's breath whistle through his teeth at her abrupt increase in pace. "Sorry," she whispered, slowing her progress to match his limp.

"Have a seat," Sam said, leading them into a second room. This one had a desk and a wall of ornate wooden shelves filled with leather-bound books.

Sam didn't strike her as a keen reader, but then she hadn't thought Esmerelda would poison kids, either.

"What did you want to discuss?" Sam said after taking a seat behind the desk.

Malikah dropped onto one of the three upright chairs before Sam's desk. They were as uncomfortable as they looked. "First, do you have a healer available? One who could take a quick look at my mate?"

Sam's brows rose to his hairline. "Your mate?" He cast a dismissive glance at Seth. "Him?"

"Yes," she said, batting down her instant anger. Seth was worth ten of Sam.

"Our healers are busy," Esmerelda said, her smile sweet even if her tone was not. She stood with a hand on Sam's shoulder.

Fluffy hovered at the side of Sam's desk. She twisted and pulled at her black jacket, slipping her hands into the pockets before removing them seconds later. A woman with a guilty conscience? Malikah intended to find out.

Unable to remain still, she stood, the action taking care of some of the angst pinballing inside her. She didn't make the same mistake as Fluffy, not wanting to give away any of her fury in her body language. She glanced at Seth, who sat slumped in his chair. Iain sat sprawled as if his seat was the most comfortable piece of furniture ever. He reminded her of a relaxed cat, but she knew better.

"Clock is ticking," Esmerelda said, her tone snide.

"Fine," Malikah said. "I have told you before about our sick children. You refused to help, which is your right."

"What has this got to do with me?" Esmerelda snapped.

"Everything," Malikah fired back. "Let me finish. The dragon healers have discovered the cause of the stasis and reversed the symptoms."

"I'm pleased to hear it," Sam said. "But what is this to do with us?"

"The children received a dose of poison," Malikah said. "It was in the packet of sweets from your colony."

"What?" Esmerelda screeched, her features turning sharp with anger. "How dare you?"

Sam appeared equally furious. "We gave you food because you have nothing. You would bite the hand that fed you?"

Malikah continued as if they hadn't interrupted her. "A lab tested the sweets for us. Only some held poison, so the result was random. Through a chance meeting, I learned the children who hang out in front of your colony with their skateboards also received a packet of sweets. These kids are streetwise and didn't trust the person who gave them this treat. This saved their lives since a gargoyle's constitution is stronger than that of a human."

"Why are you telling us?" Sam asked, and he sounded puzzled.

Malikah didn't think it was an act. He hadn't known. She turned to scrutinize Esmerelda. The woman's features reminded her of a mask. She was giving nothing away.

Fluffy, however, was nowhere near the actress that her best friend was, and she wrung her hands, her gaze darting toward the door.

"I'm telling you because it was Esmerelda who handed out the sweets. They identified her to me today."

"What utter rubbish," Esmerelda said in a bored tone. "You'd take the word of a bunch of street rats over mine?"

"Yes," Malikah said. "I retrieved that packet of sweets from the trash bin where the kids dumped it. A scientist analyzed random contents for me. When she found six out of six contaminated with the poison, she tested every piece." Malikah glared at Esmerelda. "Every item in the packet contained poison."

"This is slander," Esmerelda said, her cheeks blazing red.

"How do you know the sweets came from here?" Sam asked.

"Don't listen to them," Esmerelda snapped. "They're trying to blame us for something we didn't do, and we shouldn't entertain their accusations. I would never condone something like this. Never."

"And if someone gave your children poisoned sweets?" Iain asked. "What would you do to ensure the culprit paid?"

"This has nothing to do with you, wolf," Esmerelda spat. "You're only here because we are polite hosts and agreed to speak with you. Your father is dead, and you lost your right to rule when William beat you in a fair fight."

Unperturbed, Iain focused on Sam. "Your mate is protesting, but you're not saying much."

Malikah watched Sam and saw his gaze was on Fluffy.

His face twisted before it resettled into impassive.

Malikah was tired of talking and went for the throat. "Fluffy, did you and Esmerelda give those children a packet of poisoned sweets?"

"No, of course not," Fluffy cried, but everyone saw it was a lie.

Seth released a wolfish growl, and Iain echoed the angry rumble.

Malikah whirled to face Sam. "Your wife maliciously poisoned my kids. They've been so sick and in extreme pain. They're children. Innocents."

"They're lying," Esmerelda snapped.

The gargoyle wasn't willing to admit a thing, and she tried to glare Fluffy into submission.

Attack the weak point. Malikah whirled back to Fluffy. "You willingly poisoned gargoyle children who'd done nothing to you."

"I didn't know," Fluffy sobbed. "Not then."

"Shut up!" Esmerelda snarled, her gargoyle bleeding through her voice, making the order deeper and more guttural. "Don't say another word."

Sam rose, jerking away from Esmerelda. "Fluffy, when did you learn about the poison?"

Fluffy cast a guilty glance at Esmerelda. Another snarl and a muttered curse had her staring at her feet.

"Fluffy?" Sam prompted.

"Esmerelda didn't like those street rats making our residence untidy. At first, she asked nicely, but they jeered at her."

Malikah snorted because the kids had already told her

what had happened. Esmerelda had been drunk, and she'd almost run over them. Ever since, it'd been a verbal battle. Her peace offering of sweets had pricked their self-protection radar.

"The kids kept using our street as a skateboard track," Fluffy whispered. "Esmerelda... Esmerelda told me she would put them in their place and gave them the packet of sweets. She told them it was a peace offering and asked if they could skate elsewhere. She walked to her car and unlocked it, and she was laughing. I didn't understand until she told me she'd injected poison into them." Fluffy wrung her hands, her face so pale Malikah wondered if she might faint.

"You didn't think to tell me?" Sam asked.

"I... Esmerelda is my friend," Fluffy whispered.

"Which makes you just as guilty," Seth snapped. "You knew, and you did nothing to stop her. Do you know how much pain those kids were in before the healers discovered the cause?"

"I didn't know," Fluffy repeated. Tears streamed down her cheeks and dripped onto her fashionable pale pink blouse.

"You attempted to poison the street kids because they annoyed you. Why did you add poison to the food you gave to us? You hadn't even met our kids," Malikah said, working hard to push back the heat in her chest. Now was not the time to lose control.

Everyone focused on Esmerelda and waited for her to answer.

"Esmerelda?" Sam prompted. His voice held a note of

steel.

Esmerelda swallowed and, for the first time, seemed more vulnerable.

Malikah held her breath, waiting for the truth.

"Esmerelda!" Sam barked. "Answer the question. I won't ask you again."

The glare Esmerelda shot Malikah held pure loathing and venom. "Because of her!"

"Me?" Malikah pressed a hand to her chest. She'd been nothing but friendly to Esmerelda. When Sam had informed her she and her group couldn't stay with them, she'd left without complaint, even though the feeble excuses had stung.

"What has Malikah ever done to you?" Seth demanded.

"She made a pass at my mate. I'm tired of women trying to take my man from me. She had to pay," Esmerelda hissed.

Malikah gaped at the gargoyle woman. "I did not. I've never flirted with Sam. All I wanted was a safe place for my people." She shifted to glare at Sam, anger a heavy, hot weight on her chest. "Did you tell her that?" She didn't give Sam a chance to answer. Sam had been the one to proposition her. Many times. Heck, he was messing around with his secretary. Not that she intended to tell Esmerelda. "I have not, nor will I ever, have a sexual relationship with Sam. I do not poach from other women. Besides, I have a mate. I'm not available to any other man. Do you hear me?"

"The entire colony and the neighbors heard that screech," Esmerelda said, calming a fraction. But while serener, she treated Malikah as if she was the one to blame for this fiasco.

Malikah fought for calm. "Esmerelda has admitted to poisoning the sweets, and we know she gave them to the children. I want her punished."

Sam's gaze went from her to Esmerelda and back. Instead of disgust, smugness crawled across his face, and in that moment, she understood he didn't intend to do a thing. He was fine with Esmerelda's actions. Fury exploded in Malikah. She took half a step toward Esmerelda, and wisely, the woman positioned herself behind Sam.

"Fine," Malikah spat. "Every time I see Sam, and you're not present, he propositions me."

Esmerelda laughed. "I don't believe you."

Malikah's fists clenched and unclenched as she struggled to control her rage. These two were as bad as each other. She stared at Sam, silently willing him to do the right thing. It was a sinister act of attempted murder, not a trivial offense.

"Sam," she prompted, giving him one last chance.

He grinned with arrogant smugness. "It's time for you and your group to leave. Don't return because you won't be welcome. Don't ask me or my people for aid again because you won't receive it. You're on your own."

Malikah allowed his words to settle. Her nostrils flared. Her lips pulled back to reveal her teeth, then she leaped at him, quickly clearing his sturdy wooden desk. She pulled back her fist and punched Sam in the face, using every ounce of her strength. She took Sam and Esmerelda by surprise and got in a second punch that sent Sam to the floor.

Sam shook himself while Esmerelda recovered faster. She swung at Malikah, but Malikah had learned a thing or two and dodged the blow. Esmerelda screeched in frustration and came at her again. The woman was so angry that she didn't think. She merely reacted with tunnel vision.

Malikah was ready and stuck out her foot. The simple trip was Esmerelda's undoing. Esmerelda wasn't used to fighting or self-defense, despite her status. Malikah jumped out of the way as Esmerelda crashed into the desk. She added insult to injury by booting Esmerelda in the arse.

Malikah stood back, unimpressed by the volley of curses and threats from the woman. She glanced at Sam, wary of him jumping to the defense of his mate, but the gargoyle male didn't move.

She realized neither gargoyle cared about the consequences of Esmerelda's actions. They considered her and her people inferior. Nothing Malikah said or did would change their narrow minds.

Malikah crouched beside Esmerelda and yanked on her hair, forcing the gargoyle to turn her face. Esmerelda spat in Malikah's direction but missed her target.

Malikah stared at the snarling gargoyle with distaste. "I intend to report what you've done to the ruling paranormal council, and if they don't listen, there are other ways to get out the truth. Sam is just as guilty. He must know what you're capable of." A flash of insight struck her. "This isn't the right way to gain Sam's attention. Your mate won't change. He'll always chase other women. That's his problem. Not yours. If I were you, I'd kick him to the curb. If he's capable of cheating, it's obvious you're not true mates."

"You know nothing!" Esmerelda spat.

"Maybe," Malikah conceded. "But I understand loyalty and friendship. Decency."

With that, she wheeled around and stalked toward the door. Seth and Iain fell into step, and they swept from the office. They passed servants and residents, but not one gargoyle tried to detain them.

They didn't speak until they exited the main gates.

"What's next?" Iain asked.

"I'll report them to the paranormal council. I doubt anything will happen. They won't face any consequences," Malikah said with bitterness.

"What will hurt is the loss of their reputation," Iain said with certainty.

Seth nodded. "Once they hear what happened and Sam's lack of action, the dragons won't do business with them. Sam is a businessman, and once word gets around, his reputation will suffer. The truth will filter down to human businessmen. No one likes anyone who harms a child."

"At least we've learned not to trust Sam or his people. I know not to ask them for help. Not that we need to now. Iain, your mother-in-law has been helpful. I'll never be able to repay her kindness. Everyone in my group is happy, especially since the children are recovering."

"Yeah, Fiona is amazing. She and Dougal have been brilliant with me and Elspeth. I'm sure they didn't expect a wolf son-in-law, yet they've welcomed me and my brother. I'll do anything for either of them."

"That makes two of us," Malikah said. "I vote we forget Sam and let karma sort him out. Besides, I punched him in the nose, and damn, that felt satisfying." She shook her right hand with a rueful grin. "My fist hurts now, but I don't regret a thing."

"You also sent Esmerelda flying," Seth said, reaching for her hand. He squeezed her fingers but kept the action gentle. "My warrior."

"Yeah," Malikah agreed and met his gaze. "Your warrior."

25

BACK AT DOUGAL AND Fiona's home, Seth limped directly to the healer. Neither he nor Malikah had put a full stop to their problems, but after discussing the issue with Iain, they'd decided to report Raoul to the paranormal council. Raoul's experiments were dangerous to citizens. With things volatile between the humans and the paranormal, the council needed to stop Raoul, or at least hinder his progress.

"Hmm, interesting," the elderly female healer said. "Where does it hurt most?"

"Everywhere." Seth reassessed his aches and pains. "My leg is the worst. I thought I'd broken my arm, but it's not as sore now."

"You told me you're half-wolf and half-gargoyle. Is that correct?" the healer asked.

"Yeah. My healing abilities are pathetic." He'd fallen off a building and was lucky he wasn't dead.

"Well, the good news is you've healed most of your injuries."

Seth felt his mouth drop open and pressed his lips together so he didn't resemble a fish. "I have?"

The healer smiled, revealing a missing front tooth. "My theory is because you're mixed race, your abilities have taken longer to manifest. We can do tests, but you should consult gargoyle and wolf healers for second and third opinions. Sometimes, our emotions trap us in a state of flux. If you've been in a stressful situation, young man, that might've restricted your abilities. Mental well-being is as vital as physical health.

Seth considered her words. "I found my mate, which I didn't expect."

"That would do it," the healer agreed. "Have you suffered any unusual medical problems?"

"Because of my half-gargoyle status, I kept going into stasis. Huge chunks of time went missing that I couldn't account for."

"Is that still happening?"

"No," Seth said in surprise. "I haven't gone into stasis since spending more time with Malikah."

"Hmm. Interesting," the healer said, cocking her head like a curious bird. "Have you been together physically?"

Seth fought hard to stop fidgeting, and the healer barked a rusty chuckle at his expense.

"Come now, young man. I have seen and heard it all."

"We haven't done anything more than kiss."

"Ah," the healer said. "A physical relationship will change everything. If I were to guess, I'd say it will strengthen—is your lover a gargoyle, wolf, or something else?"

"A gargoyle."

"Yes. Yes." The healer's gaze went distant. "Since your mate is a gargoyle, that side will likely take precedence. Heal. Make love to your beautiful mate and return to see me next week." She consulted her battered diary. "On Thursday morning at ten."

Seth nodded, but his mind darted to Malikah. He imagined flying with her, soaring through the evening sky, backlit with stars, and his happiness flared. Healing himself was huge. Given his failure as a shifter, any late enhancements he manifested thrilled him.

"Thank you," he said, remembering his manners.

"Next Thursday, young man. Don't be late."

"Yes, ma'am." Seth left her treatment room, a spring in his step.

Once outside, he headed toward Fiona's gardens. He dropped onto a seat beneath a tall totara tree and pulled out his phone to call the council. He had to report Raoul.

After he'd explained what he wanted, the secretary put him through to the security department. He repeated his story, giving the investigator full details.

"Thank you," the man said. "I'll contact you if we require further information."

"What will you do?" Seth asked.

"We'll check the shifter treatment centers. We might get lucky and scoop him up for questioning. If you see him again, call me on my direct number. I'll send it to you now."

Seth's phone beeped. *Wow, this guy was efficient.* "I've got it," Seth said. "Thank you."

The man hung up, his manner abrupt, but he'd sounded sincere. Satisfied with his morning, Seth pushed to his feet, his muscles barely whimpering.

He found Malikah in the office with Iain and Elspeth. Seth walked to Malikah's side, experiencing an urge to touch her. He took her hand and checked it for bruising.

"You must have iron fists," he said, surprised at the lack of damage.

"Oh, it hurt. A lot, but I refused to show my weakness." Her hand clenched his painfully tight, her fury flashing in her eyes.

Iain leaned back in the office chair, making it creak alarmingly. "Esmerelda claimed or implied she was jealous. She accused you of targeting Sam. We know he's sleeping with his secretary. What if we use a friend and create a honey trap? Esmerelda is off balance. I say push her."

Malikah pulled a face. "I don't want anyone else in the firing line. Esmerelda is a loose cannon, and Fluffy will do anything Esmerelda asks of her. I'll tell my people the truth about what happened and why. Karma will get Esmerelda. Sam, too, since he's as guilty as his wife. He knows she did it, yet he's not taking steps to punish her. Nor is he bothered about the consequences. No, I intend to move forward instead of backward."

Pride rose in Seth. From what Malikah had told him of her time in England, she'd been a pampered rich girl. She'd grown since arriving in Auckland, although he doubted she'd agree with him. "You reported them to the council, though?"

"It's on record, but they told me they couldn't act because we lack physical proof."

Seth's phone rang before he could reply. "Seth Walsh speaking."

"This is Investigator Simmons," a man said. Seth recognized the voice. "We have Raoul in custody and will investigate further. He doesn't like you much, Mr. Walsh."

"The feeling is mutual. You won't release him without charge?"

"He'll remain with us for some time. We scooped up his employees, and they're singing like a tree full of tuis. Charges will be pending."

Seth grinned, relieved he wouldn't need to keep looking over his shoulder. "Thank you."

The man hung up without a farewell, but Seth didn't care.

"That's fantastic news," Iain said, having heard the entire conversation. "That wolf deserves everything he gets."

Elspeth released an enormous yawn, and Iain cast a worried glance at his mate.

"You need to rest," he said.

Elspeth awkwardly rose from her seat. Her belly was huge, and Seth would bet Iain had helped with her shoes because he doubted she'd manage on her own.

"Would you like to walk in the garden with me?" Seth asked, offering Malikah his arm.

"That sounds lovely." She kissed his cheek before resting her hand on the crook of his elbow. "I feel as if we haven't had much time together."

"Tonight," Seth said, winking at her.

"Yes," she agreed.

By common consent, they walked through Fiona's herb garden and ambled toward the rose beds where they'd had dinner the previous night. It seemed a lifetime ago.

A pungent wash of rosemary filled his senses, the aroma making his nose twitch and bringing an urge to sneeze. He held his breath for three seconds before letting it ease out. The basil and coriander didn't bother him as much, but he was still relieved to enter the portion of the garden containing flowers. The pansies were in full bloom, their multi-colored faces turned to the sun.

Seth squinted and pushed his glasses farther up his nose. He paused, finding no glasses, and recalled the cracking sound of the frames crunching under a werewolf's foot. Sighing, he headed for the shade.

"The healers must've helped," Malikah said. "Your limp is barely perceptible."

"They gave me a tonic to take and used magic to help my leg, which was the worst of my injuries." He grinned. "But the healer told me I healed most of the injuries myself."

"I thought you were slow to heal?"

"According to the healer, my half-breed status made me slower to manifest my powers, but she is positive one of my sides will show dominance soon."

Malikah wrinkled her nose. "That sounds painful."

"But it might mean my flying improves. I'd give anything to experience a night flight with you, one where I'm not terrified I'll dive-bomb into the ocean or, worse, hit land."

Malikah placed a hand on each of his shoulders and met his gaze. "I love you now, Seth Walsh. You're kind and loyal, a fantastic friend, and I can't wait to learn more..." She trailed off, a charming blush highlighting her cheekbones.

Seth's pulse jumped and ran faster. His gaze swept over her face and settled on her lush lips. "I'm your mate," he whispered. "The sex between us will be amazing."

Her eyes danced with laughter. "I hope you're right."

He drew her closer and kissed her, starting slowly, sipping at her lips before gradually turning the kiss toward carnal territory. Sexual hunger swept over him, sucking him down until only Malikah existed in his world. The curvy shape of her pressed against him. Her sweet scent, with a hint of oranges and lemons, filled his breath. The soft murmurs she made as they kissed thrilled him. *His future.*

Seth gradually pulled out of the kiss and pressed his forehead against hers. "I'm sorry we couldn't prove Esmerelda hurt the kids."

"Yeah, that will haunt me, but I truly believe karma will catch her. Sam wasn't impressed with her behavior. Mostly, he controlled his expression, but I saw his disgust. He and Esmerelda don't have children, and I'm sure that's a sore point with Sam. As the leader, he'd want an heir. I'm not thinking about them. It's a waste of energy."

"You're not wrong." Seth glanced toward the sun, glad it had shifted behind a cloud.

An eerie shriek split the air, grabbing their attention. He

and Malikah halted, scanning, assessing the risk.

"Esmerelda," Seth breathed.

She barreled toward them in her gargoyle form, her face a rictus of fury.

"Mine. I'll deal with her." Malikah shifted rapidly, her clothes melting into her warrior form. With a powerful push of her legs, she soared into the air.

Esmerelda attacked, claws extended and her mouth a great maw of violence. She shrieked, an ear-splitting wail that echoed across the garden. She was a woman crazed. Determined. And she wanted to pulverize Malikah.

Malikah met her blow for blow. Esmerelda snarled, raked her claws across Malikah's shoulder. Before Seth could wade in to help, a form darted across his peripheral vision. Fluffy. She hovered at tree level, her chest heaving, her expression worried.

Not wishing to distract Malikah, Seth edged toward the tree where Fluffy lingered. When she spotted him, she flitted back, eyes wide as if she might flee.

"I want to talk," Seth said, keeping his voice low. "I promise not to hurt you."

Fluffy hesitated, then floated downward, landing gracefully in a manner he had yet to emulate.

"What's up with Esmerelda?" he asked.

Fluffy bit her lip, the action strange in her gargoyle form. "Sam and Esmerelda had a private meeting after you left. Usually, they shout, but there was none today. Afterward, Esmerelda ordered me to leave her alone." She nibbled her lip again. "Esmerelda is my friend, but she's moody and not the easiest gargoyle to hang around."

A triumphant scream interrupted their conversation. Horrified, Seth watched Malikah tumble and strike the ground hard. She jumped up and shook herself, and when he glimpsed her face, her eyes glowed red.

"*Uh-oh*," Fluffy said. "Esmerelda shouldn't have done that."

"You think?" Seth snapped, angry at this ditzy gargoyle.

"Your mate wasn't trying before. She was holding off Esmerelda easily," Fluffy said.

Hadn't appeared that way to Seth, and his worry doubled. "What happened after Esmerelda retreated to her room? Wait, do she and Sam not share a room?" The more he learned, the better. Esmerelda had become unhinged. Someone needed to stop the woman.

"They have an extensive suite that has several rooms. Esmerelda likes to be alone."

Fluffy was right. The battle intensity had ratcheted up a gear. Malikah was pounding on Esmerelda, toying with her. His woman—a true warrior. Malikah punched Esmerelda in the stomach, the blow brutal, and he winced.

"Okay. What happened after that?"

"Sam held a meeting with his security team. He told them Esmerelda was leaving, and after today, they should deny her entrance. He told them she stood accused of poisoning children, and while there was no proof, he hated to put his people at risk."

"Wow," Seth said in an understatement. He hadn't thought Sam would act with such finality.

"Sam is a terrible mate," Fluffy said. "He was never faithful. He even tried to wriggle his way into my bed, but I've known Esmerelda since we were younglings. She doesn't share. I'm cautious with her."

"Bitch!" Esmerelda shrieked.

Iain skidded to a stop near them. The racket had attracted the attention of the adults from Malikah's group. They hovered nearby, two adults settling in the branches of a towering totara.

"Wow, Malikah is fierce," Iain murmured.

"My warrior," Seth said.

Malikah slashed with her talons, leaped nimbly aside to avoid Esmerelda's punch, and kicked out with her right leg. The blow caught Esmerelda's hip, and the gargoyle female howled when she crumpled. Everyone watched with bated breath. Slowly, Esmerelda rose to a sitting position. Her features contorted, her pain visible. Malikah backed up, and when Esmerelda didn't move, she turned her back and strode toward Seth.

Seth only had eyes for his mate. She was magnificent, with her wings in full spread and her gaze wild and resolved.

"Watch out!" Fluffy screamed, and her terror galvanized them.

Seth gasped, and Iain stepped forward, but it was too late.

26

MALIKAH'S CHEST ROSE AND fell with exertion, adrenaline pumping through her veins. Fluffy screamed, and the horrified shriek had Malikah whirling.

A fireball smacked her in the face. It burned, searing her eyes, the sulfur stinging her nostrils. She slapped her face until the flames died. Fury tore through her, but before she could react to the cowardly attack, a knife arced toward her. She backed up in a defensive crouch. *Too slow.* The sharp blade slid into her shoulder, slicing easily through her leathery skin and scales. The pain struck seconds later, and Esmerelda's triumphant cry rang out.

"Malikah!" Seth shouted.

Incensed, Malikah braced herself and ripped the knife out of her shoulder. She flung it aside, ordering herself to shrug off the pain. She sucked in a fortifying breath and charged.

Malikah tackled her, and they hit the ground in a

tangle of limbs and wings. Esmerelda cursed and shrieked, her powerful body bucking beneath Malikah's. This time, Malikah didn't hold back. She punched Esmerelda despite her waning power. She slashed the gargoyle's face, ripping free a chunk of flesh. Esmerelda headbutted her, attempting to gore Malikah with her horns.

Malikah pummeled Esmerelda, panting now. Damn the woman! The wound on her shoulder shrieked in agony, but she refused to stop.

This battle had one outcome.

Death.

She'd tried. She'd tried the right way. So far, she'd controlled the power her parents and January had warned her she was never to use lightly. *Only a matter of life or death*. Her ability meant she'd always have a guardian because only one gargoyle per generation received this power.

Other gargoyles assumed her power a myth. Malikah knew better.

She understood the cost. Each time she used this so-called gift, she lost ten years of her life. The last gargoyle with the power had lived longer than most, and she wanted to emulate him, by the gargoyle gods!

Esmerelda released a crazed cackle and freed one arm. She lobbed another fireball.

"Stop!" Malikah cursed and released Esmerelda, using her hands to smother the flames. Her eyes stung, and her shoulder throbbed, the wound leaking her life force despite her rapid healing powers.

Esmerelda thought she'd bested her.

Malikah forced herself to move, springing to her feet. *Ten years was nothing*. This woman deserved punishment for her crimes. A child should have the chance to prosper and grow into adulthood.

"Not so smug now, bitch," Esmerelda taunted.

Carefully watching the other woman, she dug into the heart of her soul, burrowing past the myriad shields her guardian had helped her weave to protect from unintentional use. The heat in her chest and mind grew, and her sight grew sharper.

Esmerelda charged again, a fireball spinning on her fingertips. Malikah batted it away, the sizzling heat no longer bothering her.

Using this power of hers would leave her weak, but she'd heal at an accelerated rate using the ten years of life as it did so. Energy flared in her bones, on her skin. It shimmered through her.

Malikah scrutinized Esmerelda. Beautiful on the outside, she was ugly inside where it counted, her aura—a black mass of hatred.

A hand gripped her shoulder. "Malikah?"

She knew it was Seth without looking and risked a glance at him before averting her gaze. But what she saw made her heart sing. He was everything decent. She'd acknowledged this, but this close to the edge let her see his soul. His aura was fiery pink with a hint of copper, and his wolf heritage made her smile.

A fireball slapped at her, and she gently shrugged off Seth's touch.

"Stand back." Her voice was gravelly low, barely

SHELLEY MUNRO

recognizable as hers.

Another fireball struck her, this one in the face, and Esmerelda released a victorious cry.

"Enough!" Power surged within Malikah, and she didn't try to hold it back. She let rip, her gaze connecting with Esmerelda's. The gargoyle froze, her eyes widening. She tried to run, but Malikah sprang and gripped her shoulder with one hand and her chin with her other. Esmerelda struggled and thrashed. Malikah held her firmly and released the chains imprisoning her superpower. One by one, they fractured until she'd almost reached the point of no return.

The fiery light shrouded her sight, killing all color, muting it into black and white. The heat was fierce, and she hesitated. Her guardian had told her she was the executioner, but she must behave fairly because not only would she lose years of her life but also sap her strength. It might take a week to regain what she lost. *She must be certain before she zapped her prey.*

Esmerelda sneered, disgust and arrogance emanating from her in waves.

Bitter anger filled Malikah as she stared into Esmerelda's eyes. Still defiant, the gargoyle glowered, suffering no remorse. The children didn't matter to her, and she would repeat her actions in a heartbeat. Malikah refused to let another child suffer.

"You have me," Esmerelda ground out, her voice rougher in her gargoyle guise. "But you don't have the guts to finish me."

"You don't care that you hurt those children."

"They were a tool."

Disgust filled Malikah, along with an inner calmness. "I don't do this lightly, and I pay a forfeit for using this power, but if anyone deserves this, it is you."

Esmerelda scoffed. "You can't hurt me. You're weak."

"Then why did Sam want me?" Malikah retorted. No sooner had she formed the words than she regretted them.

Esmerelda released a snarl. "You dare to proposition my mate?"

"I didn't say Sam interested me. I rejected his advances. Many times."

"Release me." Esmerelda's entire body quivered as she fought Malikah's grip.

Esmerelda wouldn't change. Didn't want to change, which made her choice easy. Decision made, she began the final ritual before she loosened her grip on the power that tingled across her skin, hungry for release.

"I call on my guardian to bear witness. I call on January."

The air tingled, and Malikah heard gasps, but she paid them no mind, merely relieved her summons had worked. January was an old gargoyle with sweeping horns and chiseled features. A long steel-gray braid hung down his back. He frowned, taking in the situation in one glance.

"Are ye sure, lass?"

"Yes." Malikah held sorrow, but the rightness of her actions gave her backbone steel. "I'm aware of the consequences and will live with this taking of a life on my conscience."

January gave a heavy sigh. "Go ahead, lass. Do not prolong the pain in her soul."

SHELLEY MUNRO

Malikah nodded, sympathy warring with certainty. She shifted her attention back to Esmerelda. "I am sorry your life has not progressed as you wished. I am sorry for your bitterness and need for revenge."

Then Malikah dallied no longer. She centered herself with a deep inhalation. As she slowly released the breath, she unfastened the last two golden chains holding her power at bay. Heat rushed through her, centering in her eyes. She went blind as the power exploded, slicing toward Esmerelda with deadly force. Esmerelda screamed, first in panic, then her cries were of pain.

Malikah increased the power behind her justice, and the screams cut off with a croak. The silence was worse than the screams. Malikah swallowed and gradually shut down her power.

"That's it, lass," January said, his calm manner doing much to center her and regain control.

Malikah focused on drawing the power into her chest. Once she'd finished, she took a moment to analyze. The pulse in her chest was weaker. Without warning, her legs went from under her, and she hit the ground. Malikah forced herself to a sitting position to study Esmerelda.

She took no joy in the woman's frozen form, her skin an awful shade between gray and white. Her features had frozen in a scowl, and when Malikah used her senses to probe for life, she found none. Then, as Malikah watched, Esmerelda disintegrated, turning slowly to a fine powder. Malikah winced, guilt slashing through her. She had done this—destroyed another life.

Whispers drifted in the background, filled with horror

and disgust. *Seth*. What did he think? Did he hate her? Fear her for what she had done to Esmerelda?

She sought him now, needing reassurance.

"Malikah." He approached her cautiously.

"You're fine, lad," January said. "She won't injure you since she has no power right now. She must recharge."

Seth dropped to a crouch and reached for her hand. His flesh was warm, his touch welcoming, while her skin felt clammy and unpleasant. Everything inside her chest went tight, and she struggled to breathe. What a time to understand she needed this man. He'd stolen her heart.

"Malikah," he said, using his free hand to smooth the hair off her sweaty face. "My warrior."

She gaped. "I don't disgust you?"

"Esmerelda deserved her punishment. Even at the end, she wasn't sorry. I bet she has hurt and injured others. Abused her position. This wasn't the first time. Shift, and we'll go inside and get you cleaned up."

All the aches and pains she'd collected returned in vengeance. Seth placed his arm around her waist. Something inside her relaxed because he wasn't treating her like a monster, even if everyone else kept their distance. When she trembled, he patted her shoulder.

"Shift," he said.

The simple act she usually managed with a mere thought took more energy, more effort. When the leathery scales and wings finally melted into her body, she couldn't halt the shaking of her limbs. Seth scooped her up and strode toward the house. She heard the renewed whispers and Iain following them.

"Is she all right?" Iain asked.

"I killed her," Malikah whispered.

"She didn't give you any choice," Iain said at their side. "Esmerelda held not a shred of guilt for her actions. She had you in her sights, Malikah, and she wouldn't have left you alone. I bet when I research her background, I'll find a pattern of the same behavior and more deaths."

"I agree with Iain," Seth said. "Don't waste your emotions on the gargoyle woman. She was bad news."

Easier said than done. Malikah spotted Fluffy standing by the heap of powder that used to be Esmerelda. Fluffy bowed her head, and her shoulders shook in silent grief. Again, guilt sliced and diced Malikah. Remorse. Would she do it again? Probably. Was Esmerelda's death worth ten years of her life? Malikah didn't know.

"Will Sam retaliate?" she asked.

"We witnessed what happened. Fluffy knew Esmerelda wasn't in her right mind. She didn't intend to stop," Iain said, his tone stern and confident. "Every one of us will back you. Fiona and Dougal saw what happened. They were watching from the front steps." He jerked his head in that direction.

Fiona rushed up to them. "Does Malikah require medical attention? Should I call the healer?"

"Tired." Her bruises reminded Malikah of the seriousness of what had happened.

"I will tend her," January said.

Malikah started, having forgotten January's presence. Seth didn't react, but Iain appeared wary. "This is my guardian gargoyle. Gargoyles with certain gifts require a guardian."

"Mostly, a guardian is short-term," January continued, "but I've been stuck with this one for life because of her unique power. A power such as Malikah bears can eat at the soul, and a guardian provides advice, their experience, and support."

"You are welcome to our home, Mr. Guardian," Fiona said.

January made a courtly bow. "I thank you. My name is January."

An hour later, Malikah still felt as if her knees wouldn't hold her body upright. She trembled and her stomach fluttered and danced as if she might...

Malikah staggered toward the bathroom, almost headbutting the wall. She barely reached the toilet before vomiting the glass of water she'd drank five minutes earlier.

"Malikah." Seth brushed a hand over her head, concern radiating through his voice.

She rose unsteadily.

"She'll be fine after she rests, lad. The power Malikah has exerts a cost on the body each time she uses it. Checks and balances," he added.

"Seth, I'm sorry." She pulled a rueful face. "This isn't the way I imagined our evening."

Seth sent her a gentle smile. "We have plenty of time. Rest."

"The lad is right, lass. Sleep will help you recover." January turned to Seth. "I shall return home and monitor Malikah from a distance. She'll remain shaky for up to a week and should refrain from strenuous exercise. Get her to eat small meals and keep up her fluids."

"Thank you," Seth said.

Malikah used the wall for balance and tottered toward the bed. Seth swung her into his arms. He placed her on her feet beside the bed and balanced her while he pulled back the covers. With a gentle push, she landed on the bed. She groaned as a bruise made itself known. Lifting her legs hurt, but she gave a relieved sigh once she lay flat. Seth twitched the quilt into place. Her eyes closed, sleep tugging at her with welcoming darkness.

Malikah wasn't certain how long passed before she ran into nightmares. When January had taken her aside, he'd mentioned this possibility. Using her powers had a steep cost. The monsters came at her, each with Esmerelda's face, determined to kill.

"Shush, sweetheart."

She was vaguely aware of a warm body curled against hers, chasing away the chill trying to invade her. No light entered the room, the curtains solid guardians. What was the time?

"Go back to sleep."

"Seth?"

"Yes."

"I love you. I didn't want to, but it crept up on me." Fatigue slurred her words, yet he heard because his lips brushed her bare shoulder. Her eyes fluttered and sleep claimed her.

When she awoke again, sunlight warmed the room even if the curtains still enclosed her in darkness. She was alone. Just her luck. She and the sexy man had shared a bed, but nothing had happened. Malikah stared glumly at the head impression on the pillow. At least he'd chased away her nightmares.

Malikah struggled to her feet and tottered to the en suite to take care of business. She assessed her condition. Still fatigued but no longer nauseous. Hunger stirred, a rumble emphasizing the thought. She could eat.

The door opened to reveal Seth. "You're awake."

"Yeah. Still tired, but hunger is driving me now."

"January said the worst is past once you're hungry. Do you want me to bring you something?"

"What time is it?"

"Two in the afternoon. You've slept for three days."

Her brows shot up. "No wonder I'm hungry."

"So, food?"

"Can I dress and grab some fresh air?"

"Of course! Need some help?"

She sniffed and decided to take a shower first. Glancing around the dim room, she asked, "Do I have clothes?"

"You do. We decided it would be safer if you stayed in the main house rather than a cottage. Your clothes are in the wardrobe, next to mine." He stalked across the room, tugging at the curtains and opening a window.

Malikah squinted against the brightness.

"I've been sleeping next to you, although mostly you didn't notice. I should've checked with you first, but you were out of it. January wasn't worried, so I took my cue from him."

Malikah dredged through her mind. "I told you I love you. I remember that."

Seth's smile was wolfish. "No take backs."

"I meant every word. Did January describe the cost of using my power?"

Seth sobered. "He did. I dislike trading part of your life for her death. I—"

"She deserved it," Malikah cut in, her voice terse. "I'd do the same again. A woman doesn't suddenly start that behavior."

"I'm sure you're right, but—"

"It's done. I can't change what happened. All that matters is we're safe and the kids are recovering. I don't want to dwell in the past. I prefer a future with you at my side—if that's what you want."

Seth's smile returned, reaching his beautiful blue eyes. "You're my mate, and I want to live the rest of my life with you. I care for you deeply and have ever since I saw you striding down the street."

"Has Sam contacted us?" she asked, knowing she had to face this one thing.

"Iain and I went to see him," Seth said. "Esmerelda's death hasn't fazed him. You've rid him of a problem, and you won't receive any payback from him. We got the impression Sam's people didn't hold Esmerelda in high regard. The only gargoyle who showed emotion is Fluffy. She'd like to speak with you as soon as you're well."

"What does she want?" Malikah asked, foreboding filling her with tension.

"She told Fiona she wanted to move here and live with your gargoyles. She wants to escape memories, and she hated how Sam behaved as if Esmerelda meant nothing to him."

"I'm not sure. Fluffy must've known what was happening."

"She swears she didn't. She is full of guilt because she placed the sweets into the basket along with the other contents. Fluffy claims she was unaware of Esmerelda's actions."

"Do you believe her?"

"I do. Fiona and Elspeth both say she isn't lying. She didn't know the sweets contained poison, and now she is desperate to make amends."

Malikah nodded slowly. "I'll have to discuss Fluffy with Tamaini and the others. They have the final decision."

"Sounds fair." He motioned toward the shower. "Take that shower and holler if you need help. I'll make you a cup of tea and a plate of sandwiches. I'll come back to get you when it's ready."

"Thank you," Malikah said, tottering toward the en suite.

The warm water washed away the last of her fuzziness, although, if she were honest, fatigue nagged like a sore tooth. She wandered into the bedroom with a towel wrapped around her, and Seth chose that moment to return.

"Malikah." He trained his eyes on her, maintaining absolute focus. Seth halted before her and trailed his finger over her bare shoulder. "I came close to losing you. I thought Esmerelda would kill you. Iain told me you were holding back, but you made every move look real."

Malikah shuddered. "I didn't want to kill her."

27

"I KNOW, SWEETHEART." SETH crossed to the window, turning his back to give her privacy.

Malikah scrambled into a comfy pair of sweats. She'd underestimated how tiring it would be to shower and dress. Her gaze drifted to the bed, but hunger pangs had her sucking up her fatigue. "I'm ready."

"Good. You have a visitor as well."

"Who?"

"Tamaini wishes to speak with you."

"Tamaini hates me. She still blames me for ending up in New Zealand." Foreboding rose in Malikah, and the old guilt she'd succeeded in squashing flared into blazing life. She rubbed her chest to ease the low-level burn. Tamaini would want to know why she hadn't used her power during the Stonehurst attack. She swallowed hard and forcibly removed her hand from her burning chest.

"They would've died if you hadn't warned them," Seth

said, breaking through her troubled thoughts. "Besides, she wasn't breathing fire. Her gift is herbs, right? I'd hate a surprise."

Malikah laughed, but the sound held little humor. "My gift is rare. January told me I'm the only gargoyle in this generation with this additional power."

"My mental powers seem tame by comparison."

"I like them just fine," Malikah said. "Besides, if it weren't for you, we wouldn't have communicated with the children and gained clues to help them."

They descended the stairs and entered the kitchen. Iain and Elspeth sat at the large wooden kitchen table with Tamaini and Fiona.

"Ah, there you are," Fiona said with her usual cheerfulness. "You slept so long you had us worried. How are you feeling?"

Malikah sank into the chair Seth pulled out for her with relief. The walk down the stairs had exhausted her. "Tired," she confessed. "But hunger drove me downstairs. My stomach is rumbling."

"Loudly," Seth said, and everyone laughed, even Tamaini. He shunted a plate of ham and salad sandwiches at her while Fiona poured her a cup of tea.

The conversation was general while Malikah ate.

"Would you like more?" Seth asked.

"Yes, please." She felt as if she hadn't eaten for a month.

"Malikah," Tamaini said. "I've come to apologize. I and the other adults blamed you for things beyond your control." Her face was serious, and her enormous eyes, usually full of anger, bore apology and sorrow. "You've found us a safe place to live. We love living and working in the countryside. You helped our kids, and they're on their way to recovery. And thanks to you, the person responsible will never hurt another child. We owe you and understanding this has taken me a long time. You saved us from certain death, and I realize it wasn't your fault we ended up in Auckland. My behavior was inexcusable when you tried so hard to build us a home. I blamed you because Samarak Ironwing refused to welcome us into his colony. In hindsight, he did us a favor because we would've been at Esmerelda's mercy."

"You don't need to apologize," Malikah said. "We've all made mistakes. I keep thinking I should've used my power when the Stonehurst clan attacked."

"No!" Fiona said.

"No," Seth said at the same time.

"They're right. You would've been one against many, and they would've killed you and the rest of us. No, you did the right thing, and I understand why you'd keep this power secret. It's a heavy burden you bear. The truth is I resented you taking leadership," Tamaini said, "yet I doubt I could've managed as well as you."

Malikah issued a startled laugh. "I'm not any kind of leader."

"That's not true," Tamaini said, standing. "In our eyes, you are a hero. You are tired, and I will leave you to rest." She paused. "Because of you, we've decided to give Fluffy refuge. She told us everything and is already working in the orchard and pulling her weight. Thank you again. I hope you will have time to visit us. You are welcome in our home anytime."

Malikah stared after the older gargoyle until she vanished. "She apologized. I thought she'd hate me forever."

"Several of the gargoyles witnessed your fight with Esmerelda," Iain said. "They saw what happened."

Seth's phone rang. He glanced at the screen and answered it. "Yes," he said. He listened for a few minutes before a slow, delighted smile crossed his face. "Yes, that sounds excellent. I can visit you tomorrow. Eleven o'clock. I'll be there. Thank you."

"Good news?" Iain asked.

"That was the head of Auckland Hospital offering me a job. From what he said, I'd work on disease prevention discoveries for human and paranormal species. I get to continue my research and help people." Seth glanced at Malikah. "Once you've recovered, would you prefer to work here or in the city?"

Malikah's heart beat faster. Was he telling her...? No, he loved her. He'd told her so. Despite her sudden qualms, she ran with her gut and told the truth. "Stay here and work with the gargoyles and dragons. I enjoy the fresh air and working outdoors."

Seth nodded decisively. "All right. We'll look for a property nearby, somewhere close to Iain, Elspeth, and your people. I like the countryside. Fewer people to see me practicing my crash landings while attempting to fly." He grimaced as Iain cackled.

Malikah stared at him, her mouth slightly agape. "You'd do that for me?"

"You're my mate. I want you to be happy." He leaned closer and took her mouth in a gentle kiss.

"I am—happier than I've ever been. This year has sucked, but the difficulties have strengthened me. I was a spoiled brat. You wouldn't have liked me if you'd met me in England." It was true. She'd changed.

"You look tired," Fiona said. "The healer ordered plenty of rest. That mysterious guardian gave similar advice. He said you were mentally and physically strong but required time to recover. Seth, help her upstairs." She smiled at Malikah, the corners of her eyes crinkling in humor. "You can come down for dinner. We're having roast beef tonight."

"Thank you." Malikah stood, pleased to find her legs stronger, her balance more certain. But she didn't reject the comfort of Seth's arm around her waist. His proximity soothed her, and she loved his scent.

Upstairs, sunlight streamed through the bedroom windows, lifting her mood.

"Did you mean it about finding somewhere to live near here?"

"Of course. My goal is to build a life with you. Spend time together. Return home to you at the end of a workday. I want to laugh with you, play with you." He reached for her hands. "Make love and hold you in my arms throughout the night. I want everything with you."

Malikah's lips parted in wonderment, her heart full. "Yes," she whispered, and her gaze slid to the bed. "I'm not too tired to start on your list."

His brows rose. "Is that so?"

"Yes." She nodded vigorously to underscore her point.

His smile was slow but heartfelt. *He wanted the same things.* Seth lifted her and headed toward the double bed. He set her down and smiled, his eyes glowing. "I can't believe you want me."

"Why? I'm no catch. Right now, I have scant possessions and no money. I have a power that can annihilate anyone I choose. That alone would make most people fear me."

"But you have a respected guardian, and you have me. We're a perfect team." Seth held her gaze as he toed off his shoes and removed every stitch of clothing.

Uncertainty claimed Malikah. "Should I undress too?"

"No." Seth joined her on the bed. "I want to unwrap my present slowly, one item at a time." He pulled her close, kissing her leisurely. No longer so tired, Malikah met each kiss, each touch and caress until she became breathless. He had a deliciously sinful mouth and tortured her with kiss after kiss, some soft and others sensual, until her heart thumped in an uneven rhythm.

"Let's take off your clothes," he said.

His stroking hands sent heat flaring across her skin until she trembled, but it was a pleasant warmth rather than her ominous power surfacing. Malikah raised her arms, and Seth whisked her sweatshirt over her head. The skin-tight tee she wore underneath went with the sweatshirt, leaving her bare from the waist up.

His nostrils flared. "Beautiful." He touched a fingertip to one of her nipples.

She gasped, feeling the brief, tantalizing contact clear to her toes. Her nipple pulled tight as they watched. He gave her a light pinch, and the twist of sensation burrowed deep, teasing her and loosing a whimper of pleasure.

"More," she pleaded.

He grinned and pulled off her sweatpants, leaving her dressed in a skimpy pair of lacy black panties. Her skin prickled, but it wasn't with cold. Each of his caresses was a phantom assault. He ran his fingers from her shoulder down her rib cage to her hip. She released a purring sound of approval, every part of her wanting to return the delight.

She hesitated before she brushed her fingertips over his shoulder and smoothed her hand down his back. He shuddered, so she repeated the move, glorying in the firm muscles beneath her fingers. Seth might be a scientist, but his lean body held strength and coiled power. He trailed kisses down her neck, pausing at the intersection of neck and shoulder. He sucked at her flesh, and she gasped at the sensations flooding her body.

Seth lifted his head, and she saw his wolf shining in his eyes. "Do gargoyles mark each other?"

"No. They exchange rings."

"Wolves do," he whispered. "My wolf wants to bite you badly. He's pushing hard."

"Would the bond work with me?"

Seth snorted. "My wolf is adamant, and too bad what you think. He's biting you."

Malikah swallowed, analyzed her feelings. "I'd like that."

Seth growled, the vibration animalistic and unlike him. She blinked. "Wow."

"Yeah." His agreement was rueful. A trifled bewildered. "Will you bite me now?"

"Not right now. It will hurt. The bite typically occurs during lovemaking."

"Oh." An insistent heat settled at the juncture of her thighs and firmed into an unrelenting throb. She stirred restlessly, gripping his shoulder. She forced every muscle to relax, smiled up at him, and raised her mouth for another of his addictive kisses.

He wasn't slow in accepting the invitation, his tongue tangling with hers in a demanding kiss that drove everything except him from her mind. He kissed down her neck again, and the pulse at her throat beat in a frantic tattoo. Yet she wasn't scared. She'd noticed a scar on Elspeth's neck and guessed this was a wolf mark. If it worked on a dragon, it would work with her, and she wasn't averse to a visible badge of belonging. She wanted Seth to wear her ring in the gargoyle tradition.

Seth lapped at the spot on her neck, sucking before he moved on. One of his hands curled around a breast, distracting her. Then his mouth replaced his fingers, the soft suction morphing into something edgier, sending lustful messages coursing through her body.

"Seth, I ache." She craved his possession and the feel of his shaft as it pierced her flesh.

"I want you crazy with wanting first." He nipped the side of her breast, the hint of pain followed by the soothing stroke of his tongue making her writhe against him.

It was time to drive him to the point of no return. They'd go crazy together. Have fun. She explored his body more thoroughly, seeking pleasure points because she was determined to return the enjoyment tenfold. She cupped his butt and pinched. His entire body jerked, and he glared balefully at her.

She giggled, loving that this act between them could hold humor and love and a little danger, too.

She spread her thighs in a silent hint and canted her hips upward in demand. The prod of his cock against her belly thrilled her, even if she wanted him to hustle.

"We didn't talk about pregnancy," he said. "I want children, but not straight away. Should I use a condom?"

"Yes, please."

With a nod, he separated their bodies, but his hand remained on her breast. He grinned and rolled one of her nipples while she stared at him in a stupefied daze. This man. He meant everything to her, and she couldn't believe she'd tried to send him away at one point.

Seth smoothed the back of his fingers over her cheek before opening a bedside drawer. He pulled out a strip of condoms, separated one off, and rapidly donned it while she admired his body.

"You don't wear your glasses as much."

"They broke when Raoul and I fought. My spare pair seemed fuzzy. My vision was better when I wasn't wearing them. The sun doesn't bother me as much, either." He reached for her and halted. "Malikah, sweetheart, you're wearing too many clothes."

She tried to wriggle from her panties, and he stopped her with a hand on her breast.

"Let me." He smoothed the black lace down her legs, humming with approval once she was fully naked. "Beautiful." He paused and sent her a quizzical look. "Can we make love in our gargoyle forms?"

"I believe so, given we have the requisite parts in those forms."

"Well, that will be interesting," he whispered, and his grin was wicked. It brought a blush to her cheeks.

He winked, and seconds later, his lips crushed against hers. Their breaths mingled, and he splayed his fingers across her ribs, drawing their bodies closer. His thick thigh parted her legs. She'd expected him to hurry, but he didn't.

He ran his hand over her hip and lower. She could've told him she was wet and so very willing, but he checked for himself. One finger glided along her slit, stopping shy of her clit. Malikah trembled at the blissful sensations whispering through her—a promise of pleasure. He stroked her carefully until fiery flames of enjoyment licked up her middle. Every one of her muscles locked tight, and she sobbed out his name, a silent plea for him to push her over the edge.

But Seth wasn't finished, and a whimper escaped once she understood he wanted to use his mouth on her. At the first touch, her hips bucked. A sharp jolt of bliss had her gasping. Her hands sank into his hair, and she tugged, silently demanding he hustle.

He licked her again and gave her nub a light suck before lifting his head and grinning at her.

"Seth." She poured everything she felt into his name.

Without uttering a word, he skillfully pleasured her, alternating between gentle licks and a warm, wet suction. A curl of arousal spiraled low in her belly, and each breath came with a hoarse rustle of air.

Seth smiled up at her, his expression full of joy. "You taste amazing, sweetheart. I wanted our first time to be memorable, our joining one to set the gold standard."

"No pressure or anything," she said, and he laughed.

He pressed a kiss to her mound, erotic vows in his gaze. His face was stark, and she blinked at the raw, male desire that flickered across his features.

"I'm a lucky man," he whispered.

He rose over her body and guided his shaft to her entrance. He pushed, pausing with his tip barely inside her. The sensual stretch thrilled her, and she wriggled, impaling herself a fraction more.

"So impatient," he chided. "We've waited so long that I intend to enjoy every sensation, every moment."

Malikah understood, but she tottered on a precipice, ready to fly into freefall. "Please, Seth. The anticipation is unbearable."

Laughing, he propelled his hips forward, forcing his shaft deeper. Seth retreated, and in his next thrust, he slid deep.

"Feels good," he said.

"Yes," she agreed. "Move. *Please.*"

Seth pulled back and surged inside her again, the head of his cock sliding against her swollen nub. The next stroke hit her perfectly, and the coiled power inside her unraveled. She grasped his shoulders, lifting into his thrusts.

His sinful mouth covered hers before sliding down her throat, and she sighed, moving with each drive. He sucked the fleshy part where neck and shoulder met, his teeth grazing the sensitive tendons and zinging bursts of enjoyment down her torso. Three plunges later, satisfaction exploded inside her, rippling through her body and stealing her breath. Seth bit down, the sharp pain bursting her buzz. She tried to jerk free, but his tongue lashed out, soothing the throbbing discomfort. Another stroke of his tongue had her sighing, every muscle relaxing and tingling, pleasure soaring again.

So good.

Whenever she was with Seth, an inexplicable closeness suffused her, one she'd never experienced before. Now, the bond seemed deeper.

More.

Perfect, as if he were her other half.

Her mate.

He gave a lazy thrust, still hard inside her, and aftershocks struck her as his tongue swished back and forth over the spot where he'd bitten her. She bucked against his solid body, reveling in every sensation. Seth rocked into her with another slow thrust before lifting his head to give her a sweet kiss. Malikah sighed, replete and so happy she fizzed with emotion, the sense of belonging.

Seth escalated the pace of his strokes, and she clasped him tightly as his climax claimed him, his muscular body shuddering with the force of his orgasm.

As their heartbeats slowed, they lay quietly together, limbs entwined.

"Heavy," Malikah mumbled after a while.

Seth laughed and parted their bodies. He rose to deal with the condom, and she watched him stride toward the en suite, her heart so full she thought she might burst.

"You truly want to live with me?" she asked when he returned.

"It's what mates do." He frowned as he stalked toward the bed. "Have I not shown you how much I desire you? How much I care for you? Love you?"

"You have, but I was double-checking." As she spoke the words, her heart fluttered with excitement, knowing he was the one she wanted to share her life with. "I love you."

"Excellent. Glad to hear it." He winked at her. "Because August spoke with me while I was in the bathroom. Get dressed. We're going to the sanctuary for a visit."

Malikah scowled down at her nakedness. "I need a shower."

"Hustle then, sweetheart. We can't keep a guardian waiting."

28

THE SANCTUARY BUSTLED WITH a strange energy not usually present. Malikah's steps slowed, her gaze sweeping the mountains and the monastery grounds. The occupants rushed, completing various errands, but everyone smiled.

Malikah's wings fluttered in agitation. Her steps slowed. "Something is wrong. That couple smiled at me. Normally, the gargoyles *tsk* because I speak too loudly."

Seth reached for her hand and tugged her back into motion. "August is expecting us. He told me his schedule is tight this week, and we should arrive on time."

"Why does he want to see me? January didn't say anything."

Seth shrugged. "August mentioned your guardian would be present. Perhaps they're busy. August told me this would be my final briefing."

"That's fantastic. August believes you'll thrive on your

current path."

Seth snorted a laugh. "My flying is still abysmal and haphazard. It's probably more him washing his hands of me."

They entered the monastery courtyard and found a gargoyle page waiting for them.

"Good afternoon. Please follow me," the young gargoyle said, his voice breaking halfway through his sentence. His face heated but dignity intact, he gestured for them to follow.

Mystified, Malikah exchanged a glance with Seth. "You don't seem surprised," she whispered.

"I have my suspicions."

"What?" Malikah demanded.

Their guide knocked on a door, and a female elder opened it.

Her wrinkled face burst into a smile, and she rubbed her hands together. "You're here. This is so exciting. Come. Come. We must prepare." She grasped Malikah's arm and tugged her over the threshold. "We have one hour, but you are a beautiful woman. One hour will be ample." She drew Malikah farther into the room and slammed the door.

Three other gargoyle women stood waiting.

"What's going on?" Malikah asked, eyeing them with suspicion.

"Your mating ceremony," one woman said with a happy sigh. "You and your mate are the talk of the gargoyle world. Finding a mate is rare, and we're celebrating this marvel."

"Oh," Malikah said, overwhelmed with a sense of wonder.

The gargoyle beamed. "It is an honor to help you prepare for your mating ceremony."

"Oh," Malikah said again in an understatement when her emotions collided like gargoyle youngsters playing a rambunctious game.

Bemused, she submitted to their ministrations, donning a flowing silver gown designed to accommodate her wings and sturdier gargoyle form. They dressed her hair with miniature red roses and a sheer veil and sprayed glitter on her wings, making them sparkle in the sunlight.

Finally, all four gargoyle women stepped back.

"Beautiful," one pronounced.

The others nodded, hands pressed together.

A gong rang, echoing throughout the sanctuary.

"It's time," the gargoyle in charge said. "Let's go. You wait here," she said when Malikah would've followed. "Your guardian will collect you."

They hustled out the door before Malikah could ask further questions. She inhaled several times to steady herself, unaccountably nervous. A swift tap on the door had her starting. The door opened, and January stepped inside, appearing more regal than she had ever seen him in a black suit with silver accessories. Approval shone on his lined face.

He offered his arm. "It is time for us to leave."

"How did you arrange this without me knowing?"

"Your young man asked August about ceremonies and rituals. August and I observed you together, and it was easy to spot the magical spark. You have brought joy and honor to August and me. We're proud of you and Seth. You give others hope, and your younger age brings a vitality to the sanctuary that spreads throughout the gargoyle world."

"Wow." Malikah didn't know what to say to this effusive speech by her typically somber guardian. This smiling gargoyle guardian was a little scary. She surreptitiously pinched her inner forearm. The pain jolted her, but the reality didn't change.

January led her to the sanctuary chapel, and when they entered the sacred building, it bulged with gargoyles, all turned expectantly toward her. Music began, the beat and swirl of it joyous and infectious.

January halted and turned to her. "I am proud of you, Malikah. Very proud. Your power is a heavy burden, and you have conducted yourself admirably."

Malikah blinked several times. "I should've tried to stop the tribe that killed my family and our gargoyles."

"You did the right thing. You were one amongst many. The enemy would've overpowered you, then you wouldn't have helped the children. Those gargoyle children have a bright future, one they wouldn't have had if not for you and your mate. You saved as many as possible, and they've adjusted to their new life. I commend you."

Praise indeed, coming from her normally taciturn guardian.

He surprised her by kissing her cheek before tucking her arm in his and walking the length of a red carpet.

The music swelled, the tempo changing, and excited whispers drifted from the gargoyles sitting in the chapel. Malikah grinned when she spotted Seth walking alongside August. Seth wore a black shirt and trousers and a gold-trimmed scarlet cloak that swirled around his legs.

When Seth and August reached them, January took her hand and presented it to Seth. Seth's warm fingers curled around hers, and she noticed his wings. The cloak held strategic slits for them, and they stirred the air with lazy sweeps.

"You look beautiful," Seth whispered.

"Shush," January said before she could reply.

A stooped gargoyle limped from a side room, his carved wooden stick tapping on the tiled floor. One of his horns had broken during his lifetime, giving him a lopsided appearance. His wings were midnight blue. When he came to a halt, Malikah stared into his blue eyes and surprisingly unlined face. He gestured for Malikah and Seth to approach him.

Seth took her arm and guided her forward.

"It is an honor to welcome you today and join these two young gargoyles with the mate bindings." The gargoyle elder spoke in a deep, rich voice that resonated in the chapel.

"Today, you witness the first ceremony for true mates in over two hundred years. History unfolds as I conduct the ceremony for Seth and Malikah. Who has the rings?"

"We do," January said as he and August stepped forward.

January handed her a ring while August presented one to Seth.

"Seth, please place the ring on Malikah's finger and repeat after me."

"In stone and sky, our spirits unite,

With wings outstretched, our hearts take flight.
I vow to cherish you forevermore,
Through darkness and light, we'll soar."

Seth repeated the words without hesitation, his gaze capturing hers and holding it.

"Malikah, please give Seth your ring and say after me," the elder said.

"In ancient artistry, our love blooms,
Carved in stone, dispelling gloom.
I vow to stand with you, side by side
In stone or flesh, our bond won't hide."

Malikah pushed the solid gold ring on Seth's finger and repeated the elder's words. Her gaze caught in Seth's and emotion shimmered in her words.

"Now repeat together."

Seth squeezed her hands as they spoke the final words.

"With wings entwined, we pledge this day,
Our love as timeless as the Milky Way.
In gargoyle form, our hearts will dance,
Eternal mates, a lifelong trance."

"By the powers of the gargoyle guardians, I declare you mates and wish you great joy." He turned his attention to the gargoyles witnessing the ceremony. "I present to you, Seth and Malikah."

Applause broke out, and the notes of a song swirled in the air. Everyone started singing, their happiness and excitement contagious. The joy swirled through the air as Seth drew Malikah closer.

"I love you, my mate. You have made me happy, and I can't wait to see what our future holds."

Malikah patted his cheek, words swelling in her throat. "Seth," she whispered, standing on tiptoes to kiss him, showing him in the best possible way how contented she was with their status.

Once the song ended, cheers rang out, but Malikah didn't move. She was right where she wanted to be—in her mate's arms.

THANK YOU FOR READING Seth and Malikah's story. If you'd like to read more about this world please check out Sarah's Huge Scoop, a special bonus read just for you. (https://dl.bookfunnel.com/3gh5c99gc6)

Happy reading!
Shelley

About Author

USA Today bestselling author Shelley Munro lives in Auckland, the City of Sails, with her husband and a cheeky Jack Russell/mystery breed dog.

Typical New Zealanders, Shelley and her husband left home for their big OE soon after they married (translation of New Zealand speak - big overseas experience). A twelve-month-long adventure lengthened to six years of roaming the world. Enduring memories include being almost sat on by a mountain gorilla in Rwanda, lazing on white sandy beaches in India, whale watching in Alaska, searching for leprechauns in Ireland, and dealing with ghosts in an English pub.

While travel is still a big attraction, these days Shelley is most likely found in front of her computer following another love - that of writing stories of contemporary and paranormal romance and adventure. Other interests include watching rugby (strictly for research purposes), cycling, playing croquet and the ukelele, and curling up with an enjoyable book.

Visit Shelley at her Website
www.shelleymunro.com

Join Shelley's Newsletter
www.shelleymunro.com/newsletter

ALSO BY SHELLEY

Middlemarch Shifters
My Scarlet Woman
My Younger Lover
My Peeping Tom
My Assassin
My Estranged Lover
My Feline Protector
My Determined Suitor
My Cat Burglar
My Stray Cat
My Second Chance
My Plan B
My Cat Nap
My Romantic Tangle
My Blue Lady
My Twin Trouble
My Precious Gift